Only one life

ALSO BY ASHLEY FARLEY

Home for Wounded Hearts
Nell and Lady
Sweet Tea Tuesdays
Saving Ben

Magnolia Series

Beyond the Garden
Magnolia Nights

Sweeney Sisters Series

Saturdays at Sweeney's
Tangle of Strings
Boots and Bedlam
Lowcountry Stranger
Her Sister's Shoes

Scottie's Adventures

Breaking the Story
Merry Mary

Only one life

ASHLEY FARLEY

LAKE UNION
PUBLISHING

Text copyright © 2019 by Ashley Farley
All rights reserved.

Published by Lake Union Publishing, Seattle

www.apub.com

Amazon, the Amazon logo, and Lake Union Publishing are trademarks of Amazon.com, Inc., or its affiliates.

ISBN-13: 9781542093842
ISBN-10: 1542093848

Cover design by PEPE *nymi*, Milano

Printed in the United States of America

To Cameron, Ned, and Ted

Live all you can; it's a mistake not to.
It doesn't so much matter what you do in particular
so long as you have your life.
If you haven't had that what have you had?

—Henry James, *The Ambassadors*

PART ONE

CHAPTER ONE

JULIA

Present Day

Julia felt as though her belly might explode wide open, even though the baby wasn't due for another two weeks. She smiled at the thought of giving birth on the tile floor in the kitchen of Duke's Diner as Duke hovered over her, coaching her through the labor pains and delivery.

Propping her elbows on the prep counter, she lifted her face to the oscillating fan, relishing the feel of cool air on her clammy skin. She longed to rest her swollen feet, but the lunch crowd had just begun to trickle in, and hours remained before her shift ended.

"Order's up, Jules!" Cook called, sliding a large tray of food and drinks across the counter toward her.

She eyed the tray, debating whether she had the energy to lift it.

Cook, tall and lean despite his profession, observed her from behind the griddle as he flipped burgers. "You all right, sweetheart?"

Brushing a damp strand of hair off her forehead, Julia fanned her face with her order pad. "The heat is killing me. This is the tenth day in a row the temperature has broken a hundred."

"The weathermen are calling it the hottest July on record," Cook said as he transferred the burgers onto buns prepped with lettuce and tomatoes in red plastic baskets lined with gingham waxed paper.

"They say that every year," Julia said and doubled over at the sudden gripping pain in her side. *Breathe, Julia,* she mumbled to herself as she sucked in a deep breath and counted to three.

Duke burst through the swinging door from the dining room. "Here. Let me help you with that." He elbowed her out of the way and hoisted the tray onto his shoulder.

With a crew cut, hard gut, and bulging tatted-up biceps, her boss fit the part of an ex-marine. And he had no patience for female drama. He grumbled incessantly when his waitresses took maternity leave and told them to suck it up when they called in sick with menstrual cramps. But he'd softened toward Julia in recent months. After nursing her through a series of miscarriages, the entire staff at Duke's—waitresses and busboys and bartenders who'd worked together for years—was cheering her on.

"Thank you, Duke," she said, following him to the front of the restaurant.

Little had changed in the dining room since Duke's grandfather, Duke Senior, built the place in the early sixties. Wooden booths with laminate tabletops lined one side of the room while leather swivel stools were positioned in front of the lunch counter on the other. A hodge-podge of mounted saltwater fish—from blue marlin to sand sharks—adorned the walls along with framed photographs of famous people who'd visited Duke's over the years. The food was the best in town, but the smell of the greasy burgers and fries made Julia nauseated as she placed the red baskets in front of an attractive young family of four.

As the afternoon dragged on, Julia's section of tables turned over time and again with families who vacationed on Edisto Island every summer. The queasiness intensified with each passing hour. By the time her replacement arrived at three o'clock for the dinner shift, she felt wretched. The weather forecast was calling for afternoon storms, and the air was so thick with humidity she struggled to catch her breath when she exited the diner on her way to her car.

She was rummaging in her purse for her car keys when she spotted an unmistakably familiar figure—an elegant woman wearing a floral sundress with her chestnut hair tied back in a low ponytail—watching her from across the street. Shielding her eyes from the blinding sun, she called out, "Mama!"

Her mother stared back at her, seemingly frozen in place.

Gripping her purse close to her body, Julia moved to the edge of the parking lot. A stream of cars passed in front of her from both directions, and by the time the traffic had cleared, her mother was speeding off in the same silver Volvo wagon she'd driven the last time Julia had spoken with her fifteen years ago.

Julia's spirits plummeted as she walked back to her car and took off down Jungle Road toward home. The street name conjured up the image of a dirt road lined with wooden huts surrounded by tropical trees with barefoot children playing hopscotch in dirt front yards. But Jungle Road was quite the opposite. It was a primary road on Edisto Beach, flanked on both sides by quaint gift shops, eateries, and weathered beach houses.

As she drove, her mind drifted back to her mother. *Why did she take off so suddenly? Surely she noticed I'm pregnant. Surely she'll want to know her grandchild.* The hurt and anger from the past that faded from time to time but never truly went away gripped her chest. With her baby's arrival imminent, Julia missed Iris more than ever. Even though she'd read every book on infant care available for checkout at the Colleton County Library, she felt unprepared for being a parent. There were certain times in a girl's life when she needed her mother. And having her first baby was one of them.

Julia found it easier not to think about her father and sister. Her hometown of Beaufort was deep in the heart of the South Carolina Lowcountry, only an hour-and-a-half drive from Edisto Island. Julia did her best to avoid her family's friends who summered on Edisto. But when they came to Duke's for lunch, she learned bits of gossip about her family. Enough to know her father had been promoted to executive vice president at his bank, her mother's flower business continued to thrive, and her older sister had married and divorced twice.

Julia pulled into the driveway of the tiny cottage she shared with her husband on the sound side of Edisto Beach. The house consisted of two small bedrooms with one common area that served as sitting room and kitchen. They could barely afford the mortgage on what the local real estate market deemed as waterfront property, even though theirs was a pie-shaped lot wedged between two full lots and they'd need binoculars to catch a glimpse of the sound. Thin walls coupled with their antiquated heating and cooling systems made for freezing winters and hot-as-blazes summers. Jack and Julia led a simple life, partially due to budgetary restrictions but mostly by design. Even though they lacked the money for luxuries, like cell phones and computers, she'd known more happiness here with Jack than she'd ever experienced in her family's three-story waterfront antebellum house in Beaufort.

Julia set her purse on the kitchen counter and went to stand in front of the sliding glass doors. The wildflowers she'd grown from seed around her dirt patio had wilted under the intense sun despite her having watered them that morning. From the time Julia was a little girl, her mother had groomed her to take over her flower business. Julia had been majoring in studio art and minoring in marketing in preparation for that very thing when she'd gotten pregnant with Jack's baby and dropped out of college to marry him. She'd miscarried two months after they eloped. Brokenhearted at the loss of her baby, she'd made a career out of becoming a mother, dedicating years and money they didn't have to fertility treatments that resulted in three pregnancies, all cut short by miscarriages. She'd often wondered what her life might've been like if she hadn't gotten pregnant. Would she have eventually married Jack anyway? Her love for him was never in question. He made her feel worthy, and she needed that reassurance after growing up with her sister's bullying and her father's constant scrutiny.

Removing her clippers from the kitchen drawer, Julia went out to the patio and cut a large bunch of wildflowers. She brought the flowers inside to the sink, filled a mason jar with water, and arranged the flowers into a pretty bouquet. Leaving the flowers on the kitchen counter, she went down the hall to her bedroom, where she stretched out on her double bed, with her feet propped on a mountain of pillows, and fell into a deep sleep.

Jack woke her when he crawled into bed beside her early that evening. "How are my wife and baby doing today?" he asked, planting a trail of kisses from the nape of her neck to her ear.

Julia snuggled in closer to him. "A little better after my nap, but today was difficult. I'm as big as a house, Jack. How can I possibly go two more weeks?"

"We have money in our savings, Jules." Jack removed the phone from his nightstand and handed her the receiver. "Call Duke and tell him you won't be able to work until after the baby comes."

She pushed the receiver away. "Put the phone back. We agreed I'd only take two weeks off. That's all we can afford. And I'd rather spend those days with the baby."

He returned the phone to the nightstand. "You're the boss, babe. Maybe we'll get lucky and the baby will come early." He got up from the bed and removed his soiled work shirt. "I met Sandy in the driveway just now. She brought over some shrimp for our supper. I thought I'd fry them up in that coconut batter you like."

Their fifty-five-year-old next-door neighbor fussed over Julia like an expectant grandmother. Nearly every day, Sandy dropped off food, baked special treats, and ran errands for them. She was the nighttime bartender at Coot's Bar and Grill and had volunteered to keep the baby when Julia went back to work. At least for the first few weeks until the baby was old enough for day care.

"That was nice of her. My appetite's been off today, but I'll try to eat a few."

She watched her husband pull on a clean T-shirt and khaki shorts. She never tired of gazing at his rugged good looks—his unruly blond hair that fell constantly in his eyes, and his broad shoulders and strong arms that protected her from life's disappointments.

She waited for him to leave the room before rolling her swollen body off the bed to her feet. She retrieved her overnight bag from the floor beside the door and placed it on the bed. She unzipped the bag and inspected the contents: two nightgowns and a robe for her, plus day clothes for mother and baby to wear home from the hospital. She zipped into the side pocket the gold cross necklace her mother had given her at her confirmation and returned the bag to the floor beside the door.

Her friends at the diner had thrown Julia an impromptu surprise baby shower back in June. Duke and Cook had combined funds for a stroller and a car seat while the other waitresses had given her an assortment of infant clothes and the usual miscellaneous paraphernalia babies required—blankets, burp cloths, bibs, and a variety of ointments and creams.

Julia's abdomen grew hard as pain tore through her body. She collapsed against the doorframe and breathed through the contraction. "It won't be long now, baby girl or boy," she said, massaging her belly. "Your daddy and I can hardly wait to meet you."

She staggered next door to the guest room Jack had transformed into a nursery. He'd painted the walls butter yellow, and she'd purchased a good-condition crib at the Salvation Army store. He'd discovered, at a yard sale, a wool carpet remnant the color of oatmeal and an old tea cart, which he'd converted into a changing table. The only thing missing was a rocking chair. If only she had the mahogany rocker with the intricately carved arms from her childhood bedroom. She'd spent untold hours in that chair as a child, reading her cardboard books and rocking her dolls to sleep.

"Don't worry, baby," she said, hugging her belly. "We'll have Daddy move the glider in from the porch. Your room is all ready for you, whenever you're ready for it."

She turned out the light and waddled down the hall to the kitchen, where she found Jack peeling shrimp at the sink.

"I saw Mama again today," Julia said as she set two places at the counter separating the kitchen from the main room.

Jack looked up from his shrimp. "Did you talk to her?"

She shook her head. "It was Iris, though. I'm sure of it. And when I called out to her, she hightailed it out of there."

"I don't understand why she's stalking you," he said as he transferred the shrimp by handfuls to a plastic bag filled with flour.

Julia gave his arm a playful slap. "She's not stalking me. She's . . . I don't know what she's doing. Checking up on me, I guess."

"Why would she drive all this way to check up on you and not talk to you?" He shook his head as if trying to understand.

Julia removed a pitcher of sweet tea from the refrigerator. "You know why. Max won't let her communicate with me."

He let out a sigh. "Does your father really hate me that much? You'd think that, after all this time, he'd get over it."

"Don't take it personally. I've told you a thousand times it's not about you. My parents don't even know you. You're just not what they had in mind for their daughter."

"You mean a redneck boat mechanic from a poor family."

Jack spoke the truth. Fifteen years ago, Julia had gone to her parents for help when she'd discovered she was pregnant. Her father had disowned her, banished her from his house. Julia had expected that kind of treatment from Max, but she'd been surprised and disappointed when her mother supported his decision.

She prepared two glasses of sweet tea and set them on the counter beside their place mats. "My father is a bank executive. Everything is about money for Max."

"Never mind that most of the money in that bank is his," Jack said under his breath.

"Who knows? Maybe Mama is on Edisto for a reason other than checking on me. She could be doing flowers for a wedding or a big cocktail party."

"That's a logical explanation." He cracked an egg and dumped it into a bowl. "I know how much you miss her. And I've gotta believe she misses you too." He added more flour and the remainder of the beer he'd been sipping to the bowl and stirred the mixture with a fork. "Maybe you should try writing to her again."

After her father had kicked her out of the house, Julia wrote a letter to her mother, begging for forgiveness and understanding. Much to her dismay, she never received an answer. As a result, over the years, her feelings for her mother had turned cold.

"She knows where to find me, and unless she's gone blind, she knows I'm pregnant. If she wants to miss out on the chance to know her grandchild, then that's her problem."

Julia wrapped her arms around Jack from behind, pressing her belly against his back. "Did you feel that?" she asked when the baby kicked.

"Mm-hmm. He's a strong one. My boy's gonna be an all-state baseball player like his father."

"Or be a ballerina if it's a girl," Julia said.

"As long as she's not a pole dancer."

Julia giggled. "She'd better not be."

She ran her nose along the skin in the crook of his neck, inhaling his scent—motor oil mixed with sweat—as she watched him dip each shrimp in batter and then roll it in coconut flakes.

When a sudden sharp pain caused her to gasp, he dropped the shrimp in the batter and turned to face her. "Are you all right?" he asked, taking her by the shoulder.

She nodded, biting her lip until the pain stopped. "Just another Braxton-Hicks."

Steering her over to the couch, he stacked the throw pillows at one end and held her arm as she lowered her cumbersome body. "Now, lie here and don't move until dinner's ready."

She saluted him. "Yes, sir!" Her gaze shifted, and she noticed the sky darkening through the sliding glass doors. "Storm's coming. I hope it gives us some relief from this heat."

"I'm afraid we're gonna get more than that," he said, tucking a lightweight blanket around her body. "I heard the weather report on the radio on my way home from work. This is a dangerous system with potential for tornadoes."

She snuggled deeper beneath the blanket. "Good thing we don't have to go anywhere tonight."

When he started to walk away, she grabbed him by the arm. "Does it bother you that our child won't know his or her grandparents?"

Jack knelt down beside the couch. "Not as much as it bothers you. My parents have been gone for so long, and you and I are used to being on our own." A faraway look settled on his face, and he snickered. "But my parents would've made awesome grandparents. They would've been doting and kind. They would've spoiled this kid rotten."

CHAPTER TWO

A boom of thunder startled Julia awake from her snooze. She sat bolt upright and swung her legs over the side of the couch. "Good grief! That was close."

"I know, right?" Jack said from the stove, where he was frying shrimp. "You should probably move away from the glass doors."

As she got to her feet, she felt a pop, followed by a gush of warm liquid between her legs. "Oh my God, Jack!" she called out. "My water just broke!"

"Are you serious?" he asked, metal slotted spoon suspended in midair.

"Why would I lie about such a thing?"

"Woo-hoo!" He punched the air with the spoon gripped in his fist. "Mark the calendar! It's July twenty-fifth. We're gonna have ourselves a baby tonight." He dropped the spoon in the spoon rest, turned off the stove, and moved the iron skillet to the back burner.

"Leave it to our kid to be born during the worst storm of the summer." Julia pressed her knees together to stop the flow of amniotic fluid as she made her way through the room to the hallway.

"We'll call him Stormy," Jack said, following her into the bedroom.

She smiled at him over her shoulder. "You're going to be awfully disappointed when your *him* is a *her*." She opened the closet door and flipped through her few maternity dresses.

"What're you doing? Your bag's been packed for weeks," he said, pointing at her overnight bag by the door.

"I'm changing my clothes. I have no intention of wearing my uniform to the hospital." She stepped out of her wet underwear and slipped her waitressing dress over her head, tugging on a pale-pink loose-fitting shift.

"We need to hurry, babe." Jack tapped his watch. "We've got an hour's drive to Charleston as it is. And the storm will slow us down."

"I'll be ready in a minute." She slipped on a pair of dry panties and went into the bathroom. At the sink, she teased the top layer of her blonde, medium-length hair and pinched color into her cheeks.

"What's with all the fuss?" Jack asked, watching her from the doorway. "You're about to deliver a baby."

"I want to look nice when I meet our child." Julia smeared on clear lip gloss and smacked her lips together. She locked eyes with her husband in the mirror. "You realize our lives are about to get crazy."

"Bring it on! We've waited a very long time for this baby. I don't care if he, *or she*, is a little demon who puts us through hell." Taking Julia by the hand, he led her out of the bathroom. "Where're your keys?"

Her car was only slightly more reliable than his pickup truck. Jack did a good job of keeping the 2001 Toyota Camry her parents had given her when she went off to the College of Charleston in good working order, but it still had its issues.

"In my purse on the kitchen counter." A strong contraction took her breath away, and she doubled over in pain.

"Breathe through it," he said as he stroked her hair.

She took several deep breaths until the pain passed. "We need to hurry," she said, straightening.

Jack grabbed a pillow from the bed and her overnight bag. He ran to the kitchen for her purse and met her in the hallway. He opened the front door and quickly slammed it shut again. "It's a bloody monsoon out there." He retrieved an umbrella and their raincoats from the coat closet, slipping his on before helping Julia into hers.

He kissed her hard on the lips. "I love you, Jules, more than you'll ever know. You're the best thing that's ever happened to me."

"And I love you," she said, pinching his chin. "But I'm about to be the second-best thing that's ever happened to you."

"There's enough room in my heart for two best things. Are you ready?" he asked with his hand on the doorknob. "On the count of three. One. Two. Three."

As they stepped out into the storm, the wind whipped the umbrella out of Jack's hand. "Make a run for it," he hollered over the howl of the wind. He flung open the back car door, tossing her bag onto the floorboard and the pillow onto the seat. "You'll be more comfortable back here." He helped her get settled before closing the door and running around to the driver's side.

They drove slowly down Jungle Road, turning left once they reached the highway. The wind roared, the rain pounded the roof of her car, and the wipers swished back and forth on the windshield at top speed. When the contractions hit, Julia chomped down on her lip so as not to cry out in pain and distract Jack from driving. From the radio, the announcer reported the sighting of a tornado near Palmetto Road and Fishing Creek in the direction they were heading. They'd driven down the highway several miles and were beginning to pick up speed when she heard a loud crash, the car jerked to an abrupt halt, and everything went black.

CHAPTER THREE

Julia's eyes opened wide, and she let out a piercing scream at the realization she was trapped in the back seat of her car. The back windshield was shattered, the roof of the car was inches from her face, and the engine was hissing. She sniffed. What was that burning smell? Was the car on fire?

Panic set in. "Jack, are you all right? Can you hear me?" Light from the dashboard flickered, and she saw his head, his sandy hair matted with blood, resting at an unnatural angle on the side of the driver's seat.

"Oh my God, Jack!" She pounded the roof with her fists. "Help! Somebody, please help us. We're trapped in here!"

There was a knock on the passenger-side window behind her head, and a beam of light illuminated the interior of the car. A man shouted, "Try to remain calm, ma'am. I've got the 911 operator on the line. They're sending help now."

"Tell them to hurry! My husband's unconscious. I'm afraid he might be—" Pain tore through her abdomen, and she clutched her belly. "Oh my God! My baby!"

"Is there a child in the car with you?" he asked in an alarmed voice.

When she craned her neck to get a look at him, she saw his concerned brown eyes peering in at her through the rain-streaked window.

"I'm pregnant!" Another pain ripped through her body, and between gasping breaths, she cried, "In labor. This baby. Is coming. Now!"

"This woman's in labor," the man yelled to the 911 operator. "Get someone here fast!"

"Hang on tight, ma'am. I'm going to stay with you until help comes. My name's Clint. What's yours?"

"Julia," she yelled.

Clint's voice was muted by the window, but she was grateful for his presence. "Trust me, Julia. I know all about childbirth. I've been through this four times myself. Signal to me when your next contraction begins, and we'll count together."

The acrid smell was now burning her nostrils. "The car's on fire! It's gonna explode. You've gotta get me out of here!"

"The car is not on fire, Julia. It's the airbag. It smells like gunpowder when it deploys. There's nothing to worry about. For your baby's sake, I need you to calm down."

A labor pain hit her hard, and she screamed.

"Inhale through your nose and exhale through your mouth. Find the rhythm that works for you."

Julia closed her eyes and tried not to think about what was happening to her. To Jack. To their baby. Help was on the way. Soon they would be out of the car and at the hospital, where she and Jack would deliver their baby. She thought back to her childbirth classes. She could feel Jack's strong arms around her, his voice near her ear encouraging her to take slow, deep breaths. The air in the car was thick, and her body was damp with perspiration. She breathed and counted through the contractions that came every couple of minutes.

Her eyes shot open at the sound of sirens approaching from the distance. "Clint!" she called out. "Are you still here?"

"I'm right here, Julia. Can you hear the sirens? A fire truck is pulling up now."

The glow from red flashing lights filled the car. "Tell them to help my husband first. He's hurt worse than me."

"We'll let them make that decision."

She couldn't see the firefighters, but she could hear their voices as they discussed with Clint how far along her contractions were.

A tap on the window, and one of the new male voices said, "An ambulance will be here momentarily, ma'am. We're going to pry open the door. I need you to move as far away from the door as possible. Close your eyes and cover your face if you can."

Julia inched over on the seat until her bent knees were jammed against the roof of the car. Squeezing her eyes shut and folding her arms over her face, she cowered in response to the loud creaking and screeching noises near her head as the rescue workers ripped the door off the car. Hands, multiple sets of them, braced her head and supported her body as they pulled her from the car and set her down gently on a gurney.

She grabbed a firefighter by the arm. "My husband! You have to get my husband out."

"We're doing all we can, ma'am."

"Where's Clint? I need to talk to Clint."

He called out, "Anybody here named Clint?" and a man, whose warm brown eyes she recognized, appeared at her side.

"You saved my baby's life," Julia said. "Thank you."

He dipped his head in a solemn nod. "I'm glad I came along when I did."

Another contraction gripped her belly, and she wailed, "Oh. My. God."

Clint leaned down close to her ear. "Breathe, Julia. Count and breathe."

"I can't do this without Jack," she said with fear in her slate-gray eyes. "Please, can you stay here with Jack? I don't want him to be alone.

Find out where they're taking me. Make sure they bring Jack to the same hospital."

Sadness crossed Clint's face. "I'll do what I can. For now, you need to concentrate on yourself, on bringing that baby into the world safe and sound."

Paramedics on either side counted to three before lifting the gurney into the back of the ambulance. Two paramedics in their early twenties—a male and a female, both with brown hair and eyes—climbed into the ambulance with her. The doors slammed shut behind them, and she felt trapped again.

The female crouched down beside the gurney near Julia's head. "I'm Kate, and that's Mike. I need some information from you." Her fingers danced across the screen of an iPad as Julia provided answers. "Name? Doctor? Due date? How far apart are the contractions?"

Julia clenched her jaw when another contraction twisted her insides. The pressure in her pelvis was unbearable, and she gripped Kate's arm. "I need to push!"

The paramedics exchanged a look of terror and said in unison, "Don't push!"

The pain subsided, and Julia's eyes shifted between them. "Please tell me one of you has delivered a baby before."

They both shook their heads. "But we've had plenty of training, if it comes to that," Kate said.

Mike nodded. "For your sake and the baby's, it's better if we can make it to the hospital. If we have to pull over on the side of the road and deliver your baby in the ambulance, our driver will know how to handle the situation. He's our crew leader. He's seen everything."

"Then why isn't he back here with us?" Julia hollered as she felt another contraction coming on.

"He's behind the wheel, where he needs to be right now," he said. "He's the safest and fastest driver on our squad."

Kate sat down on the built-in bench seat and leaned in close to Julia. "We're not going to let anything happen to you, Julia. We're going to get you through this."

Julia looked up at the young woman with pleading eyes. "Can you give me some drugs? Please? Anything."

"They'll have plenty of drugs for you when we get to the hospital. For now, let's concentrate on breathing."

"Breathing doesn't help, you bitch!" she cried as the pain reached its peak, and when it subsided, she apologized. "I'm so sorry. I didn't mean to call you that."

Kate smiled at her. "You can call me anything you want, if it helps."

During the remainder of the drive to Charleston, Julia panted and sweated and let out a string of expletives that had never before crossed her lips. She tried her best not to push, but when the ambulance reached the hospital and they wheeled her gurney into the emergency room, she could no longer hold back.

"This baby. Is coming. Right now!" With knees bent and legs spread, she bellowed in agony as she pushed with all her might. A team of medical personnel—some in white coats, others in blue scrubs—swarmed her as they gently glided the baby out of her body.

A young doctor with a scruffy face and wire-rimmed glasses held up the slimy, naked baby for Julia to see. "You have a fine, healthy baby boy. Would the daddy like to do the honors of cutting the umbilical cord?"

The daddy? Jack? Where's Jack? Her eyes darted from face to face in search of Jack's. "Where's my husband? What hospital is this? Did they bring Jack here?"

Mike, who'd been watching the delivery from over their shoulders, stepped toward the doctor. "I'm one of the paramedics from the scene. This woman and her husband were in a horrible accident on the way to the hospital. Her husband didn't survive," Mike explained in a lowered voice, but Julia heard him anyway.

"Liar!" she cried. "Jack's alive. Help him. Don't leave him stranded in that car." She broke into a hysterical fit of crying. "I know my husband's alive."

The doctor called out orders to give her a sedative.

"No! Jack needs me. Let me up." When she tried to get off the gurney, two nurses held her down while the third injected a clear liquid in her IV. Seconds later, Julia felt herself slipping away.

CHAPTER FOUR

Julia woke with a start. She was confused at first, but as her eyes darted about the room, the haze cleared, and she remembered she was in the hospital. The reality of the accident came crashing back to her, and she stifled a sob. She struggled to sit up. She saw Sandy sitting in a recliner near the bed cradling a blanketed bundle in her arms. Julia's baby. Her son.

"Is Jack really dead?"

Sandy looked up from the bundle, and Julia saw that her blue eyes were red rimmed and swollen. "Oh, honey, there's no easy way to say it. That poor sweet man. I loved him like a brother. I hope you'll find comfort, like I do, in knowing he didn't suffer. I don't know how much you remember about the accident, but a tree fell on your car, killing him instantly. You're lucky you got out alive. And that the baby wasn't hurt."

Julia bit down on her lip until she tasted blood. She knew Sandy was only trying to help, but Julia would never find comfort in anything about the accident that had killed her husband. She wished she'd died with him, because a life without Jack was a life not worth living. Spotting her overnight bag on the floor beside Sandy, she realized someone had retrieved it from her wrecked car.

Sandy babbled on. "I never wanted to get married, never wanted to get stuck with some grumpy old fart." She clucked her tongue at the baby. "But not having children is my biggest disappointment in life. Your baby is so beautiful, Jules. It's hard to say for sure with the scrunched-up face of a newborn, but I think he's the spitting image of Jack." She moved to the edge of the recliner. "Are you ready to hold him?"

Tears filled Julia's eyes and slid down her cheeks. "We were never meant to be parents. God tried to tell us that with the miscarriages, but we wouldn't listen. And now he's punishing me. If not for that baby, Jack would still be alive."

"You're talking nonsense, Jules. Accidents happen. God didn't punish you; he blessed you with this beautiful baby. Here." Sandy got up from the chair and stood beside the bed. "Hold your baby. You've waited so long."

Julia raised her arm, her finger pointing at the door. "Get that baby out of my room. I don't want to see him."

Sandy flinched at her angry tone. "You've been through an ordeal. I understand you need some rest. I'll take him back to the nursery for now." She walked backward toward the door. "Get some rest, honey. Let the nurses take care of him while you're here. I have to work tonight, but I'll be back to pick you up first thing in the morning."

Once she was gone, Julia punched the call button on the side of her bed to summon the nurse. While she waited, she watched patients and their visitors—relatives who'd come to meet the newest member of their family—pass by her doorway in the hall. Snippets of their conversations reached her—discussions about naming their babies and breastfeeding and making preparations for going home.

Ten minutes passed by on the wall clock before a bone-thin nurse with sunken cheeks and gray hair arrived. She introduced herself as Elsie.

"I'm in a lot of pain," Julia said. "Can you give me something?"

"It's not time for your pain meds." Elsie used the remote control to raise the head of the bed. "After we get you cleaned up, we'll go for a little walk in the hallway. Then, if you're still hurting, I'll get you something for the pain."

Julia pulled the covers up under her chin. "I'm not getting out of this bed. I want my pain medicine now," she said in a demanding voice that sounded foreign to her ears.

Elsie's chin dropped to her chest. "I beg your pardon. I don't take you for the prima donna type."

Julia's face grew warm. "I'm sorry. I'm not myself today. My husband, Jack, was killed in a car accident last night on the way to the hospital. I want to go to sleep and never wake up. Please, can't you give me some medicine?"

Elsie's face softened. "Oh, hon, no one told me." She sat down slowly on the edge of the bed. "I'm so sorry for your loss. I understand what you're going through, but no medicine will take away that kind of pain."

Julia gasped for air. "This is real pain, Elsie. I feel like I'm having a heart attack. My chest aches, and I'm having trouble breathing."

The nurse patted Julia's thigh beneath the blanket. "That's anxiety, sweetheart. Which is totally understandable in your situation. Getting out of bed will help."

Julia studied Elsie's face. Lines creased her forehead and the skin around her warm brown eyes. The nurse's calm demeanor reminded Julia of her mother. "If you say so."

"Good. How about we start with a bath?" Elsie rose from the bed and gently peeled the covers away from Julia's body.

Julia leaned against the nurse for support as they made their way into the bathroom. Elsie adjusted the water temperature in the shower and helped Julia out of her soiled hospital gown. She left the bathroom while Julia showered but was waiting with a towel and the blue cotton gown and robe Julia had brought from home when she got out. After towel drying and brushing Julia's hair, Elsie squirted toothpaste on Julia's toothbrush and stood close to her while she brushed her teeth.

"Now," Elsie said as they exited the bathroom, "how about that walk?"

Julia eyed the hospital bed and noticed the sheets had been changed. She wanted to crawl beneath the covers and hide for the next thirty years or until it was time for her to be with Jack in heaven.

"I'm tired from my shower. Maybe later." She made her way back to the bed without Elsie's help.

"All right, then. We'll wait until after your nap." She lifted the menu from the bed table. "Let's order you up some lunch so it'll be here when you wake up."

Julia's stomach rolled, and she shook her head. "I'm not hungry."

"You have to eat to keep your strength up for the baby." Elsie's eyes traveled the menu. "What about a grilled chicken sandwich? Everybody likes grilled chicken sandwiches."

"Whatever," Julia said to make the nurse go away. Mealtime had been Jack's favorite time of day. She would never again enjoy the taste of food.

Julia nodded off while Elsie was placing the call to the cafeteria. When she heard the nurse's squeaky shoes leaving the room, she called out in a soft voice, "Please turn off the light and close the door behind you."

She dozed off and on for the rest of the morning and much of the afternoon. The few times she fell into a deep slumber, she was startled awake by nightmares of falling trees and crashing cars.

Elsie entered the room and turned on the lights a few minutes past four. "Rise and shine, hon. Your doctor's on the hall. She's gonna have my job if she finds out I haven't taken you to walk today."

"Look, Elsie, I'm exhausted. Don't worry. I'll take the blame. I'm not afraid of Dr. Carr. She's been my obstetrician for years." She closed her eyes and rolled over on her side with her back to Elsie.

Elsie yanked the covers back. "I gave you a break by letting you sleep all afternoon, but we're going to walk. Now. This is nonnegotiable."

"Geez. Anything to get you off my back." Julia sat up straight in bed and swung her legs over the side. When she hauled herself to a standing position, the room began to spin. Fortunately, Elsie was there to catch her.

"That's what happens when you get up too quickly." Elsie eyed the untouched lunch tray. "Why didn't you eat your lunch?"

"I wasn't hungry," Julia mumbled.

"You're going to have to eat sooner or later." Elsie draped Julia's robe over her shoulders. "Can you manage on your own, or do you want to use a walker?"

"I'm fine," Julia said, and took off out of the room.

Elsie caught up with her and took her by the arm. "Let's walk down this way to the nursery."

Julia spun on slippered feet and headed in the opposite direction.

Elsie hovered close to catch her if she fell. "Do you have family, hon? Someone who can help you when you get home?"

"My friend Sandy's going to help me."

"Does Sandy live close to you?"

Julia nodded. "Next door."

They passed a gray-headed grandmother jiggling her crying grandchild in her arms. "What about your mama? Is she still alive?"

Julia thought about her mama. She longed to curl up in her lap and bawl her eyes out like she'd done as a child when she'd fallen off her bicycle or gotten stung by a bee. But her mother's soothing voice and butterfly kisses couldn't make this boo-boo go away. "Yes, but we haven't spoken in fifteen years."

Elsie cast her a sidelong glance. "Was it something you did or something she did?"

Julia kept her eyes fixed on the floor in front of her. "My parents didn't approve of Jack, but I married him anyway." She swallowed back tears. "He was the love of my life. The best person I've ever known."

"Shame on your mama," Elsie said, her lips pressed thin. "Every day a mother gets to spend with her child is a blessing."

Julia had already squandered the first day of her child's life. Maybe, in her genetic makeup, she'd inherited a flawed chromosome from her mother that made casting one's children aside easy.

Julia and Elsie turned around when they reached the elevator. The doctor was waiting in the room by the time they got back.

Dr. Carr rose from the chair and said, "Julia, I'm so terribly sorry about Jack." Her enormous brown eyes, behind her round black-rimmed glasses, had inspired Jack to refer to her as the Owl.

"Thank you, Dr. Carr," Julia mumbled.

"I used to look forward to chatting with him at your appointments. He was one of the good guys. He was the most enthusiastic daddy-to-be that I've known in all my thirty years of practicing medicine."

Julia would never get used to people talking about Jack in past tense. "And he never got to see his child."

Dr. Carr motioned her to the bed. "Shall we?"

Julia lowered herself and lay back against the pillows while Dr. Carr examined her.

"Physically, everything appears in good order," Dr. Carr said, tugging her stethoscope from her ears when she finished. She dragged a straight-backed chair close to the bed. "But frankly, Julia, I'm worried about your unwillingness to bond with your baby. I understand you've been through a terrible ordeal, and we've made an exception because of your circumstances. But it is our hospital's policy for newborns to stay in the room with their parents. That practice is in place for a reason. It allows you a chance to grow accustomed to caring for your baby while you have our trained staff to guide you."

"Parent, Dr. Carr. Not parents."

The doctor shook her head as if to clear her ears. "I'm sorry. I don't understand."

"You said a newborn should stay in the room with his parents. My baby only has one parent."

"A slip of the tongue." Dr. Carr inhaled and exhaled slowly as if summoning her patience. "My point is, breastfeeding can often be frustrating while mother and baby are getting to know one another. I won't be able to release you tomorrow until I'm satisfied your breastfeeding is going well. I've just come from the nursery. Your baby is hungry."

"Then give him a bottle."

The doctor's owl eyes grew even larger. "But you seemed so excited about the prospect of breastfeeding during your last office visit."

Julia pulled the blanket up over her aching breasts. No one ever warned her they'd hurt so much. "You're aware of my finances, Doctor. You know I can't afford to stay here another day."

"I understand, Julia. But just so you know, if we give him a bottle now, you run the risk of him rejecting your breast later."

Jack had been the one gung ho about breastfeeding. Julia had argued that bottle feeding would afford them more flexibility with her having to go back to work so soon.

"Okay. I get it. Now, if you don't mind"—she waved her hand at the door—"I'd like to try to get some sleep."

~

Julia lay awake for most of the night, mourning Jack and worrying about how she'd survive without him. This baby was meant to be *their* baby—the baby they would raise together. She never would've opted to have a baby on her own. Although she admired women who could raise a child alone, she wasn't one of them. She wasn't as strong as Jack had given her credit for. Her financial situation without his income caused her considerable angst. She had no idea how she'd pay the mortgage, let alone the hospital bills. And what about the funeral expenses? Even if she had a simple service, she would still have to pay for cremation.

She needed to see Jack. Where had they taken him? She imagined his beautiful body lying cold in a morgue somewhere. She would never again feel his muscular arms around her body or his soft lips against hers.

Her eyes were like waterfalls; she couldn't stop crying, and the night nurse had to change her soppy pillowcase three times. Just before daybreak, after giving up on sleep, she dressed in her street clothes and pushed the recliner over to the window to watch the sunrise.

When Elsie entered the room around seven, Julia whispered, "I've decided to leave the baby here."

Elsie set Julia's paper cup of pills on the bed table and crossed the room to her. "I'm not sure I understand what you mean."

"I mean," she said in a louder voice, "I can't take the baby home with me."

"Is that what you think Jack would want?" Elsie said, resting against the windowsill. "For you to abandon his baby at the hospital? To give his son to someone else to raise?"

A sob caught in Julia's throat. "No!" Jack would be ashamed of her for even considering it. "But it's the baby's fault Jack is dead. He picked the worst night to be born. If we hadn't been on the way to the hospital, we wouldn't have gotten hit by a tree and Jack would still be alive." Julia realized she sounded like a raging lunatic, but she didn't care. She felt like a raging lunatic.

Shaking her head, Elsie said, "Julia, that's just crazy talk. That's as ridiculous as me taking the blame for my daughter's husband beating her to death."

Julia gasped. "Your daughter's husband beat her to death?"

A faraway look settled on Elsie's face. "I was supposed to be there that night. She'd invited me over for dinner. But I was too tired from working a double shift to go. If I'd been there, I would've called the police, cracked him over the head with an iron skillet. Something. I would've done something to save her life. The what-ifs will destroy you if you let them, Julia."

Julia, her grief momentarily forgotten, reached for Elsie's hand. "How'd you do it, Elsie? How'd you survive losing your child?"

"Surviving is all I'm doing. I gave up living a long time ago. You're suffering now, but you *will* survive. And you'll live again. Because you have something to live for." She aimed her thumb down the hall. "That sweet baby in the nursery. And he is a sweet one. I've been loving on him every chance I get. There is no greater joy than a mother's love for her child."

Julia swiped at her eyes. "I have little money and no husband. My baby deserves a life better than the one I can give him. There are plenty of fine folks, who have more to offer than I do, waiting to adopt a newborn."

"Life deals us a hand, honey, and it's up to us to decide how we want to play our cards. You can either fold or you can put on your poker face and greet each day as it comes. Don't give up on this baby just yet. You need him as much as he needs you. He will be your salvation." Elsie pushed herself off the windowsill. "At least meet him before you make your decision. Will you let me bring him in?"

Julia hesitated. She'd carried the baby in her womb for nine months, and her body ached to hold him. But she knew that once she saw him, she would never let him go. She was terrified of an uncertain future, but she couldn't let Jack down. She would do as Elsie suggested. She would put on her poker face and greet each day as it came. She sucked in a deep breath. "Yes. Bring him to me, please."

CHAPTER FIVE

Julia fell head over heels in love with her son the minute she laid eyes on him. His resemblance to Jack broke her heart and, at the same time, filled her with warmth. "I'm going to name you after your daddy. You'll be John Eric Martin Jr., but I'm gonna call you Jackson," she said, kissing the downy hair on top of his head. Jack had been adamantly opposed to having a namesake, but Julia thought it would help keep her husband's memory alive.

On the way home from the hospital in Jack's truck, with Sandy at the wheel and Julia in the back seat beside the baby, Julia said, "Good thing Jack put off installing the car seat in my car. It would've been destroyed in the accident."

Sandy looked at Julia through the rearview mirror. "That blasted car seat. I had to take it to the fire station to get them to install it. But I met a sexy fireman while I was there, so all was not lost. He's taking me out for drinks next week."

Julia rolled her eyes. "Only you."

Sandy rarely left Julia's side during those first days home from the hospital. She cooked Julia's meals, made multiple trips to BI-LO for supplies, and slept on her sofa to help with the baby during the night.

She made arrangements with the funeral home to have Jack's body cremated and organized an informal memorial service on Sunday of the following weekend.

The attendees, dressed in casual attire, gathered at dusk on the end of Sandy's dock. The air was still, the tide low, and the no-see-ums swarmed their heads. After reading several passages Jack had marked in his tattered leather Bible, Julia gave his friends and coworkers the opportunity to speak about the man they'd all loved so much. They told anecdotes Julia had never heard about fishing adventures and escapades at the boatyard.

Jack's boss, Rick, was the last to speak. "It's true what they say about the good dying young. Jack Martin was one of the good guys. He was always the first to lend a helping hand or bail out a friend in need." Rick turned to Julia. "We took up a collection for you and the baby." He pressed an envelope in her hand. "If there's ever anything you need, all you have to do is ask."

As twilight turned to night, Julia dumped several handfuls of Jack's ashes into the Wadmalaw River but left most of her husband's remains in the pewter urn. She would return the urn to its position of honor on the top shelf of her bookcase, where it had been since Sandy brought it home from the funeral home. Having the urn nearby comforted her. Aside from their son, the ashes were all she had left of Jack.

When Sandy, who'd been holding the baby during the service, invited everyone up to her house for a cookout, they all processed up the narrow dock in single file, their heads lowered and minds preoccupied with thoughts of Jack.

Duke, five people ahead of Julia, slowed his pace to wait for her. "I want you to take all the time you need, Jules. Your job will be waiting for you whenever you're ready to return."

"That means a lot coming from you, Duke. But if it's all the same to you, I'd like to return sooner than I'd originally planned. I was thinking next week. I could really use the money."

Relief crossed his face. The first two weeks of August were the busiest of the summer, and being short staffed would be a hardship on all of them. "Fine by me, if you want to give it a try. We'll take it one day at a time. If you realize it's too soon, you just let me know, and we'll figure something else out."

She gave him a half hug. "Thank you, Duke. I don't know what I'd do without my friends."

"I ditto what Rick said. If you need anything at all, just ask."

One by one, her friends pulled her aside during the cookout to offer their support. Money was the thing she needed the most, but she couldn't bring herself to ask any of them for a loan. Especially not the guys from the boatyard, after they'd been so generous with their gift. Their money would come in handy in paying the funeral home and the medical deductible for her hospital stay. Her friends were honest, hardworking people who lived paycheck to paycheck. They didn't have spare cash lying around. But now, without Jack's income, she didn't know how she would be able to keep the lights on in their tiny cottage. Because of the exorbitant cost of formula, she was already regretting her choice to bottle-feed the baby.

~

Julia's new reality set in when she returned to Duke's the following week. She moved through her days in an exhausted stupor. Business was booming, and she couldn't complain about the tips, but she was dead on her feet when she got off work most afternoons. Jackson was a good baby, sweet and even tempered, but he was still an infant with constant needs—changing and bathing and feeding. She thought a lot about the things Elsie had said to her in the hospital. *Life deals us a hand, honey, and it's up to us to decide how we want to play our cards.*

Two weeks after Labor Day, Sandy slipped on a wet floor at work and broke both bones in her right forearm. She needed surgery to pin one of the bones to allow for proper healing. Julia took the day off to drive her to Charleston for the procedure.

Sandy sat with Jackson in the back seat of Jack's truck on the way home. "I'm so sorry, Jules," she said, still loopy from the drugs. "I love taking care of this little sweetheart. Maybe after my arm heals . . ."

Julia risked a glance at her in the rearview mirror. "I've taken advantage of you for far too long. It's time for Jackson to go to day care."

She'd done her research before the baby was born. Mimi's Day Care was the only suitable childcare that fit her budget. Mimi had raised eleven children of her own and considered herself an expert at child-rearing. At seventy-two, she was physically fit and had a no-nonsense attitude toward life that Julia admired.

The main living room at the front of Mimi's small ranch house served as the play area, while a bedroom with an assortment of cribs and playpens down the hall offered a quiet place for the young children and babies to nap.

When Julia dropped Jackson off at Mimi's for his first day, she was surprised to see toddlers crawling all over each other on the gray stained rug. "I see you have a full house. I wasn't aware you kept so many children at once."

"Some days we have more than others. I have several other sitters who help out. One of them is due here any minute." Sensing Julia's hesitancy to leave, Mimi took Jackson from her and walked her to the door. "Don't you worry. We'll get along just fine."

Fighting back a flood of guilt and uncertainty, Julia hurried to her car and drove away. She cried all the way to work and called Mimi every chance she got during her shift to check on Jackson.

The arrival of autumn had driven vacationing families back home to school, and with the consequent decrease in tip money, even the cheapest day care on Edisto Island proved to be more than Julia could afford. More than ever, she regretted not finishing college. If only she had a real career. For the first time in her life, Julia experienced real hunger. *You can either fold or you can put on your poker face and greet each day as it comes.* She forced a smile and endured the constant rumbling in her tummy.

"Whoa! Somebody's really hungry today," Cook said when he caught her scarfing down an untouched half of a ham-and-cheese sandwich she'd taken from a customer's plate. It was mid-October, and Julia had dipped below her prepregnancy weight. He gave her the once-over. "You're looking thin, Jules. Are you feeling okay?"

Julia's cheeks burned. "I'm fine. With the baby and all, I've been too busy to eat."

"Uh-huh." His terse reply and skeptical look told Julia he'd seen through her lie.

From that day on, he made certain she ate at least one hot meal for every shift she worked. Sometimes he'd say, "I miscounted and cooked too many omelets," or "The customer asked for medium rare, but I accidentally cooked this burger well done." The excuses he created made it clear that he didn't want to embarrass her.

In addition to the meals she ate at work and the cup of dry cereal she allowed herself for dinner, she managed to survive by bloating her belly with water.

When Thanksgiving rolled around, Julia stole several large potatoes and a slab of butter from Duke's kitchen and made mashed potatoes for Sandy's potluck dinner. Sandy's doctor had removed the cast from her arm the week before Halloween, but Sandy had not offered to help out with Jackson. She'd been spending all her free time with Marty, the sexy fireman who'd helped her with Jackson's car seat, and Julia was happy for her.

Julia bundled her son up against the chilly afternoon and dragged herself next door. Sandy's Thanksgiving dinners were popular affairs. She invited the same group of locals, give or take a few every year, who lacked other family obligations for the holiday. Julia had once looked forward to spending the day preparing and eating a delicious meal with their closest friends. But on this first Thanksgiving without Jack, she was as interested in being with a crowd of people as she was in staying at home alone. If only she could escape the here and now for just one day.

The aromas of cinnamon and rosemary greeted her when she let herself in the front door. She worked her way through the crowded living room to the kitchen, where she found Sandy carving a ham and Marty basting the turkey. Julia stopped in her tracks in the doorway. Roasting the turkey had always been Jack's responsibility.

Sandy took in a quick breath when she saw Julia's haunted expression and hurried over to greet them. "It's weird for me too," she said, kissing Julia's cheek. "We just have to get through the day." She turned to the baby, cooing, "How's my sweet baby boy?"

Jackson smiled and flapped his chubby arms at her.

"I swear he's grown since I saw him on Sunday." She took the car seat from Julia, set it down on the linoleum floor, and lifted the baby out. "Come here, you." She planted her face in the folds of his neck and blew on his skin. He giggled in response.

Julia made herself step across the threshold into the kitchen. *You're being ridiculous, Julia. We can't not have turkey because Jack's gone.* She slid her casserole dish into the oven and took off her coat.

"You need a drink," Marty said and placed a cranberry margarita in her hand.

Julia tasted the margarita. The combination of bitter and sweet puckered her mouth.

"We've got everything covered in here." Sandy dropped the baby in her arms. "Why don't you go in the other room and show off this handsome young man."

With baby on hip and drink in hand, Julia returned to the living room. "Let me see that baby," one of her friends said, snatching Jackson away from her. Julia stood off to the side, sipping her margarita, while the women in the group passed her baby around. The men were oblivious to the baby, their eyes glued to the television as they cheered the Cowboys on. Jack's team. Except for Jack's absence, everything was just as it was every year—same food, football, and friends—yet nothing felt right without him. The margarita hit her empty stomach, making her dizzy, and she thought she might be sick.

She retrieved her son and went back to the kitchen for their things. "I'm sorry, Sandy. I can't be here right now." Flustered, she dumped the baby into the car seat and grabbed her coat.

"Please don't go, Jules," Sandy said, following her out of the house. "I know this is hard, but you really shouldn't be alone today."

"I'll be fine," Julia called to her, and with Jackson bouncing in the car seat, she ran across the yard to the safety of her home.

After feeding Jackson a bottle, she put him down for his nap and spent the remainder of the afternoon curled up on the sofa in a fetal position, staring at the urn of ashes on the bookcase.

Her mind drifted to Thanksgivings past, to the traditional feast her mother always prepared with turkey and stuffing, garlic mashed potatoes, and Julia's personal favorite—tomato pie. She wondered how her parents spent their Thanksgivings now. Did they go to a restaurant, or did her mother still cook? Did her sister still eat with them? Did Alex and Iris sip wine together in the kitchen while they basted the bird?

While holidays with Jack had been happy times, she'd occasionally thought over the years about her family, while trying not to dwell on how much she missed them. She'd made her choice to be with Jack— rather, her parents had made that choice for her. And now, struggling to keep her head above water, she'd never felt so alone. It would be so easy to pick up the phone and call home. But her pride prevented her from doing that.

Hell will have to freeze over before I go crawling home.

CHAPTER SIX

Her husband's presence in their house comforted Julia through the long winter nights that passed at a snail's pace. She imagined Jack at the stove scrambling eggs or browning hamburger meat for chili. His scent on his pillow had grown faint, but she didn't dare wash it. His toiletries occupied the medicine cabinet in the bathroom, and his clothes hung in their closet, but she couldn't bring herself to clear them out.

She talked to Jack constantly. "Bobby and Teresa are having a party tonight. They didn't include me, but I don't blame them. They know I'm busy with the baby." It was the second Friday night in December, and she was stretched out on the floor beside the baby, who lay on his belly on a blanket, gumming a plastic rattle.

"Sandy's the only person I want to see, but she's always with Marty. His pickup truck is perma-parked in front of her house. Duke's Christmas party is next weekend. I haven't decided if I'll go. I can't afford a sitter, and it seems foolish to take Jackson with me. All those people with their germs wanting to touch and hold him." She moved in closer to the baby, stroking his cheek. "You can tell from his chubby little body there's nothing wrong with his appetite. But he picks up every virus that sweeps through day care. I probably shouldn't take him to the doctor every time he gets a sniffle. I certainly can't afford the bills.

"I'm a big fat loser without you, Jack. I can't even take care of our child. I know how to do two things—wait tables and arrange flowers. All those hours I spent in Mama's flower shop were wasted. Edisto doesn't even have a florist, if you can believe that."

Jackson struggled to roll over, and when he finally managed to succeed, Julia sat up cross-legged and cheered.

Jackson flashed her a toothless smile in return.

"Did you see that, Jack? He has the cutest little personality, and I love him so much, more than I ever thought possible. He *is* my salvation, just like that nurse in the hospital said he would be. Look at him, Jack. Isn't he amazing? He has your crystal-blue eyes that light up when I enter the room. Oh, how I wish you were here with us."

Jackson babbled, "Da, da, da."

"Can you hear him, Jack? He misses you too."

On a cold and rainy night in late January, she was awakened by the splatter of water on her face. "Please, no, Jack. Not now. Can't you wave your angel's wand and fix the leak? You patched our roof for years. Why didn't we ever replace it? I know. Don't answer that. There was always something more urgent that needed repairing."

By the end of an exceptionally wet February, buckets and pots and pans covered the floors in the main room. Part of the ceiling collapsed in the nursery and forced her to move Jackson's crib into her bedroom. When her heat pump died during a late-season cold front in mid-March, Julia faced the reality that she would have to sell the house. She hadn't made a mortgage payment since Jack died, and for months she'd been tearing up past-due notices and avoiding urgent phone calls from the bank.

"I can't wait any longer, Jack. It's better to sell now than have the bank foreclose."

She called Angela Brown, the Realtor whose name she saw on the majority of FOR SALE signs around town, and set up an appointment for Monday of the following week.

Julia spent the next five days cleaning up the house as best she could. Praying the dark sky wouldn't break while the Realtor was there, she stored the buckets and pans in the closet right before Angela arrived.

The Realtor's lip curled the second she entered the house. "Do you have a mildew problem?"

"I have a leak in my roof," Julia said, shifting the baby from one hip to the other.

"You'll have to get that fixed. And your walls could use a fresh coat of paint. Buyers in this market aren't looking for fixer-uppers. They want turnkey."

Julia's heart sank. She didn't have the money for repairs.

She followed Angela as she paraded around the house, opening cabinets and testing faucets, and then out onto the dirt patio.

"How much do you have in the place?" she asked and gaped when Julia told her.

"When we bought the house ten years ago, it was listed as water-front," Julia explained.

Angela shielded her eyes against the sun as she looked toward the water. "I practically need binoculars to see the river from here. I'm sorry to say, you'll never get your money back."

Sensing her distress, the Realtor sat down with Julia and explained her options—none of which were viable without the money to make the necessary improvements.

"Think it over and call me in a few days," Angela said when Julia walked her to the door. "I'm happy to help you in any way I can."

As Julia watched the Realtor's Toyota sedan back out of her drive-way, she felt the first jab of real fear. She was going to lose her home. And all her memories of Jack along with it. She closed the door and leaned against it, holding her baby close to her chest. If the bank fore-closed, she'd be homeless, and social services would take her child and put him in foster care. And she couldn't let that happen.

She tossed and turned all night and had worked out a plan by morning. Julia would ask Sandy if she and the baby could live in her spare bedroom for a few months while she saved money to start a new life. As much as she loved Edisto, her house, and its memories of Jack, she needed to move to a bigger town that offered better opportunities. Going back to school was out of the question, but in a foodie town like Charleston, she'd at least be able to get a better waitressing job than the one she had.

Optimistic her luck would soon change, she refused to let the poor conditions at day care dampen her spirits when she dropped Jackson off on her way to work. Business at Duke's had picked up with the arrival of springlike weather. After hustling through the late breakfast crowd, she was delivering burgers to a table of golfers early that afternoon when she glanced up and saw her mother standing just inside the doorway, looking ever so elegant in a wide-brimmed straw hat and formfitting black sundress.

Their eyes met, and Julia mouthed, "Mama."

Longing, mixed with fear and uncertainty, crossed Iris's face.

"Give me a minute," Julia called, but she wasn't sure Iris heard her over the noise in the diner.

She served the lunch baskets as fast as she dared, but by the time she'd finished, her mother had disappeared. She set the tray on the bar and dashed out the front door. Neither Iris nor her car were anywhere in sight.

She spent the rest of her shift confused and perplexed by her mother's visit. She'd never ventured inside Duke's before. She obviously wanted to speak to Julia, but something had changed her mind. Had something spooked her?

Julia left the diner a few minutes early, hoping to catch Sandy before she left for work. Feeling the sun on her face and the cool air on her skin, she picked up her pace on the way to the parking lot. Spring was the season of rebirth, and for the first time since Jack's passing, she felt hope for the future.

She climbed into Jack's truck and fastened her seat belt, but when she turned the key in the ignition, the engine wouldn't start. She pounded the steering wheel. "Dang it, Jack! Of all the days for your engine to give out."

Duke's face appeared at her window. "Sounds like you have a dead battery. I have some cables in the van. I'll give you a jump."

"You're a lifesaver, Duke," she said, popping the hood of her truck. "This is the last thing I need right now. I'm trying to get home in time to talk to Sandy before she leaves for work."

He held up a finger. "I'll be back in a flash."

Less than a minute later, his van pulled up beside her. He got out and attached the jumper cables to both batteries. When she turned the key, it took longer than it should have for her engine to fire.

"You're probably gonna need a new battery soon," Duke said as he disconnected the cables. "Run the engine a good long time if you can."

She thanked him and waved goodbye as she sped out of the parking lot toward day care. She did as Duke suggested and left the engine running while she dashed up to Mimi's front door. Mimi was waiting for her with a screaming Jackson on her hip. Julia took the baby from her. "What on earth happened?" she asked when she saw the goose egg on his forehead.

Mimi's face turned a bright shade of crimson. "One of the older children walloped him with an Etch A Sketch board."

"What was—" Julia started and then stopped herself. She felt her temper rising. "You know what, it doesn't matter. I've had enough of your so-called 'day care.' This place is filthy, and judging from the persistent diaper rash on his bottom, he's not getting the attention he deserves. And no wonder. I've never once seen any of the other sitters you claim work for you. Consider this our last day."

The consequences of her actions set in as Julia stomped off to her car. "I've really done it now, baby boy," she said as she fastened him into his car seat. "How am I supposed to work without someone to take care of you?"

Jackson screamed bloody murder on the short drive home. By the time she stopped alongside the mailbox at the end of the driveway, Julia's nerves were frayed and she was near tears. She opened the box and removed the stack of mail. Fear gripped her chest at the sight of the envelope marked FORECLOSURE NOTICE. She'd been fooling herself to think she could get out of this mess. No home, no day care, a truck that barely ran. Even if Sandy agreed to keep Jackson while she worked, Julia still barely made enough money to feed and clothe her growing boy. She'd been fooling herself to think she'd ever be able to save enough money to start a new life. Jack was her guardian angel, and he'd been sending her signs all day. Only one of them mattered. Her mama.

When she saw Sandy emerging from her house, Julia waved her over.

Sandy eyed the pink envelope in her hand. "What're you gonna do?"

"What I should've done months ago."

Hell has frozen over, Jack. I'm going home.

PART TWO

CHAPTER SEVEN

IRIS

Present Day

Iris felt blue, as she usually did after spending the day on Edisto Island. Not the depths of depression like she'd known before but a melancholic sadness over lost loves and things that might have been.

Across the mahogany dining table, she watched her husband slice his meat so as not to leave a morsel of lamb on the bone. Max controlled every detail of her life in the same precise manner he controlled his fork and steak knife. And she let him. It was easier to obey his wishes than to argue with him. Any trace of joy that had ever existed in their marriage had died when . . .

Stop, Iris! Don't go there tonight. The day has been hard enough as it is.

Iris typically made the trip to Edisto twice a year, once in late summer and once in early spring. She felt an urgent need to set her eyes on her youngest. Although she mostly wanted to make certain Julia was healthy and happy, her visits also served as a reminder whenever her memories faded. Whenever her guilt lessened.

But her trip to Edisto today had been her second in a week. She'd worried all weekend after Friday, when she'd noticed how much weight

Julia had lost and seen the look of sadness on her face. She'd even dared to follow Julia from her cottage to that awful day care. How she longed to hold her grandbaby in her arms. She was determined to talk to her daughter. She'd gotten so close that afternoon, but then she'd run away. What was wrong with her, freaking out like that?

"Do we have any more rolls?" Max asked, interrupting her reverie.

Like a dutiful wife, she went to the kitchen for more bread. Iris worked from sunup to bedtime—in the garden, at the shop, at home. Max insisted they adhere to the same routine in the evenings. National news at six thirty, followed by whiskey and a cigar on the veranda, followed by dinner at seven thirty on the dot. Traditional fare only—meat, potatoes, and a starchy vegetable. But Iris didn't mind so much. The structure was the glue that held her emotions together. Whenever she veered off course, she felt her grip on reality begin to slip.

After filling her basket with warm rolls from the oven, Iris returned to the dining room. As she was passing the nearest of two built-in corner cupboards, she noticed the assortment of contemporary china pieces where her extensive shell collection had once been. Her home was packed with priceless antiques, but her shell collection, her mementos from her day trips to Edisto, was the only thing she valued.

She turned her back on the cupboard and faced the table. "What'd you do with my shells, Alex?"

Her oldest daughter, nearly forty years old and twice divorced, sat to Max's right, cutting her meat into tiny pieces and biting them off her fork with her pointy teeth. Alex had inherited Iris's long limbs and chestnut hair, but she was her father in every other way. A female Max, strong willed and confident and self-absorbed.

"I boxed them up and put them in the attic," Alex said without looking up from her plate.

Iris's heart raced. *Don't say anything. Just get a hold of yourself.*

Iris loved her daughter dearly despite her flaws. She had been difficult as a child and unmanageable as a teenager. Not only had she experimented with alcohol and drugs, she'd made herself available to any boy who expressed interest. She'd been truly happy with her first husband, but that happiness had morphed into anger and bitterness when Phillip had a public affair with his secretary. To get back at Phillip, Alex had fallen for the first man who came along. Eighteen months after she married Tom, she cheated on him with his law partner. As if her ruined love life weren't enough, she'd run her home furnishings boutique into bankruptcy by purchasing extravagant goods too upscale for her small-town clientele.

When she'd moved into their guest cottage six months ago, Max had taken pity on Alex and hired her to redecorate their house.

"I'm giving you carte blanche to work your magic," Max had said one night over dinner during her first week back at home. "The place is a dump. The marble is cracked, and the pipes are rusty in all the bathrooms. Your mother has allowed the house to deteriorate to the point of embarrassment."

Iris had glared at him. "That's not fair, Max. I've been asking you for years to make improvements."

"Now that we have our very own live-in decorator, I can hardly say no. Alex will make all the choices. With my approval, of course."

"What about my approval?" Iris hadn't waited for him to respond. Her approval never mattered to him. "I'm not denying that Alex has great flair, but her style is contemporary. Are you prepared to get rid of all your Oriental rugs?"

"She can do whatever she wants. Brighten up these old rooms. I feel like I'm living in a tomb."

The only brightness in the now-gray rooms were accents of color in pillows, lamps, and artwork. Iris felt like a visitor in her own home. She'd shown her daughter photographs in magazines of fabrics and wallpapers she liked, but Alex had ignored most of her suggestions.

While Iris could live with that, her daughter had overstepped her bounds by removing Iris's shells from the cupboard. Enough was enough. It was time for Alex to vacate their guest cottage and get on with her life.

Iris handed the bread basket to Max and reclaimed her chair at the table. "Did you have any job interviews today, Alex?" she asked in an offhand manner.

Her daughter cut her golden eyes at Iris. "We've talked about this ad nauseam, Mother. There aren't any jobs in this town for a designer of my caliber."

"Maybe it's time to make a change, then," Iris said. "You can't hide out in the guest cottage forever."

Alex dropped her fork to the plate with a clatter. "Where else would I go?"

Iris placed her linen napkin in her lap and smoothed out the wrinkles. "Why not move to Atlanta or New York? Didn't you say the most successful design firms are in the big cities? I'm sure your father would be willing to offer financial support while you look for a job." She cast a nervous glance at her husband.

Max looked first at Iris and then at Alex. "If that's what she really wants."

Alex stared down at her plate. "I couldn't ask you to do that when you've already done so much."

Iris knew her daughter well. The sad voice was intended to evoke pity from her father. After seeing Julia working so hard at the diner, her patience with her spoiled oldest was wearing thin. "Well then, why not see what's available in Charleston? It's close enough for you to drive back and forth while you're interviewing."

"I guess I can do that," she said with a nod and a sniffle.

Max winked at Alex. "Don't rush into anything. I've grown used to having you around." He gulped down the rest of his whiskey and slid his glass toward her. "Now, be a good girl and get your daddy a refill."

When Alex scurried off to the wet bar in the adjacent family room, Iris pushed back from the table. "I'll get dessert."

In the kitchen, she removed the blueberry cobbler she'd made that afternoon from the oven, scooped healthy portions into two blue speckled ceramic bowls, and added a dollop of vanilla ice cream on top. Returning to the dining room, she placed the bowls in front of her husband and daughter and gathered up their dinner plates.

Alex's face registered surprise. "You're not having dessert, Mother?"

"My doctor has me on a low-sugar diet, remember?" Every night Alex asked the same question, and every night Iris gave her the same answer. Iris wondered if her daughter was a poor listener or if she simply didn't care. She suspected the latter.

She left her husband and daughter to carry on their evening rant. They drank scotch and argued political and social issues she cared nothing about. While she boiled water for tea, Iris rinsed the dinner dishes, placed them in the dishwasher, and stored the leftovers in the refrigerator. She prepared the coffee maker for the next morning and assembled the ingredients for the lemon poppy seed muffins she planned to make for breakfast. When her tea was ready, she took it up to the second-floor veranda and made herself comfortable on the hanging bed with her book. She was engrossed in Mary Alice Monroe's recent release an hour later when she heard the screen door bang shut downstairs.

"Night, Mother!" Alex called up to her on her way out to the guesthouse.

Iris abandoned the daybed for the railing. "Night, honey. Sleep tight," she said, watching her daughter until she was safely inside the two-story guest cottage at the rear of their property.

She stood for a few minutes, watching the lights from a sailboat twinkle in the distance and the breeze rustle the Spanish moss dangling from the live oaks in their backyard. How could a home that offered such a peaceful setting be so full of turmoil?

She turned out the light on the veranda and ran into Max in the hallway as he was coming upstairs. "We need to talk about Alex. It's been six months, Max. She needs to move on with her life. Someplace other than Beaufort."

"There's nothing wrong with Beaufort. It's her home." He brushed past her, nearly knocking her off-balance. Her husband was a bowling ball—barely five and a half feet tall and forty pounds overweight. Iris suspected his cholesterol and blood pressure were dangerously high, but he refused to go to the doctor for a physical.

Iris followed him into his bedroom. They hadn't shared a bedroom in decades, and she entered his masculine sanctum only to put away his laundry. "Seriously, Max. Two failed marriages and a ruined business. A fresh start would do her good."

"She can have a fresh start here. I'll give her the money to start her own design firm if that's what she wants." He went into the adjoining bathroom and squirted toothpaste on his toothbrush. "She'll be a success. Good taste comes from good breeding. Thanks to me, Alex has it."

Her eyes met his in the mirror. "And I don't? Is that what you're saying?"

He smirked. "Something like that."

"It always circles back to my upbringing. Why'd you marry me, Max, if you're so ashamed of me?"

"You don't really want me to answer that," he said with a mouthful of toothpaste.

He was right. She didn't want him to answer that. No doubt he had another snide remark at the ready. When was the last time he'd said anything nice to her? "Why can't we just get a divorce and be done with it?"

He gargled with mouthwash, dried his lips with a towel, and turned around to face her. "You know why, Iris. We've been through the reasons a thousand times." He folded the hand towel in half and hung it neatly on the towel bar.

She didn't want to argue—a fight was rare these days as they mostly avoided each other—but on the heels of the emotional day, he was pushing all the wrong buttons. "You're a damn hypocrite, Max Forney. You banished our daughter from our lives for marrying a man you don't approve of. Yet you did the same thing in marrying me. In case you're interested, I went to Edisto today. I saw Julia. And our grandson."

His head shot up. "Why were you on Edisto, Iris? Looking for something you lost?"

CHAPTER EIGHT

December 1976

Iris met Max at Tapp's—the oldest homegrown department store in Columbia, South Carolina—on a Wednesday afternoon a week before Christmas in 1976. She was working the perfume counter, and he, a senior at the University of South Carolina majoring in finance, was purchasing a bottle of White Shoulders for his mother. In the center of the store, a few feet away from the perfume counter, a little boy no more than three years old was throwing a temper tantrum over being made to sit on Santa's lap.

"Something's wrong with this picture, if you ask me," Max said. "Parents teach their children not to talk to strangers, yet they force them to sit on the lap of an odd-looking character dressed in a red suit with a white beard."

The giggle that escaped her mouth sounded foreign to Iris. Flirting didn't come easy for her. "I've never thought about it before, but you're right." She sprayed perfume from the bottle onto her wrist and held it out for him to smell. "This is Tatiana by Diane von Furstenberg. It was all the rage last year and is still going strong this season. Perhaps your mother would like to try something new."

"Nice," he said as he pressed his nose against her wrist. "What else is popular this year?"

She spritzed a number of different fragrances up her arm for him to sample. Each time, his nose lingered longer against her skin, sending tingling sensations across her body. His teeth were too small and his eyebrows too bushy for her to think him handsome, but his blue eyes, as pale as a summer sky, and the dimple in his chin added character to his face.

"Which one will it be?" she asked, running her fingertips across the tops of the bottles lined up on the counter.

"Hmm, I'm not sure." He flashed her a naughty grin. "How about if we try them out again on your other arm?"

She offered him a shy smile. "I'm not sure my boss will approve."

"You're probably right," he said with a disappointed sigh. "I've taken up enough of your time, and I wouldn't want you to get in trouble on my account. I should stick with the White Shoulders, since my mother doesn't like change."

"White Shoulders it is," she said, removing a packaged bottle from the cabinet beneath the display case. "Shall I gift wrap this for you?"

"That'd be great." Max leaned against the counter, with his feet and arms crossed, and chatted her up while she wrapped the gift.

She was conducting the credit card transaction when he said, "Have dinner with me tomorrow night."

It was a statement more than a question, and even though she was wary about having dinner with a virtual stranger, she found his confident yet playful personality irresistible.

She handed him his credit card receipt. "I'm working late. I would have to meet you there."

"Name the time. I know a wonderful little French bistro." Borrowing her pen, he scrawled the address on the back of the receipt and handed it back to her.

"Is eight thirty too late?" she asked, slipping the receipt into her skirt pocket.

"Eight thirty is perfect." Taking her hand in his, he lifted it to his nose and sniffed all the way up her arm one last time. "Until then."

"Until then," she repeated, the words soft on her lips as she watched him exit the department store through the revolving doors.

~

Maison Mabelle was charming and intimate with low lighting, white tablecloths, and a harpist playing soft melodies in the corner.

Iris wore a simple black knit dress that accentuated her slim figure, showed off her long, shapely legs, and brought a smile of approval to Max's lips when she was shown to his table.

He rose to greet her. "You look enchanting."

Iris thought it an old-fashioned thing for a young man of their generation to say, but she blushed at the compliment nonetheless.

She realized during dinner—escargot appetizers and boeuf bourguignon for the main course—that everything about Max was old fashioned, from his gentlemanly manners to his blue blazer, starched white button-down, and creased khaki pants. He smelled of old money, and she decided over crème brûlée that she would follow that scent to a better life.

When she was eight years old, Iris's life had changed in the blink of an eye when her parents were killed in a tragic car accident. Her parents left no will and no life insurance. The judge sent Iris to live with her aunt Ethel, her mother's much-older sister and only surviving relative, in Columbia, South Carolina. Aunt Ethel was also granted control of the money Iris received from the sale of her parents' home in Augusta, most of which was gone within a year.

"If I'd wanted children, I would've gotten married and had my own," Ethel reminded Iris nearly every day.

During the day, Ethel worked as a receptionist in a hair salon. At night, she watched sitcoms, like *M*A*S*H* and *All in the Family*, and drank herself into a stupor on cheap bourbon. A heavy smoker from a very young age, Ethel had developed emphysema, which prevented her from doing most physical activities.

Except for school, Ethel had never allowed Iris to venture far from home. "Your mama left you in my care, and I don't have time to go chasing after you. Lord knows I don't need no trouble." Iris's classmates occasionally invited her over after school, but because her aunt's house reeked of cigarette smoke and cat pee and her bedroom was the size of a large closet, she never invited them back, choosing to be lonely rather than embarrassed.

She'd worked part-time jobs from the time she was old enough to be hired. The jobs allowed her freedom outside of school and home, and Ethel never complained about the extra income. When Ethel finally had to go on round-the-clock oxygen, Iris dropped out of the eleventh grade and went to work full time. Her organizational skills and eagerness to please earned her a quick promotion from sales clerk to manager of the perfume counter, but without a high school diploma, she'd reached her performance peak by the time she turned twenty.

Iris envied Max his education. If only she'd had the chance to go to college. Like most women, she wanted to get married and have children, but her aspirations went beyond that. She wanted to be an entrepreneur, a trendsetter, a woman with the means to stand on her own two feet.

Max left Columbia the day after their dinner date to spend the holidays with his family in Beaufort, but he called her on the phone most nights after she got home from work. She dragged their one phone with its extra-long cord into her tiny room and talked to Max, stretched out on her lumpy mattress, until the early hours of the morning. Iris kept the conversation geared toward his favorite topic—himself. He told her about his life growing up in the Lowcountry—their big house, servants, and boats with multi purposes and sizes. His wealth and privilege terrified her as much as it excited her. The only thing she felt she had to offer a man of his upbringing was her virginity. Sex meant love from her perspective, and love meant commitment. But would it mean the same to Max?

On the Friday night at the end of the first week of January when Max returned to campus, he took her to see the movie *A Star Is Born*. He bought her the soundtrack from the kiosk in the lobby, and she daydreamed all the next day that Max was Kris Kristofferson and she was Barbra Streisand.

They dated several times a week throughout the rest of January. Whenever he offered to pick her up, Iris always had an excuse as to why it would be better to meet him at the restaurant or movie theater or in front of the gym for a basketball game at the university. She became an expert at evading his questions about her personal life. She would eventually have to tell him the truth, but she worried that once he found out about her poor upbringing, he would end their relationship. And she cared about him way too much to let that happen.

When he invited her to his fraternity's formal on Valentine's Day, she bought a red velvet dress, marked down 50 percent due to a tiny tear in the fabric, and asked him to pick her up in front of Tapp's after work.

"You're the prettiest girl here," he whispered in her ear as they entered the party.

She'd never been to a fraternity party, and she felt out of place among the sorority girls who were already drunk and making fools of themselves by dancing provocatively on stage with the band.

Struggling to mask her discomfort, she was relieved when Max said, "This is a drag. Why don't we go back to my place? We can watch a movie and drink some wine." He wrapped his arm around her waist and drew her near. "My roommate's gone to Chapel Hill to see his girlfriend, and I have the apartment all to myself."

Sex had been at the forefront of Max's mind for weeks, and she knew she wouldn't be able to hold him off much longer. Knowing her virginity was at stake unnerved her.

Iris kissed the dimple in his chin. "Can we get something to eat first? I'm starving."

He appeared dejected and hopeful at the same time. "Why don't we just eat here." His eyes traveled the room before landing on a food table littered with empty pizza boxes. "On second thought, there's a new little seafood joint in Five Points called the Half Shell. I heard the oysters are decent."

"Sounds perfect." She'd never eaten raw oysters before and the thought made her nauseated, but at least it would buy her some time.

Her first experience turned out to be unforgettable. Within minutes of eating her first slippery oyster, she became violently ill. Max drove her home, stopping three times along the way so she could vomit on the side of the road.

"Who lives here?" he asked, both bewilderment and disgust on his face when he pulled up in front of Ethel's cinder block house on Park Street.

Iris knew she was busted. "This is where I live, Max, with my aunt Ethel. My parents died when I was a child. My life couldn't possibly be any more different than yours." She clambered out of his Wagoneer, leaving him speechless, and hurried into the house to the bathroom, where she hugged the toilet for the rest of the night.

Iris managed to pull herself together enough to show up for work the following morning. She'd just finished up with a customer when Max called her late that afternoon. "We need to talk. What time do you get off?"

She glanced at the wall clock. "In an hour. Can't it wait until tomorrow?" she asked, hoping to postpone the inevitable breakup.

"Meet me at Bagels and Brew on Harden," he said, and hung up.

She stared at the receiver in her hand. *That's it? You're not even going to ask how I feel?*

She was tempted not to show up, but at the last minute she decided to go. If there was any chance of salvaging their relationship, she had to at least try.

"You owe me an explanation," he said when she sat down at his table for two by the window. "And an apology for keeping the truth from me."

She cocked a neatly plucked eyebrow. "Seriously, Max? If I'd told you the truth, you wouldn't have given me a second glance."

He was silent for an excruciatingly long few minutes while he sipped his coffee. "I have to admit, you had me fooled. You seem so educated, and you carry yourself with such grace. I assumed your family had money."

She stared down at her hands, clasped tightly in her lap. "I don't even have a high school diploma. I had to drop out of the eleventh grade to take care of my aunt, who has emphysema. I learned how to carry myself from studying Audrey Hepburn in *My Fair Lady*, which I've watched about a hundred times." Raising her chin, she looked him in the eye. "I'm sorry I misled you. I like being with you more than any man I've ever met. I thought that maybe . . ." She swallowed past the lump in her throat. "I realize now how foolish I've been." She got to her feet. "Goodbye, Max." She ran a finger down his cheek before hurrying out of the restaurant. He made no attempt to stop her.

The next evening when she got off work, she was shocked to find him standing in front of Tapp's revolving door with a bouquet of exotic orchids in hand.

"I care about you, Iris. As long as you promise there will be no more secrets between us, I'd like to try to make our relationship work."

CHAPTER NINE

Once Iris's past was out in the open, she shared her innermost thoughts with Max and they grew closer. Although he didn't like it, he respected her when she confessed she was a virgin and wanted her first time to be special. Around the first of April, Max seemed distracted, and Iris sensed he was working up the nerve to ask her something important.

They were leaving the stadium after a Gamecock baseball game the Wednesday night before Easter, when he blurted, "I know this is last minute, but will you go with me to Beaufort to have Easter brunch with my parents on Sunday?"

The thought of meeting his parents terrified her, but she couldn't very well decline his invitation when he was making such an important step.

"Of course! I'd love to meet your parents."

Iris was a nervous wreck by the time Sunday morning rolled around. Determined to make a good impression, she'd used her employee discount to buy a conservative dress in pale-lavender linen from the women's departments and a box of Godiva chocolates for Max's parents.

Max spent much of the two-hour drive to Beaufort assuring her that his folks were harmless. "Once they get to know you, they'll love you." He almost had her convinced by the time they arrived.

They pulled into the brick driveway of a stately home with extensive grounds overlooking the Beaufort River. "This is where you grew up?"

He put the car in gear and turned off the engine. "Home sweet home. Welcome to Live Oaks."

She blinked hard, not trusting her bedazzled eyesight. "I was expecting a big house, not a plantation with its own name."

Max chuckled. "It's not a plantation, Iris." He glanced at the clock on the dash. "We have a few minutes before my parents get home from church. Let's walk down to the river."

Iris stared up at the massive columns and double-decker porches as they walked around the side of the house. "What style architecture would you call this?"

"Greek Revival. My ancestors built it in the mid–eighteen hundreds."

They continued around to the water side of the house where a sweeping lawn, flanked by manicured gardens, led down to the Beaufort River. Iris fell instantly in love with the breathtaking scenery—boats, their sails flapping in the wind, gliding gracefully across the open water, and oak trees with branches hung low and wide. By the time they started back up to the house, his parents had arrived and were headed down the brick sidewalk to greet them.

On the outside, Max's mother was exactly what Iris had envisioned—dowdy in a green brocade suit and matching pillbox hat. But when Iris presented the box of chocolates and Mrs. Forney accepted it with her kid-gloved hand without so much as a thank-you, Iris knew this woman was not the modern-day version of June Cleaver she'd anticipated.

Edgar Forney, Max's father, greeted Iris with a warm embrace. He smelled of lime aftershave and sunshine, and his love of the outdoors was evident by the golden tan on his long, graceful limbs.

Mrs. Forney motioned for Iris to enter the house ahead of her. "I admit I was surprised when Max called to say he was bringing a friend for brunch. I didn't realize he'd been seeing anyone."

Iris hesitated. *What does that mean?* "Do you know all these people?" she asked of the oil portraits lining the wide center hallway.

Mrs. Forney arched an eyebrow. "Of course, dear. Why would we have portraits of people we don't know hanging in our home?"

"Well then!" Mr. Forney exclaimed with a clap of his hands. "What're we waiting for? It's Easter. Let's get a drink and celebrate the day."

Iris and Max trailed his parents down the hall, through a comfortable-looking sitting room, to the covered porch they referred to as the veranda. Two uniformed servers—a male and a female of indiscriminate ages—appeared with silver trays bearing tall glasses of Bloody Marys and raw oysters on the half shell. Iris accepted a Bloody Mary but passed on the oysters, having no interest in ever trying them again.

As she stood at the porch railing, sipping her drink, she spotted a tiny two-story cottage with dormer windows tucked away behind the shrubbery. She hadn't noticed it on their walk down to the water. "Who lives in that cute little house?" she asked Mrs. Forney beside her.

"That cute little house is a guest cottage," she said in a haughty tone. "Guests stay there when they come to visit."

"Oh." Iris let out an awkward giggle. "That makes sense."

Mrs. Forney angled her body toward Iris. "And who are your people, dear?"

Iris gulped. "My people?"

"Yes, dear, your family. I don't know any Johnsons from Columbia."

Mrs. Forney's point was clear. She didn't know any Johnsons from Columbia because there weren't any Johnsons she deemed worth knowing. Iris didn't stand a chance against a shrewd woman like Max's mother. She decided it was best to be herself and hope that, over time, she could win her over.

"I don't have any people, Mrs. Forney. Only a person—my aunt Ethel, who raised me after my parents were killed in a car accident when I was eight."

"How tragic," Mrs. Forney said, and lifted her glass to her lips.

They finished their Bloody Marys in silence. When the male server announced that brunch was ready, Max and his father followed him inside, but Mrs. Forney held Iris back. "If I may have a word with you, dear."

"Of course," Iris said, stepping back onto the veranda.

"My son has a passion for projects. You're not his first. As a boy, he was always building forts and restoring old boats. And I dare say you won't be his last. He'll eventually get this"—she flicked her wrist in the air—"whatever it is going on between you, out of his system. He has certain obligations to his family. One of them is to marry someone of means."

Mrs. Forney turned and left Iris standing on the veranda alone, biting back tears. Her instinct to flee was squashed by the realization she had no means of getting away. She inhaled a deep breath and followed the others inside.

Max was waiting for her in the doorway to the dining room. "There you are. I was wondering where you'd gone."

Iris smiled sweetly. "Your mother and I were getting better acquainted."

"Good! I'm glad to hear it." He showed Iris to her seat.

A sea of brown wood separated Iris and Max from his parents across the table. Built-in cupboards occupied two corners, wallpaper with birds and trees and butterflies adorned the walls, and an enormous crystal chandelier hung above a silver bowl of white flowers in the center of the table.

"What kind of flowers are these?" Iris asked. "They smell so sweet."

"They're lilies," Mrs. Forney said. "Easter lilies."

Max leaned toward her, his forearm touching hers. "Mother's something of a whiz with flowers."

"I can see that," Iris said, removing the linen napkin from her plate and draping it across her lap. She stared down at the place setting in front of her. Three crystal goblets stood next to a dinner plate rimmed with a band of cobalt and gold surrounded by ornate silver flatware—three forks, two spoons, and two knives—on top of an intricate lace place mat. Aunt Ethel's collection of dinnerware and eating utensils consisted of three sets of bent and mismatched silverware, four plastic plates, and two ceramic cereal bowls.

A third server appeared with the first course, a salad of romaine lettuce and sugar snap peas. Iris lifted the small fork closest to her plate, praying it was the right one.

Mrs. Forney cleared her throat, and Max rammed his elbow in her side. "We haven't said the blessing yet."

"Oops. Sorry," she said, and set the fork back down.

After Mr. Forney offered the blessing, Iris waited for Mrs. Forney to take her first bite before once again lifting her fork. Iris felt the woman's scrutinizing gaze on her as she took tiny bites of her salad, gulping her food down past the lump that had settled in her throat. During the next two courses—cold potato soup they called *vichie*-something, followed by crab quiche and buttery ham biscuits—Mrs. Forney quizzed her son about his upcoming job interviews and graduation festivities. As the others were finishing their strawberry shortcake, Iris, desperate for escape, excused herself to the restroom. After conducting her business in the tiny powder room across the hall, she spent a few minutes roaming around the downstairs, admiring the twelve-foot ceilings, heavy wainscoting, and vast rooms. She was in the hallway, returning to the dining room, when she heard Max say, "But I care about her, Mother. You don't have any say in who I marry."

Iris's ears perked up. He'd never mentioned marriage before.

"Yes, we do, son," Mr. Forney said. "As your parents, it's our duty to make certain you find a suitable wife."

Traitor, Iris thought. Max's father had been so nice to her earlier.

"She has no upbringing," Mrs. Forney said. "That much is obvious in her lack of table manners. She's not for you, son. Be patient. You'll find the right girl."

"But Iris *is* the right girl," Max argued.

"You stand to inherit considerable wealth. If you want to throw that away—"

Mrs. Forney stopped in midsentence when Iris entered the room, and Max's face turned the same dark shade of red as the sugared strawberries on his plate. When the servers cleared the table and offered coffee, Max made an excuse about needing to get back to campus to study for exams.

Little conversation was exchanged during the drive back to Columbia, and when they neared her street, Iris said, "You can drop me off here." Aunt Ethel's cinder block house would serve as a reminder to Max of his argument with his mother. Iris would never be good enough for her son.

"If you're sure." He pulled over to the curb and parked. "Iris, I . . . ," he started, but his voice trailed off.

A sense of dread settled over her. "You what, Max?"

He stared at his hands on the steering wheel. "I'm going to be busy the next few weeks with job interviews and exams."

"Why don't you just admit the truth? Your parents don't think I'm good enough for you."

"It's complicated," he said, refusing to meet her eyes.

"It's less complicated than you think." She got out of the Wagoneer and slammed the door behind her.

She never expected to see him again but was heartbroken when days and then weeks passed without a word from him. She couldn't sleep, didn't want to eat, and cried over the smallest things. As April drew on, she picked up extra work shifts in the evenings to occupy her lonely hours. The first Monday in May passed with no tears. And then Tuesday, followed by Wednesday. She was beginning to think she might survive, and then he showed up on Aunt Ethel's doorstep one exceptionally hot Saturday afternoon in mid-May, still dressed in his black cap and gown from graduation.

"Pack your bags! We're getting married." He dropped to his knees and presented her with a black velvet ring box. "I can't live without you, Iris Johnson. I have a college degree, and I've been offered an excellent job with a bank in Beaufort. We can make this marriage work. That is, if you'll have me." He squeezed her fingers around the ring box. "Go ahead. Open it."

She peeked inside the ring box at the small diamond.

"It's not much now, but after I make my first million, I'll buy you the biggest diamond I can find." He took the ring out of the box and slid it onto her finger.

She lifted her hand, admiring the way the diamond sparkled in the sunlight. "But what about your parents?"

"They'll come around eventually."

CHAPTER TEN

Aunt Ethel was none too happy to see Iris go, more perhaps because of the loss of income than companionship. To put her aunt at ease, Iris promised to send spending money as soon as she got some extra cash. She assumed she'd get a job in Beaufort to help pay for household expenses.

After packing her meager belongings and the contents of his apartment in the back of the Wagoneer, Max and Iris drove to Asheville, North Carolina, where they were married by the justice of the peace and spent their wedding night at the Grove Park Inn. After months of anticipation, the loss of her virginity was a disappointment—a fumbled and short-lived coupling that left Iris neither satisfied nor eager for more.

"You'll get better with time," Max said offhandedly.

I'm the newbie, Iris thought. *Shouldn't you be the teacher?*

After a hearty breakfast in the hotel's dining room the next morning, they made the four-and-a-half-hour drive to Beaufort. Max grew more reserved with each passing mile, and Iris suspected he dreaded breaking the news of their elopement to his parents.

"They're home," Max said as he parked behind a station wagon and a sedan in the driveway. "You should probably wait here."

He entered the house through the side door but was back before Iris could freshen up her makeup. He opened the door on her side of the car.

"That was fast," she said. "What happened?"

"They're mad as hell, of course. They need a little time to cool down. We're to stay in the guest cottage until they do." He pulled her out of the car and into his arms, spinning her around in circles.

"Wait! Stop!" She smacked him on the back. "I don't understand why you're so happy when your parents are so angry."

"Because I was expecting them to disown me," he said, waltzing her around the driveway.

She tilted her head back and laughed. "Well then, by all means, let's celebrate the victory."

They spent the rest of the afternoon moving into the guest cottage and shopping for groceries at the Piggly Wiggly. Several times during her many trips to the car, Iris spotted Mrs. Forney watching her from the second-floor veranda. When she risked a smile and a wave, Mrs. Forney returned her greeting with a steely glare.

The guest cottage offered a small sitting room and kitchen downstairs with a master bedroom and bath on the second floor. Dormer windows overlooking the Beaufort River in the bedroom and french doors leading onto a brick terrace made the interior seem more spacious. Iris felt like royalty residing in a palace after living in Ethel's cinder block shack for fifteen years.

Tired from unpacking, Max and Iris stretched out on chaise longues on the terrace, sipping chardonnay and nibbling on brie while watching the orange ball of the sun sink below the river's horizon. The wine did little to take away their inhibitions, and their second attempt at lovemaking proved more awkward than before. After Max fell asleep, Iris tiptoed down to the kitchen to get the *Cosmopolitan* magazine she'd picked up at the Piggly Wiggly and hidden in the pantry. Curled up on the sofa in the sitting room, she skimmed articles about how to cope with men's worst sexual fears and why men are terrified of intimacy.

Iris fell asleep on the sofa and was startled awake early on Monday morning by a loud knocking on the french doors. Wrapping her robe around her, she opened the door to a thin woman with caramel skin and a cropped head of gray hair carrying a breakfast tray.

"You must be Max's new missus. I'm Estelle. I've been with the Forney family since before Max was born." The housekeeper eyed Iris from the top of her dark bedhead to her bare feet. "You sure are a pretty thing."

"I must look a sight." Iris giggled and raked her fingers through her hair. "I'm Iris, and it's very nice to meet you. Please come in." She opened the door wider.

"Is that you, Estelle?" Max came bounding down the stairs and greeted her with a sloppy kiss on the cheek. "God, it's good to see you. You're looking as pretty as ever." He took her tray and carried it to the small table in the corner. He lifted the lid on one of the plates. "Check this out, Iris. We have eggs Benedict, bacon, and freshly squeezed orange juice. I don't know about you, but I'm ravenous."

The smell of bacon wafted toward Iris, making her stomach growl. She turned to Estelle. "Thank you so much for the breakfast. We're still getting settled. I haven't even checked to see if we have a pan to scramble eggs."

"The kitchen should have everything you need," Estelle said.

"I'm glad someone's happy to see us," Max said as he shoveled food into his mouth. "Mom and Dad are mad as fire at me."

Estelle planted a fist on her bony hip. "You know your mama don't agree with nothing that ain't her idea. And your daddy always does what she tells him to do. Just try to be patient. In the meantime, if you need anything, you ask old Estelle."

Iris cast an uncertain glance at Max and lowered her voice so he couldn't hear her. "If there's anything you think I should know, Estelle, please feel free to tell me. I'm a little out of my element here."

"Don't you worry none. You're a sweet girl. You'll do just fine. I'll leave you to your breakfast now."

Iris closed the door behind Estelle and joined Max at the table. "She seems nice."

"She's the best. She'll be a good ally for you," Max said without looking up from his plate.

Iris removed the linen napkin from the tray and placed it in her lap. "Ally? That makes it sound like we're at war."

"We're at war, all right. I guaran-damn-tee it. Question is, how many battles do we have to fight with Mother before she surrenders?"

Iris took a tiny bite of eggs Benedict. "Your family is complicated, Max."

"You're part of that family now, honey," Max said, slurping down half a glass of juice. "Watch and learn. The sooner you understand my mother's strategies, the better off you'll be."

After breakfast, Iris dressed in bermuda shorts and a T-shirt, returned the tray of clean dishes to Estelle, and went for a stroll through the neighborhood. She admired the wide, columned porches and the branches of moss-draped trees meandering across the roads. Everyone she passed greeted her with a smile—young mothers pushing baby strollers and elderly distinguished-looking couples navigating the sidewalks with canes.

Invigorated by the cool morning air, Iris ventured farther along Bay Street to the downtown area. The disco craze had taken the country by storm, with kids of Iris's generation dressing in platform shoes and synthetic glittery fabrics. But in Beaufort, men wore khaki pants, blue blazers, and penny loafers, while the women donned sensible dresses that covered their knees.

Nearly two hours later, Iris returned to an empty cottage. She dropped to the chaise longue on the terrace to wait for Max. She'd been dozing in the sun only a few minutes when she heard loud arguing coming from inside the house—Max's angry voice matched by his mother's indignant tone.

Iris went inside the cottage and closed the door to block out the sound. She was spreading Duke's mayonnaise on bread for ham sandwiches when Max came sauntering in. He planted little kisses on her neck from behind. "I declare the first battle a victory."

"Congratulations," she said, turning her head to meet his lips. "How many battles do you think it'll take?"

"Another seven. Maybe ten. In two weeks' time, I'll have her eating out of my hand."

Two weeks seemed like an eternity to Iris, and she panicked when Max left her alone to start his new job the following Monday. He'd argued with his mother every single day, and there was still no sign of a reconciliation. *Is it even possible?* she wondered.

"What if she comes after me while you're gone?" Iris asked Max when she walked him to the driveway that morning.

"Come after you?" He chuckled. "My mother's not going to beat you up, Iris." He got in his Wagoneer, started the engine, and rolled down the window. "Keep yourself busy. Do whatever it is housewives do."

"That's just it. I don't know what housewives are supposed to do."

"You'll figure it out. Play bridge or tennis or have lunch with a friend."

"I don't know how to play bridge or tennis. Maybe I should get a part-time job."

"Why bother? You'll be busy raising our children soon enough. In the meantime, I'm sure you can find something to occupy your time," he said, blowing her a kiss as he backed out of the driveway.

Busy raising our children? Am I even ready for that kind of commitment? She and Max had never discussed the timing, but she'd assumed they would wait a few years. Until then she wanted to use her time constructively, maybe take classes at the local community college. If there even was a community college in Beaufort. But what would she study? Iris decided to discuss it with Max over dinner. Her bigger concern was how to get through this first day on her own.

She considered going to the kitchen in the main house to visit Estelle. The housekeeper had brought them treats every day—a pan of warm corn bread, a plate of sliced ripe tomatoes, a platter of fried flounder. She'd also dropped helpful hints about Mrs. Forney's high expectations and finicky ways. At the risk of running into her mother-in-law, Iris decided instead to return to the guest cottage for more coffee.

She took her refill out to the garden and spent most of the morning wandering the gravel paths and admiring the manicured beds of shrubs and flowers. The fragrance and velvety petals of the blooms boosted her spirits, and she decided to try her hand at gardening. After all, wasn't gardening one of those things housewives did?

She discovered three cast-off terra-cotta containers in the potting shed behind the detached garage and dragged them over to her terrace, positioning the two larger ones on either side of the french doors and the smaller one between the two chaise longues. She grabbed her purse and set out on foot to buy plants at the local hardware store she'd passed a dozen times on her walks. She selected six different varieties in the store's outdoor lawn-and-garden section for her containers and began her trek home. Balancing the cardboard tray of plants in one hand and tucking the small bag of potting soil under the other arm, she admired the hanging ferns and containers spilling over with blooms on the porches of the houses she passed.

Iris felt discouraged when her bag of potting soil filled only the smallest of her containers and the plant she'd chosen looked lost, a lone pink flower surrounded by a wasteland of dirt. She sprinkled water on the plant and sat back on her haunches.

Iris raised her gaze when a shadow crossed the terrace in front of her, and she was surprised to see her mother-in-law looming over her.

"I see you helped yourself to my pots." She touched the terra-cotta planter with the toe of her black rubber-soled lace-up shoe.

Iris clambered to her feet. "I'm sorry, Mrs. Forney. I found them behind the shed. I just assumed you weren't using them."

"Even so, next time ask before you help yourself." She eyed her container. "So, you like gardening, do you?"

"Yes! I mean, I guess. I don't know much about it."

"That much is obvious. Snapdragons won't last in the summer heat. They like cooler weather." She plucked the snapdragon out of the dirt and knelt down to inspect Iris's other plants. "Now, petunias are a good choice for summer." She dropped the purple creeping flower into the hole and tamped the dirt down around the plant's base. "It'll get plenty of sun here. If you water it every day, it will spill over the sides of your pot in no time." Mrs. Forney removed the yellow plant from the cardboard tray. "Lantana do nicely in the heat as well." She looked around the terrace. "Where's your potting soil?"

"I ran out." Iris held up the empty bag.

Mrs. Forney's dark eyes grew large. "You bought that little bag of dirt for all three planters?"

Iris gave a sheepish shrug.

"You have a lot to learn, my dear." Mrs. Forney's lips parted in a smile that transformed her face from an old grump's to an attractive matron's. "Every southern woman should know how to grow and arrange flowers. I'd be happy to teach you, if you're interested."

"Yes, ma'am. I'm eager to learn."

Mrs. Forney gave an abrupt nod. "In that case, let's start with lesson number one. Fill the bottom half of your container with something other than dirt. Not only does it save on cost, it also helps with drainage and makes the container lighter and easier to move around."

Iris stared down at the large containers. "What kind of something?"

"Anything, really. Styrofoam packing peanuts or plastic milk jugs. I use crumpled-up Coca-Cola cans myself. Let me show you." Mrs. Forney led the way to the garden shed, where she pulled on gloves to protect her manicured nails and slipped an apron over her head to protect her white slacks and plaid blouse. She contributed some leftover annuals from her own spring planting, and the two worked together for the rest of the morning.

"All done," Mrs. Forney said, rubbing her gloved hands together to rid them of loose dirt. "All you have to do is water them daily. Morning is best." She wiped the perspiration from her forehead with the back of her arm. "I'm parched. Why don't we go inside for some of Estelle's sweet peach tea?"

"I've been wondering," Iris said as they walked side by side. "How does Estelle make her tea? She won't tell me."

Mrs. Forney laughed for the first time since they'd met. "That's because Estelle's sweet peach tea is the best-kept secret in the South."

When Iris and Mrs. Forney entered the kitchen together, a satisfied smile appeared on Estelle's lips.

"What're you making?" Iris asked, peering over Estelle's shoulder at the yellow batter in the KitchenAid mixer.

"Lemon angel food cake." Estelle gave them the once-over, her eyes lingering on Iris's dirt-smeared clothes. "Looks like y'all need some tea." She grabbed a pitcher from the refrigerator, filled two glasses, and shooed them out to the veranda.

"Sit down, Iris." Mrs. Forney gestured toward a rocker. "It's time we had a little chat."

Iris lowered herself to the rocking chair, and Mrs. Forney sat down next to her.

"I'd like to plan a party to announce your nuptials. I prefer to wait, however, until you've been married for a few months. We'll find you a pretty dress that shows off your slim figure. I can't have my friends thinking my son was forced into marrying you. Max has assured me that you're not, but I feel inclined to ask you myself. Are you pregnant?"

Iris giggled despite herself. "No, ma'am. I'm definitely not pregnant."

"Good. Then we'll plan the party for September. That'll give me plenty of time to teach you proper manners. I'd like to save you from embarrassing yourself. And us."

Does that mean the battles are over? Iris smiled. "I would appreciate that, Mrs. Forney."

CHAPTER ELEVEN

A relationship based on mutual respect developed between Iris and her mother-in-law during that first sultry summer. Iris admired Mrs. Forney's many talents, while at the same time Iris's eagerness to please impressed her mother-in-law. She taught Iris dinner etiquette—how to set a table, how to dress, how to handle correspondence, how to create elaborate flower arrangements. She enlisted Estelle to show Iris how to iron linens, polish silver, and stuff and roast a Thanksgiving turkey. "These are things every young bride needs to know how to do—even though you'll have help of your own one day."

Iris was grateful to fill the long, lonely hours of the day and evening. Max, eager to make a good impression on his new employers, worked late most evenings. Arriving home around seven, he decompressed alone with a Dewar's on the rocks before sitting down for the dinner Iris had prepared. He approached sex in much the same manner he gobbled down his food. He wanted instant satisfaction. Enjoyment was never a consideration for either of them.

It didn't help that all summer long, he'd spent his free time on the weekends either sailing or fishing or playing golf with his bachelor friends, who would come home drunk with him from the golf course. They were loud and obnoxious and spoke crudely in front of her.

"You guys need to find girlfriends so I'll have someone to talk to," she'd said in a teasing voice one night, even though she was dead serious.

"Come on, Iris, lighten up," Max said, giving her a playful shove. "We're just having a little fun."

That playful shove had been the source of Max and Iris's first argument.

"Do you have to play golf again today?" Iris asked on Saturday morning of Labor Day weekend.

"We have three whole days together," Max said, pouring the remains of his coffee down the drain. "We'll do something special on Monday, just you and me."

But when Monday rolled around, he left early and spent all day sailing with his father. The following Saturday, he headed to the golf course for an early tee time. Iris didn't mind on that particular Saturday because she needed to prepare for the party the Forneys were giving in their honor that night. When Max came home late that afternoon smelling like a brewery and slurring his words, she ordered him to shower and dress and then sent him over to the main house for his parents to deal with.

She took her time getting ready, wanting to look just right for the new friends she hoped to make. Before heading over to the party, she looked in the mirror and smiled, barely recognizing herself in a plum-colored tea-length dress with her dark hair styled in a soft chignon. She waved at Estelle, who was busy supervising the caterers, as she passed through the kitchen. Large arrangements of fall flowers adorned the dining room table, the huntboard in the hallway, and the mantels in the drawing and family rooms—every surface gleaming. Servers in black pants and crisp white shirts waited in the hallway with trays of hors d'oeuvres for the first guests to arrive. A small bar had been set up in the drawing room at the front of the house with the main bar out back on the veranda.

Her father-in-law whistled the moment he saw her. "You look stunning, my dear," he said, giving her a peck on the cheek.

While her father-in-law insisted Iris call him Edgar, Max's mother had not followed her husband's lead. Everyone called Anna *Mrs. Forney*. Even her own husband on occasion.

Max sat slumped over on the sofa with a mug of black coffee. Iris suspected his parents had given him the firm lecture he deserved.

Tonight's your night, Iris. Don't let him get to you.

When the first guests began to arrive, the four Forneys moved to the front of the hall to receive them. Iris had never seen the guest list, but Mrs. Forney had assured her that young people from the most respectable families had been invited. Much to Iris's dismay, only a small fraction of them showed up. The few who did welcomed Iris to town and exchanged a few minutes of polite conversation, but no one invited her to have lunch or join their social groups.

Iris deemed the party a failure and was distraught when her mother-in-law insisted she accompany her to her garden club meeting the Tuesday morning after the party. She wanted to meet young people, not more old ladies. Mrs. Forney was making a big to-do about Iris's first meeting, which in turn made Iris a nervous wreck. When she showed up at the kitchen door in navy slacks and a cream-colored sweater set, Mrs. Forney frowned.

"That won't do at all, Iris. First impressions are the most important impressions. Go put on your best church dress and a pair of low heels."

The meeting was being held a few blocks away at a member's home. When they entered the house, one of Mrs. Forney's friends yoo-hooed them over to the empty seats next to her. Iris sat next to the woman's daughter, a pretty girl about her age with auburn hair, creamy skin, and clear green eyes.

The girl leaned in close to Iris. "I'm sorry we missed your party on Saturday. My husband and I are die-hard Georgia Bulldogs fans, and we went to Athens for the first football game of the season. Anyway, I've been dying to meet you. We're destined to be best friends."

Iris felt a flutter in her chest. "I don't understand. I'm all for being friends, but—"

"Because my name is Lily. Lily Matheson."

A wide smile spread across her face. "Iris and Lily. I love it. How appropriate we're meeting for the first time at a garden club."

Lily let out a honking laugh that Iris found charming on a girl with such classic good looks. "See, I told you we would be best friends."

"This is my first meeting," Iris said.

"Mine too," Lily said with an upturned lip. "I'm a newlywed from Atlanta. Bernadette, my mother-in-law, says this is the best way for me to make new friends. But aside from you and me, everyone else appears to be over fifty."

As if to prove her point, the president, Gretchen Baldwin, an attractive blonde who was well into her sixties, called the meeting to order. The program dragged on with endless announcements about upcoming events and a presentation about best practices for presenting specimens at horticultural exhibits. In closing, Gretchen introduced Lily and Iris as the club's two newest members and asked to speak with them after the meeting.

"I'll see you at home," Iris said to her mother-in-law.

Gretchen pulled the girls aside. "Every year, our new members arrange the greens workshop for our December meeting. You'll find everything you need to know in here." She thrust a black binder at Lily. "Lucy Benson hosts the event in her garage. You'll find her contact information in there"—she pointed at the binder—"along with a list of members willing to donate boxwood. Of course, we'll need other greens like pine, magnolia, yew, and holly. Make sure you cut plenty and condition them well."

"Yes, ma'am," Lily and Iris said in unison.

Tucking the notebook under her arm, Lily took Iris by the hand and maneuvered them out the front door. "I was starting to feel claustrophobic in there," Lily said, fanning herself with the notebook as they strolled side by side down the sidewalk.

"Yeah, me too." Iris stuffed her finger in her ear. "I was going deaf from listening to all those women cackling like hens. But the greens workshop sounds like a fun event to plan."

Lily rolled her eyes. "What it sounds like is a drag. Do you have any idea how much boxwood it takes to make one wreath?"

Iris's face fell. "Oh."

"Don't worry. My in-laws have a hunting farm about thirty miles outside of town. We can get all the greens we need from there." When they reached the end of the sidewalk, Lily looped her arm through Iris's, and they headed toward downtown. "I'm starving. Let's go get lunch. I'm going to take you to the best restaurant in town."

Iris didn't have enough money in her wallet for a fancy restaurant and was relieved when Lily turned down a side street to a hot dog stand. Iris laughed. Her new friend was full of surprises.

"Trust me. I grew up in Atlanta. I'm a restaurant connoisseur. I've tried every place that serves food in this town, and Pappy's is hands down the best."

They ordered chili dogs and lemonade and walked to the waterfront.

"I love a good scandal. I'm dying to know why you and Max eloped." Lily's green eyes were bright over her hot dog as she prepared to take a bite.

Iris had managed to elude such questions at the party by pretending she didn't hear them and quickly changing the subject. But she sensed her astute new friend would know if she lied. "The Forneys were against our marriage at first, because . . . well, because I don't come from a wealthy family."

Disappointment crossed Lily's face. "I figured something like that. A lot of people in town thought you might be pregnant. Obviously, you're not—unless you had a miscarriage. Did you have a miscarriage?"

Iris smiled. "No, nothing like that. I don't think my husband would approve of me talking about this."

Lily's free hand went up. "Don't worry. I won't say a word."

"Do you have any skeletons in your closet?" Iris asked with a nervous giggle. "If we're going to be best friends, I should probably know."

"Sorry to say, I'm an open book. I already told you I'm from Atlanta. The only girl with three older brothers. I went to UGA. Married the love of my life. And here I am eating hot dogs with my new best friend. I assume we're about the same age. I'm twenty-three."

"Me too. Wouldn't it be crazy if we had the same birthdays? Mine's in April—the eighteenth."

"I was born on March twenty-second," Lily said. "Does that make us the same zodiac sign? I'm Aries."

Iris beamed. "I am too."

They talked on, sharing their lives as newlyweds while they finished their lemonades. Iris described her mundane existence at Live Oaks, and Lily told her about the fixer-upper she and her husband had recently purchased on Craven Street. Lily felt a twinge of jealousy. When she'd hinted to Max about getting a place of their own, he'd balked. "Why on earth would we do that when we can live here for free? Besides, Live Oaks will be mine one day."

As they walked back toward Bay Street, Lily asked, "Would you like to help me paint my dining room this afternoon? I've chosen this hot-pink color called Razzle Dazzle that's gonna blow my husband's mind."

"I'd need to change clothes first."

Lily gave her the once-over. "We're about the same size. I'm sure I can find some old jeans for you to wear."

"In that case, count me in."

They reached Bay Street and turned left. Two blocks down, Lily stopped in front of an abandoned storefront with a lime-green awning that covered double windows and the entryway. "One day, I'm going to open up a shop here."

"What kind of shop?"

"I haven't figured that out yet."

Iris cupped her eyes and peered through the windows. Aside from the dingy tile floors and lavender walls, there wasn't much to see. "What was here before?"

"A women's hat store, or so I'm told." She turned away from the windows. "Oh well. It's just another one of my many pie-in-the-sky dreams."

They'd only just met, but Iris had a hunch that Lily did more than just dream.

CHAPTER TWELVE

"Bring your husband and come to supper tomorrow night," Lily said on a Friday at the end of their second week as friends. "It'll be my first dinner party, a celebration of our accomplishment."

"Thank you, Lily. I've told Max about your knack for selecting bold hues that work beautifully together. And Max and Wiley can get to know each other better. I'm looking forward to it already."

Max complained about attending the dinner party until Iris told him Wiley was being groomed to take over his father's law firm.

They arrived at the Mathesons' fifteen fashionable minutes late with a bottle of inexpensive red wine and a bouquet of yellow dahlias Iris had snipped from her mother-in-law's garden. She felt overdressed in her cocktail attire—gold silk pants and a navy jacket—next to Lily, who greeted them in black capris and a crisp white cotton blouse.

Lily, the ever-gracious hostess, held up her hand and said, "You look gorgeous, Iris. I'm sad to say, I spilled meat juice on my dress and had to change." She took Iris's flowers and examined their saucer-size blooms. "These are amazing. Did you grow them?"

"No, I—"

"My mother grew them. Iris has yet to sprout her green thumb," Max said.

Lily smiled. "Iris has good instincts when it comes to gardening. I'm going to put these in some water." As she headed toward the kitchen, she called, "Wiley, fix Iris a glass of white wine and whatever Max is having."

Wiley showed them to the sitting room and the tea cart Lily had converted into a bar. He made idle conversation while he poured a glass of chilled white wine for Iris and a Dewar's on the rocks for Max. With brown hair and chiseled features, Lily's husband was every bit as handsome as his wife was pretty.

"I hope you don't mind if I leave the game on." Wiley's chocolate eyes traveled to the small television in the corner of the room, where the Georgia Bulldogs were playing the South Carolina Gamecocks in football.

"Not at all," Max said. "I'm a Carolina man, myself."

Wiley chuckled. "That should make for an interesting evening." He motioned them to the sofa. "Shall we?"

Iris and Max sat side by side in the center of the gray velvet sofa. Lily had set out a tray of canapés that were mini works of art. "These are too pretty to eat," Iris said as Max popped two into his mouth in quick succession, swallowing them down with a mouthful of scotch.

Iris opened one of the oversize hardbound books on the coffee table. "If only I could design flowers like these." She thumbed through the glossy pages that bore photographs of elaborate tablescapes and flower arrangements.

Wiley sat down next to Iris, taking the book and flipping to the About the Author page, where he pointed to the auburn-haired woman. "That's Lily's mother."

"She's stunning. Lily looks just like her." She read out loud the first line of Norma Stanton's bio. "*A Legend from Atlanta—The South's Flower Queen*. She's a true artist."

Wiley nodded. "And Lily has inherited her creative gene. She approaches every project as an artist would a blank canvas, including our meal tonight." He looked up as Lily entered the room to announce dinner was ready. The love on his face was obvious.

Lily served dinner at a table set to perfection in the pink dining room. The yellow dahlias, now arranged in a cut crystal vase with several stalks of poet's laurel, offered a pop of color from the center of the table. It wasn't until later, when Iris was helping with the dishes, that she noticed the bouquet of black-eyed Susans cast aside on the kitchen counter. Lily had replaced her own beautiful blooms with the flowers Iris had brought.

The food—beef Wellington cooked medium rare in a flaky puff pastry with tender new potatoes and asparagus in béarnaise sauce—was indeed a work of art against the plain canvas of the simple Limoges china.

The men monopolized the dinner conversation, moving from one topic to another. Iris and Lily exchanged a knowing look. They'd so hoped their men would get along.

They returned to the sitting room for dessert—a decadent chocolate mousse served with a fine aged brandy—to watch the end of the game. Iris was mortified when Max refilled his brandy snifter three times and gulped it down like water. On his way to being very drunk, he screamed obscenities at the television and pouted like a poor sport when his team lost.

He embarrassed her in front of her friend, and she told him so on the walk home.

"Ha. You're the one who embarrassed herself by fawning all over Lily like a lovestruck fool. She's a woman of great class, and you'll never measure up to her standards. She's using you, and you're too naive to see it. She craves attention and feeds her ego by surrounding herself with inferior women like you."

His words stung. Had she been overly eager to please? Was Lily really using her? And what if she was? Her life was far more interesting with Lily in it. Especially now that her husband had turned on her.

"I don't get it, Max. I can do no right in your eyes. Your parents have finally accepted me, but now that you've won the battle, you're pushing me away. Is that all our relationship was to you, an act of rebellion to test their love for you?"

"Careful, Iris. Don't ask questions unless you're prepared to hear the answers."

~

On a crisp day in mid-October, Lily and Iris were returning from a meeting with Gretchen Baldwin when Lily once again stopped to admire the empty store with green awnings on Bay Street.

"I keep having this recurring dream about opening up a shop in this storefront. I'm going to call the Realtor this afternoon about leasing the space."

"What kind of shop, Lily?"

"A flower shop, of course. We'll be the talk of the town."

Iris's mouth fell open. "We?"

"You and me, silly," Lily said, jabbing her elbow into Iris's side.

"But Max and I don't have the money to invest in a flower shop, not that he would ever consider it anyway."

"I don't need your money, Iris. My father's already agreed to give me the money. I'm looking for a working partner—someone to help run the business. Whenever the time is right for you financially and you'd like to buy into the business, we'll figure something out then."

"Sounds like you've thought it all through."

"I have, from every possible angle. This town is desperate for a good florist. We'll make big money on weddings and charity events. We'll be open Tuesdays through Saturdays, which will give us two days off in a row. My mother knows the best wholesale florists in Georgia and South Carolina, and she's promised to give us guidance. You and I make a good team. Please say you'll come to work for me."

Lily's enthusiasm was contagious and inspired in Iris a sense of purpose. She would have a job, make her own money. Even if it was a pittance, it was a start that could lead to something bigger.

Iris's smile lit up her face. "How could I possibly say no?"

"But shouldn't you talk to Max first?"

"Are you kidding me? Max will never even notice I've gotten a job."

"Then let's go to my house and call the Realtor," Lily said, waving her on as she scurried off.

"What're you gonna name the shop?" Iris asked, slightly out of breath when she caught up.

"I haven't decided yet. Something simple like Blossoms or Blooms."

Three hours later, after a brief tour of the storefront, Lily signed the lease and wrote a check covering two months' rent. The building's ample space offered room in the back to install a built-in cooler, metal prep tables, a work sink, and even a tiny closet for Lily to use as an office.

Much to Iris's surprise, Max wasn't angry when she told him about her new venture. "Fine by me. It'll keep you busy and off my case," he said. She was unaware of being on his case but knew better than to argue.

Iris and Lily set the opening date for the Saturday before Thanksgiving, immersing themselves in countless details. They watched with glee as an artist painted on the front window their new logo—*Lily's* written in a flowery script in a moss-green color with the stem of a pink lily underlining the name.

Lily's mother arrived the morning before the grand opening. Norma Stanton's spirited personality matched her daughter's. After touring the facility, Norma said, "Girls, you've done a spectacular job of setting up shop, but I'd like to make suggestions on ways to make your business run more efficiently." They spent the rest of the day implementing her ideas, which everyone agreed were for the better. Lily and Norma worked well together, with obvious respect for one another. Iris envied their relationship, hoping one day to have the same with a daughter of her own.

Women of all ages lined up on opening day for the chance to meet Norma, the South's Flower Queen. By the end of the day, they'd sold every bloom and flowering plant in the shop. Fortunately, they'd placed their restocking order well in advance in anticipation of their success.

Iris and Lily worked tirelessly during the weeks leading up to Christmas, selling wreaths and garlands, poinsettias, and amaryllis and narcissus bulbs they'd forced themselves. They bought a van and hired a deliveryman to deliver their flower arrangements. They even managed to pull off the garden club's best-ever Christmas greens workshop. Their success allowed Iris to send a Christmas card with a check for $300 to her aunt.

Her first Christmas with the Forneys was everything she'd hoped for. Edgar dragged home a twelve-foot cedar tree and set it up in the center hallway for Estelle and Mrs. Forney to decorate. On Christmas Eve, after a simple meal of crab bisque, ham sandwiches, and fruit salad, they attended the midnight candlelight service at Saint Peter's Catholic Church. They reconvened in the kitchen Christmas Day for pastries and coffee before moving to the family room to open gifts. Mrs. Forney and Edgar surprised Iris with a bicycle—a turquoise cruiser with a basket in the front and a rack behind the seat.

Iris clapped her hands in glee. "It's perfect! Now I can bike to work every day." Tears welled in her eyes as she gave each of them a hug, finally feeling accepted.

She'd created gifts for her in-laws that were equally as thoughtful but not nearly as extravagant—lavender sachets for Mrs. Forney and a small watercolor of Edgar's sailboat.

"You have quite a talent with the brush, my dear," Edgar said, genuinely impressed with his painting.

Iris's pride surged.

She was considerably less enthused about Max's gift—a new vacuum cleaner for the guest cottage—but he seemed pleased with the camouflage hunting jacket she'd given him. If hunting, fishing, and golfing were the way of life for every southern gentleman, spending time with her husband on weekends wasn't going to happen. She didn't mind so much, now that she worked Saturdays at Lily's. The one condition she insisted on was that he keep his guns locked up in his father's gun safe in the main house.

CHAPTER THIRTEEN

Iris and Lily provided elaborate arrangements of all-white flowers and greenery for their first wedding reception, which was hosted by the bride's family at one of the historic inns in town on New Year's Eve. Lily thereafter became known as the South's Flower Princess, and their calendar was soon booked with weddings for spring and summer.

Valentine's Day brought an onslaught of orders for red roses. It was around this time when Lily's mood shifted. She wore a solemn expression and snapped at Iris for no apparent reason. When Iris had had enough on an exceptionally warm day in early March, she brought a cup of freshly perked coffee to Lily, who was sitting at her desk tallying receipts from the previous day's sales.

"You've been out of sorts for weeks, Lily. I know something's wrong. Is the business in trouble?"

Lily looked up from her adding machine, as though surprised to see Iris standing there. "I might as well tell you," she said, getting up and taking the coffee to the sink, where she poured it down the drain. "I'm pregnant."

"That's wonderful!" Iris said, and when she noticed Lily's emerald eyes glistening with unshed tears, she added, "Are you not happy about the pregnancy?"

"I am, and I'm not. I feel wretched all the time. I'm one of those lucky women whose morning sickness lasts all day long. I don't know, Iris. I'm excited about the baby. I've always wanted children. I just didn't think it would happen this fast. This pregnancy wasn't exactly planned. We got careless one night over the holidays." Her voice broke when she said, "Our business is thriving. How will I manage with a baby?"

"You'll hire a nanny, of course. And you have me." Iris went to stand beside her friend, giving her a half hug. "When's the baby due?"

"Late September."

"That's good timing. We don't have any weddings booked from the middle of September until Thanksgiving. We'll keep the calendar open. I can manage the shop, but I don't think I could organize a wedding alone."

"My mother is planning to come for several weeks after the baby comes. She's offered to help out here if you need her." Lily removed a tissue from her jeans and blew her nose. "That's another thing. I cry all the time now. It wouldn't be so bad if I felt more like myself."

"What does the doctor say about how you're feeling?"

"That mood swings and morning sickness are part of being pregnant and that it'll get better in the second trimester." Lily buried her face in her hand. "If I live that long."

"Hang in there," Iris said, giving her arm a squeeze. "It'll all be worth it in the end."

~

April marked the beginning of Lily's second trimester. Her morning sickness subsided, which, in turn, greatly improved her demeanor.

At the end of the month, Lily's father-in-law announced he was retiring and turning over the law firm and their Edisto Island cottage to Wiley. By mid-May, Mr. and Mrs. Matheson had packed up their most valued possessions, put their house on the market, and moved to Jupiter, Florida, to live out their days in the sun.

"Have you and Wiley thought about moving into his parents' house?" Iris asked Lily. "You would have enough room for an army of children."

"Ha." Lily stabbed a stem of Queen Anne's lace in the oasis with the rest of her flowers. "I'm definitely not planning to have an army of children. After the way I felt my first trimester, I may only have this one. But to answer your question, Wiley's parents' house needs a ton of work that I'm not willing to do. At least not for that house. I'm holding out for a big spread on the water." She added a couple of sprigs of greenery to her arrangement. "I'm excited about the Edisto cottage, though. We'll have to get you and Max down some this summer."

As it turned out, Iris and Max spent nearly every weekend of the summer with Lily and Wiley on Edisto. The girls closed the shop on Saturdays and drove the hour-and-a-half drive in separate cars with their husbands. They cooked on the grill Saturday nights and spent Sundays on the water until the late afternoon, when Wiley and Max took one of the cars back to Beaufort for work on Monday. Lily and Iris stayed at the cottage for the next twenty-four blissful hours, sleeping late, reading romance novels, and dozing in the sun. Before their return to Beaufort on Monday afternoons, they changed linens and tidied up, resetting the cottage for the coming weekend.

Wiley's kind and gentle nature seemed to rub off on Max, putting him on his best behavior that summer. He helped with boat maintenance and small jobs around the cottage and took his turn at the grill every other Saturday. And he complained only once or twice about missing out on golf. Her husband's improved mood gave Iris hope that their premarital happiness might one day be restored.

The happiest summer of Iris's life ended on a sad note on Labor Day weekend. The blazing sun and heavy air had set everyone on edge.

There was no relief, not even inside the cottage, where the air conditioner struggled to keep up. Lily, in her eighth month of pregnancy, was particularly irritable.

"It's too hot to eat," Lily complained. She dropped a hamburger patty on the platter and slid it across the Formica countertop to Wiley. "Do you think you can stop drinking beer long enough to cook these?"

"Who said I had to stop? I can drink beer and cook at the same time."

Iris placed the tray of deviled eggs she'd been working on in the refrigerator. "Why don't you lie down, Lily. I can finish up." She walked Lily to the sofa in the adjoining room and handed her the latest edition of *Parents* magazine.

Iris boiled corn on the cob and cut up watermelon slices to go with the burgers, but no one had an appetite. After cleaning up from dinner, they played gin rummy and crazy eights. Within an hour, Lily was so cantankerous, Wiley insisted she go to bed. Ten minutes later, he followed her into the master bedroom. Iris and Max turned in as well, but Lily and Wiley's arguing in the next room kept them awake.

Iris turned on her side to face her husband. "They don't usually argue like this. Do you think something's wrong?"

"Something's definitely wrong. Lily is miserable, and she wants to make sure Wiley's miserable too. That's how wives operate."

Iris smacked his arm with the back of her hand. "That's not fair, Max. And Lily's not like that."

"Like hell she's not. She's a spoiled-rotten bitch who has to be the center of attention."

"Don't talk about my best friend like that," Iris said.

"Don't talk about my best friend like that," Max mimicked in a high-pitched voice.

Iris rolled over to face the wall rather than respond. She didn't fall asleep until long after Max had started snoring.

Early Sunday morning, Max sat at the table drinking coffee while Iris fried bacon. Wiley entered the kitchen and poured a cup of coffee, saying, "Lily had a rough night. I'm going to let her sleep in. I'm thinking I might head back to Beaufort early. It's too hot to be outside, and I've got a trial starting on Tuesday. I could use the time to prepare."

"If you go, I'm going with you." Max tried to sound nonchalant, but his eager expression gave him away. They'd planned to stay through the long weekend, as Monday was a bank holiday. But Max, as Iris knew, would rather die than get trapped in a cottage with his wife and a hormonal pregnant woman.

She fed them a big breakfast, helped them pack the car, and waved as they backed out of the driveway, relieved to see them go. She escaped into a Danielle Steel novel and was on the last chapter when Lily finally emerged at two o'clock.

She stared out the sliding glass doors at the darkening sky. "I hope the rain cools things off. I'm sorry for my sour mood. I'm just not myself these days."

Iris got to her feet. "I'll fix us some lemonade. We can take it out to the porch and watch the storm move in."

Lemonade in hand, they sat in silence in the rocking chairs on the screened porch, watching the first fat raindrops bouncing off the creek. "The air feels noticeably cooler," Iris said. "The baby will be here soon, and you'll settle into a routine."

"I know what you're thinking, Iris, but the baby isn't the problem." Lily placed a hand on her belly. "I can hardly wait to meet my son or daughter. I only hope that once the pregnancy is over, I'll feel like myself again. I can't explain it. I'm just so unhappy." Her voice broke and she couldn't continue.

Iris gave her a minute to compose herself. "Is it your marriage?"

"Yes and no. I love Wiley with all my heart. He's honest and considerate and a wonderful provider. But that's part of the problem. He's too perfect. He's so perfect, he's boring." Lily squeezed her eyes shut. "Oh God, Iris, I'm a horrible person for saying that about my own husband, but I can't help the way I feel. I miss Atlanta, my family, and my friends. I thought I loved Wiley enough to leave Atlanta, but I'm not so sure anymore." A tear escaped and slid down her cheek.

Lily's words hurt. *What about the business we've worked so hard to build? Does our friendship mean nothing to you?*

"I adore you, Iris," Lily said, as if reading her mind. "This is not about you or the business. Honestly, I don't know what it's about."

Patting her friend's hand, Iris said, "I'm sure it's your hormones." But Max's words echoed in her mind. *She's a spoiled-rotten bitch who has to be the center of attention.* Lily was already the center of attention. She was the center of Wiley's world. And she was the South's Flower Princess, the darling of Beaufort society. She was talented, beautiful, and charming. And in a few weeks, she would hold her firstborn in her arms. For a woman with Iris's past, that seemed like everything.

CHAPTER FOURTEEN

Charles Augustus Matheson entered the world on a bright and crisp Saturday morning at the end of September. Iris dragged Max off the golf course late that afternoon to visit the proud new parents and their bundle of joy.

"He's a lucky bastard getting a boy the first go-round," Max said as they stood looking through the nursery at baby Gus.

Iris stepped closer to her husband. "You could be a lucky bastard, too, you know." Seeing the innocent baby sleeping so peacefully created a longing deep inside her.

"You're right. I could. My dad was a lucky bastard." His expression morphed from *maybe* to *why not*. "We might as well start planning for a family of our own."

Iris embarked on a mission to seduce her husband with sexy negligees and candlelit dinners. While they didn't experience the intimacy Iris had initially hoped for from her marriage, during the next few months, they renewed the closeness they'd shared prior to their elopement. The sex continued to be brief and awkward. But she prayed the increased frequency would pay off with a baby.

Lily's mother stayed for three weeks, spending more time in the flower shop with Iris than with her daughter and new grandson. Under the tutelage of Norma Stanton, Iris became an expert at flower arranging. And the tips Norma gave—such as how to revive wilting petals, how to condition certain blooms to last longer, and how to support the weaker stems for better presentation—were invaluable.

Mrs. Forney invented excuses to stop by the shop, but Iris understood her sole objective was to talk flowers with Norma. As a result, her mother-in-law, with pride in her eyes, began treating Iris with a whole new level of respect.

On the morning Norma was to return to Atlanta, she stopped by the shop to say goodbye. "You've come into your own as a designer these past weeks. And I'm proud of you, Iris. If you continue to gain confidence, your work will take you great places."

Iris beamed. "That means a lot coming from you."

"I mean it! I'm often looking for women to help out with my larger events. I may invite you to Atlanta sometime to be my right-hand gal."

Iris imagined herself featured in one of the glossy magazines working alongside the regal Norma Stanton. Her dream was coming true. She would be a trendsetter, a Norma Stanton protégée. "I'd absolutely love that. Anytime."

Norma's vote of confidence along with the shop's steady increase in profits motivated Iris to take Lily up on her offer to invest in the business.

"We don't have that kind of money, Iris," Max said when she broached the subject over dinner one night. He gave her a monthly allowance for groceries and household expenditures, but he never discussed their finances with her. She usually sent Aunt Ethel a portion of her meager pay at Lily's and spent the rest on clothes for herself.

"I thought maybe, with your promotion and all. . ." Her voice trailed off.

He'd recently been promoted to trust adviser in the private wealth management department and was slated to take over the bank's wealthiest clients when his senior adviser retired next year. *Promotion or no promotion, I may as well forget about a loan from Max.* Max's parents had plenty of money, but her husband never shared the details of their wealth. She wondered whether any of that money would be available to Max before they died, but she didn't think it her place to ask.

"Do you think the bank would lend me the money based on our profit statement for our first year of business?"

"We don't own anything to pledge as collateral. Why would you want to burden yourself with a business when we're hoping to get pregnant soon?"

Iris didn't press the issue. She had no intention of quitting her job to be a stay-at-home mother. *No matter what he thinks, today's modern woman can have both career and family.*

The next evening before Max arrived home, Iris went over to see her father-in-law. When she knocked lightly on the door of Edgar's wood-paneled study, he called out for her to come in.

"Well now, this is a surprise," he said, looking up from behind his desk, where he sat packing his pipe with tobacco. "To what do I owe this honor?"

She took a seat in the red leather chair opposite him and slid a file with their first year's earnings reports across the desk. "I was wondering if you'd consider loaning me the money to invest in Lily's. You can see from the numbers that we're doing quite well."

He flipped through the reports and said, "Your business is doing *extremely* well with a steady incline in profits. I assume you've already discussed with Max."

"Yes, sir. He claims we're not in a financial position to invest, and I wouldn't go behind his back if this didn't mean so much to me." She moved to the edge of her chair. "I'll be honest with you, Edgar. I don't know much about money. I've never had any to worry about. But I'd like to take advantage of the opportunity now before Lily changes her mind about having investors."

Edgar steepled his fingers and furrowed his brow in thought, his silence unnerving her. "Let me start by saying how flattered I am that you felt comfortable coming to me about this." He got up and went to the cabinet behind his desk that housed his liquor. He poured a finger of scotch into two tumblers and handed one of the glasses to her. "You've changed quite a bit since you first came to Beaufort. You've developed into a fine young lady, and I admire your drive and enthusiasm for your business. You have gumption, Iris. And I like that about you. And because I believe in you, I'd be delighted to loan you the money."

She broke into a toothy grin. "Really? You will?"

"Of course I will. And when you're a huge success, I'll be the first to point out to my foolish son that he missed out on a grand opportunity. We'll figure out a payment plan that works for you. I'll have the papers drawn up for you so that your share of the flower business is yours and yours alone. You won't ever have to give Max a dime if you don't want to. That way you'll have your own money to worry about. Do we have a deal?" He held his glass out to her.

Iris sat up straight in her chair with her chin up and head held high. "Yes, sir! We have a deal!" She clinked his glass, ignoring the burn in her throat as she gulped down the brown liquor.

"Thank you so much, Edgar," she said, kissing his cheek when he walked her to the door of his study. "I promise I won't let you down."

She could hardly wait to tell Lily and hurried back to the cottage to call her. Relieved to discover Max had still not arrived, she poured herself a glass of wine and dialed Lily's number, dancing around the sitting room with wineglass in one hand and phone in the other while she waited for Lily to answer.

"I've got great news!" she blurted when Lily picked up on the seventh or eighth ring. "Edgar's agreed to loan me the money. We're finally going to be partners."

"Good!" Lily said, emitting a sigh of relief. "I can't wait to turn over half of this headache to you."

Iris was too excited to let Lily's sour mood spoil her celebration. She was babbling on about her plans for the business when Lily finally cut her off.

"Listen, Iris, this will have to wait until I come back to work. I need to go put the baby down now."

When Lily returned to work the week prior to Thanksgiving, she didn't mention the partnership until Iris finally broached the subject late that afternoon while they were reviewing their calendar of bookings.

"I've contacted my attorney. He's drawing up the paperwork for our partnership, Lily. That is, if you still want to go through with it."

Lily looked up from the calendar. "Our partnership?" Her dazed expression cleared. "Oh, right. That. I'm sorry. I've been so preoccupied with the baby and hiring a nanny. My life is so complicated, I'm tempted to turn the whole business over to you."

"You don't mean that, Lily. It's your first day back. You'll feel better once you've settled in."

Lily's dark mood showed no signs of lifting throughout the holiday season. Her pregnancy blues had transitioned into postpartum depression. She'd lost all her baby weight, but instead of wearing the glow of motherhood, she looked gaunt and tired. She sulked around the shop with her mind in some faraway place where Iris couldn't reach her no matter how hard she tried. By the time New Year's rolled around, Iris had begun to accept the fact that the vibrant Lily she loved so much was never coming back.

CHAPTER FIFTEEN

On September 7, 1979, the Friday after Labor Day, Anna Alexandra Forney was born. Max did his best to hide it, but Iris could tell he was disappointed over not getting a son. "We'll name her Anna Alexandra after my mother and grandmother," he said, standing beside Iris's hospital bed, staring down at the newborn in her arms. "But we'll call her Alex. I'll teach her to hunt, play golf, and sail. She'll be the best damn sportswoman the South has ever seen."

Iris didn't like the masculine nickname, but she was too ecstatic over the birth of her first child to argue. She was swept away by her feelings of tenderness and a pure love she had never known was possible.

The baby arrived in the wake of a difficult summer. When Aunt Ethel had died suddenly in her sleep, Iris was faced with making funeral arrangements and clearing the old woman's meager possessions out of her cinder block house. To make matters worse, she'd fought with Max incessantly about where they would live after the baby's birth.

"The guest cottage isn't an option," Iris said, time and again. "We only have one bedroom, and babies require a lot of equipment. Please, Max. We've been married for two years. Can't we get our own house?"

"Live Oaks is my home, and this is where we'll live. We'll manage in the guest cottage."

It wasn't until they spent the long Fourth of July weekend with the Mathesons on Edisto that things changed. The cranky teething baby crawling at his feet set Max on edge, and he began to comprehend their future reality. The minute they arrived home, he spoke with his parents about their living arrangements.

"You're welcome to the third floor, son," his mother said, as if there was never any question. "Honestly, I don't know why you haven't moved into the main house sooner."

Iris had given up having a home of her own and was overjoyed to get out of the cramped guest cottage. Using her income from Lily's, she converted one back corner room into a master bedroom, the opposite corner room to the nursery, and the generous hallway space in between into a sitting room. Stunning views of the river from the third floor compensated for the absence of a kitchen and the two flights of stairs she'd have to climb with a baby on her hip.

Not only did Mrs. Forney enlist her furniture repairman to refurbish the crib and Victorian rocker that had been in their family for generations, she also donated several of her prized antiques from the lower floors. The week before the baby arrived, her mother-in-law sought Iris out in the nursery, where she was folding baby clothes.

"I want you to have this for the baby," she said, presenting Iris with a full-length lace christening gown. "It would mean so much to us if you'd consider baptizing our grandchild in our Catholic church."

"Of course, Mrs. Forney. That makes perfect sense," Iris said, even though she had little experience with religion.

"Good! Then that's settled. I'll have Estelle press the dress so it's ready for the big day. I've taken the liberty of scheduling the christening for the first Sunday in November. We'll have a luncheon reception here following the service for a small group of our closest friends."

~

Iris approached her return to work with mixed emotions. As much as she dreaded leaving her baby, she didn't want to be a stay-at-home mom forever, and she took her partnership at Lily's seriously. As the shop grew more and more successful every day, she felt compelled to see it through.

As a compromise, she opted not to hire a nanny right away.

"You should've warned me, Iris," Lily said when she showed up on her first day back with Alex in tow. "This is hardly a place for a baby. Where are you going to keep her? Our workroom is too small to house a playpen."

The phone rang just as Alex began to cry for her bottle.

"Great!" Lily tossed her hands up. "This is real professional, having a crying baby in the background while I'm talking business on the phone." But later that afternoon, when Alex woke from her second long nap in the playpen Iris had set up in an out-of-the-way corner, Lily said, "I can't believe how good she is. A much better sleeper than Gus ever was. How nice it must be to have a sweet little girl."

They soon settled into a routine, and Iris often found Lily by the playpen staring down at her daughter with an expression Iris couldn't read.

"I don't know what's wrong with me," Lily said early one morning in mid-December when her requisite three cups of black coffee failed to energize her. "I can't get my creative juices flowing. You have more artistic flair than me, anyway. At least according to my mother. Why don't you take care of the creative side of the business and let me handle accounting matters, vendor orders, and building maintenance?"

Iris interpreted her friend's willingness to relinquish control of creativity as a sign that Lily was slipping deeper into depression. Hoping to provoke inspiration, Iris showed her magazine pages that featured elaborate floral arrangements, but Lily expressed no interest. Iris brought treats—Estelle's homemade fudge, blueberry scones, hearty vegetable soup—in an attempt to put meat on her bones but received in return only a murmured thank-you and a weak smile.

The day after Christmas, when Lily and Iris were going over their orders for New Year's Eve, Lily inexplicably burst into tears.

"Please tell me what's bothering you. Maybe I can help," Iris said, taking her by the hand.

"You can't help me. No one can."

"Maybe you should talk to someone. Postpartum depression is fairly common."

"This is not postpartum depression," Lily snapped, and jerked her hands away. "Or any other kind of depression. I just hate my life. And I hate Beaufort. This sleepy little town will never wake up."

Iris was stunned into silence. In her mind, Lily's life was perfect. Wonderful husband. A child she adored. Beautiful home. Prosperous business. Iris admitted that small-town living had taken some getting used to, but she'd grown to love the relaxed atmosphere, the pleasure of riding her bike to work while taking in magnificent views of the river at every turn.

Iris hoped that closing the shop for their customary week of vacation in early January would help Lily. When she went to work the following Tuesday, she was alarmed to find Wiley in the office, counting out five-dollar bills into the register drawer.

"Lily's gone to Atlanta, and she took Gus," he said, without so much as a glance in her direction.

"Good!" Iris plunked her diaper bag down on the metal worktable. "A visit with her family is just what she needs. When's she coming back?"

He swiveled in his chair and stood to face her. "This isn't a visit, Iris. I don't know when, or even if, she's coming back. We've been having some problems. I'm sure that doesn't come as a surprise to you." Taking the baby from her, he buried his nose in Alex's neck, inhaling her scent. "There's nothing quite like holding an innocent baby in your arms." Sadness settled on his face.

"I'm so sorry, Wiley. I had no idea things had gotten so bad."

"She's a complicated woman. I knew that when I married her." He drew in a deep breath, composing himself, and returned Alex to her arms. "She was going to call you, but she knew you'd try to talk her out of leaving. She doesn't want her absence to be a hardship on you, so I've agreed to take over the finances while she figures out her future." He retrieved the cash register drawer from the office and disappeared into the showroom.

"I've never prayed for anything in my life," Iris said to Alex as she set her down in her playpen. "But I'm praying to whatever God is listening to help Wiley and Lily through this crisis."

Alex began to cry, waving her arms in the air to be picked up. "Not now, little one," she said, handing her a sterling teething rattle.

Wiley burst through the swinging doors. "Two more things before I go," he said, removing his suit jacket from the back of the desk chair. "Lily doesn't expect you to manage the business alone, and she wants you to use your discretion in hiring someone to take her place."

Iris shook her head. "I'm not ready to do that yet. I can handle it for a while. January is a slow month, and I'm certain Lily will be back by Valentine's Day."

Wiley smiled. "What my wife needs is a healthy dose of your optimism."

"She'll come around soon enough."

"I hope you're right," he said, slipping on his suit jacket. "In any event, Lily insists you use Cora while she's gone. You can't take care of the business and the baby alone."

"I'm not sure I can do that, Wiley. Nothing against your nanny, but I'd rather take care of my baby myself."

"Please, Iris. Do this as a favor to Lily. At least until she figures out what she wants. If she decides to give our marriage another chance, she'll want Cora back."

Iris hesitated. "I guess it wouldn't hurt to give it a go. Now that Alex is getting older, she requires a lot more of my attention."

"You won't be sorry. Cora has a gentle but firm manner. And she can fry a mean pork chop."

Iris snickered. "No way Estelle's gonna let her in her kitchen."

Wiley crossed the room to the back door. "I'll have her stop by the shop this afternoon to go over the logistics."

~

Iris knew from the start that hiring Cora was a smart move. On warm mornings, the nanny took Alex for long walks in the stroller, and every afternoon Alex napped for three or four hours.

For the first time since her daughter was born, Iris felt like some semblance of order had been restored to her life. Without baby-related interruptions, she accomplished twice as much at work, where she got to be Iris the floral designer and shopkeeper during the day. Upbeat days then spilled over to evenings, inspiring her to be a more pleasant wife to Max and a more attentive mother to Alex. During the slow days of January, she cleaned the shop, organized the supply closet, and spent hours working on designs for weddings they'd booked for the spring. Without Lily, she was lonely and began to look forward to Wiley's late-afternoon visits. He made bank deposits and paid bills and was eager to help with manual labor. After concluding business, they enjoyed a splash from the bottle of Crown Royal that Wiley kept in the bottom desk drawer. Iris developed a taste for the fine Canadian whiskey, which went down smoothly. Over time, they began to speak of subjects other than Lily and discovered they had much in common—television programs, politics, attitudes on child-rearing.

Late one frigid afternoon at the end of January, Iris was wrapping green florist foil around the base of a peace lily when she heard him come in the back door. She completed the purchase for the customer, locked the front door, and went to the workroom, where she found Wiley standing in the middle of the room with a look of bewilderment.

Iris went to him and took him in her arms. "What's wrong? Is it Lily?"

Considerably taller than she, he stooped his shoulders and cried into her neck. "She's not coming back. She says she wants a divorce."

"I'm so sorry, Wiley," she said, rubbing his back. "I don't know what to say. This is not the outcome I imagined."

She held him while he cried. Even though she was the one doing the comforting, she felt oddly comforted herself. She felt safe in his arms in a way she'd never felt with Max. Truth be told, she'd never been in her husband's arms long enough to feel much of anything. Wiley was gentle and kind, so different than Max. He was also her best friend's husband. She pushed him away, but seeing the look of utter dejection on his face, she drew him in again for a tighter embrace.

"I'll never get to see my son," he bawled. "He'll grow up not know-ing his father."

"That's not true. You'll have visitation. I can't imagine how hard this is for you, Wiley. I know how much you love your wife."

Wiley lifted his head, giving it a solemn shake. "Not in the same way I once did. I'll never be able to please her. Trying so hard and get-ting it wrong all the time is not good for a man's ego." He dried his eyes with his linen handkerchief. "Tell me, Iris. Are you happy with your life?"

She dropped her arms and took a step back. "Happiness is a state of mind, Wiley. I learned a long time ago that it's what you make of your life that determines whether you're happy or not. I'm not talking about people who are chemically depressed, or mourning the loss of a loved one, or terminally ill, or trapped in terrible lives with no way out. I'm talking about people who have a roof over their heads and are capable of supporting themselves. But that's just me, Wiley. Lily and I come from very different backgrounds. Her standards for happiness are not the same as mine."

"Her standards are too high. As are her expectations." He stuffed his handkerchief in his suit pocket. "Thank you for sharing your thoughts. You'll never know how much I appreciate your kindness."

"Everyone needs a friend to talk to every now and then."

"Do you have someone to talk to, Iris? Do you and Max talk until late at night about the things that matter most to you?" When she looked away, he said, "I'm sorry for prying."

"No, it's okay," she said, meeting his gaze. "The truth is, Max and I don't talk about much of anything. If it doesn't have to do with money or bank business, Max isn't interested."

"Then he's a fool who doesn't deserve you."

His close proximity suddenly made Iris feel uncomfortable. "It's getting late. I should probably go. Cora is expecting me home by five thirty."

Together, they collected the day's sales slips and credit card charge forms and reset the register drawer with the appropriate amount of cash for the following morning.

"Lily insists you hire someone to take her place." He stood at the door with the leather bank deposit bag tucked under his arm. "I'll continue to take care of the finances until she decides what to do about her partnership in the business."

As she closed the door behind him, her anger at Lily escalated. Deep down, she knew Lily was suffering from depression. But she was also acting like a spoiled brat, running away to Atlanta and shirking her responsibilities to their business and her marriage. Why not call Iris on the phone instead of sending messages through her husband? They had important decisions to make, decisions Iris felt uncomfortable making alone. Lily didn't want a say in who Iris hired to replace her.

Did she plan to sell out of the partnership entirely? They had weddings scheduled for spring and summer that clients had booked with Lily, specifically requesting the Flower Princess to be in charge of the flowers.

Iris sat down at the desk, planted her face in her hands, and cried. It hurt that Lily hadn't confided in her, that Iris had to hear about Lily's plans for the future secondhand. But it wasn't all about the business. She couldn't bear the thought of Lily moving to Atlanta permanently. Lily was her best friend. The only true friend she'd ever known.

CHAPTER SIXTEEN

Iris interviewed half a dozen candidates for the full-time position at the shop, but only one possessed the enthusiasm she was looking for. She hired her on the spot, just in time for the Valentine's rush.

A recent graduate of NYU, Felicia Newman had returned home to Beaufort at her father's insistence to figure out her life. "Daddy's mad as fire at me, and I don't blame him. New York is crazy expensive. I graduated last May, and he's been paying my living expenses. I tried, Iris. I went to over a hundred auditions, but no one offered me a part. So much for my acting degree." She tossed her hands in the air flamboyantly. "I'm right back where I started from."

"Beaufort's not such a bad place, Felicia. I know your parents are thrilled to have you home."

"So is my old boyfriend," Felicia said with a mischievous grin. "I ran into him at the filling station this morning on my way to work. He's taking me to Joe's Spaghetti House for dinner tonight."

Iris figured her pretty new shopkeeper would have every boy in town chasing her before long. Felicia wore bellbottom jeans that hugged her shapely bottom and her blonde hair parted in the middle with Farrah Fawcett wings. She was quick witted and approached flower arranging with a minimalist style Iris found fresh and edgy. Within the week, Iris had turned all phone-in orders over to Felicia.

Wiley's visits became less frequent as he began preparations for an upcoming trial. The case was all over the news—a Hatfield-McCoy–type feud between two neighbors who'd lived side by side for twenty-five years, one who raised hogs and the other who bred horses. Wiley represented the horse breeder in the civil lawsuit and stood to earn a nice chunk of a large settlement, as well as gain valuable exposure due to the high visibility of the case.

Iris silently rooted him on, all the while missing him more than she cared to admit. Every evening she watched the local news coverage of the trial, hoping for a glimpse of him leaving the courthouse.

The attorneys had presented their closing arguments and turned the case over to the jury on the last Friday in March. On Saturday morning, Iris discovered on the office desk a gardenia blossom with an envelope bearing her name.

She tore open the envelope and removed the creamy embossed note card.

> Dear Iris,
> This lovely bloom greeted me this morning when I went out for the newspaper, and I immediately thought of you. I've missed our evening visits. Now that the trial is over, I'm looking forward to getting back to my normal routine. And to seeing you.
> Yours,
> Wiley

Iris clutched the note card to her chest. So she hadn't imagined the chemistry between them.

She moved through the rest of the day in a daze. She overcharged one customer by twenty dollars for an orchid plant and sent the mayor's wife a dozen pink lilies for her birthday instead of the white ones her husband had ordered. She pondered how to respond to Wiley's note.

In the end, she penned *Me too* on her notepad, tore the paper off, and folded it into one of their business envelopes, sprinkling in a handful of red rose petals. She left the envelope with his name on it in the middle of the desk in plain view.

The note was gone on Tuesday morning, and Wiley had left nothing in its place. Gloom settled over her like the storm clouds billowing in from the west.

You're setting yourself up for heartache, Iris, she reminded herself time and again as she trudged through her day. *You're a married woman, and he's a married man. Married to your best friend, no less.*

Her mood improved dramatically when, late that afternoon, the jury awarded Wiley's client $5 million in punitive damages. The case would make Wiley's career, and he deserved some happiness for a change.

Iris left for work early the following morning in the hopes of finding Wiley working at the office desk. Instead, she found another gardenia and a short note.

> Dear Iris,
> I'm in the mood to celebrate. Play hooky with me today. Meet me at the house on Edisto. I'll be waiting for you when you arrive.
> Yours,
> Wiley

She kissed the note and danced a pirouette in the tiny office. The mere thought of seeing him made her heart flutter.

When Felicia arrived twenty minutes later, Iris asked, "Can you handle the shop alone? I need to see a client in Charleston about a wedding. I'll be gone most of the day."

"I'll be fine," Felicia said.

Iris pedaled her bicycle home as fast as her legs would pump, jumped in her car, and took off for Edisto in the used Chevy Chevette her husband had bought for her when the baby had come. She argued with her conscience during the drive. She desperately wanted to be with him. To talk to him and feel the comfort of his arms around her. But was she ready to have sex with him? While her body said yes, her heart wasn't ready to be unfaithful to Max, to the life they'd created together with their precious daughter, or to Lily, the woman she still considered her best friend despite feeling betrayed by her.

She knew something was wrong the moment Wiley opened the door. His serious expression was not that of a man who'd just won a career-making lawsuit. Instead of taking her in his arms like she'd dreamed, he stared past her, refusing to meet her eyes, as he stepped aside so she could enter the cottage.

Memories of Lily assaulted her as she walked down the short hall and into the main sitting room. She suddenly found it difficult to breathe. Coming here had been a mistake.

Sensing her angst, Wiley said, "Let's go out on the porch." He opened the door and led her to the rocking chairs where she'd shared so many heart-to-heart talks with Lily.

Iris had never been to the cottage at that time of year when the marsh grasses were turning green and osprey were reclaiming their roosts on tops of channel markers. The sun was high in a bright-blue sky, and a slight breeze brought with it the stench of rotting fish and fluff mud at low tide.

Hands in lap and chin up, Iris said, "Congratulations on winning your trial. You must be thrilled." They would have a nice chat, a short visit between two friends, and then she would leave. No harm done.

The corners of his lips turned up into a soft smile. "I'd hoped to spend the day celebrating with you. But Lily spoiled my mood with her phone call this morning."

"How nice of her to want to congratulate you," Iris said, trying to sound upbeat.

"She wanted more than that. She wants to get back together. I can't say I'm surprised. She realizes what winning this case could mean for my career, and she wants to be a part of it."

"Why do you seem so glum when this is obviously the best outcome for your family?"

"For Gus, maybe. But not for me. And not for Lily, either, regardless of what she's decided she wants today. She hated living in Beaufort, but Beaufort hasn't changed, and I'm not moving. My life is here. And my career."

"What'd you tell her?" Iris gripped the arms of the rocker, steeling herself for his answer.

"All of that and more. But I want to be with you, Iris. I thought I made that clear."

Iris looked away. "I thought that's what I wanted too. But I'm not so sure anymore. Being in this house reminds me so much of her. And of Max. And it feels wrong. I'm not the type of person who cheats on her husband."

"Of course not. You're the most principled woman I've ever met. But you're not happy with Max. You hide it well, but I can see it in your eyes." He took her hand and brought it to his lips. "Don't you think we deserve to be happy, Iris?"

"If only you'd asked me that two hours ago. As much as I care for you, this isn't right." She stood abruptly. "I'm sorry, Wiley. I can't be here with you like this."

When she tried to move past him, he took her in his arms, and she collapsed against him, unable to deny her attraction to him.

"Stay with me," he said in a breathy voice. "At least for lunch. We're just two friends sharing a meal together. I prepared a picnic with all your favorites—fried chicken, potato salad, and those silver-dollar-size ham biscuits from Edith's Catering that you love so much."

Iris tilted her head back and gazed up at him in surprise. "How'd you know those are my favorites?"

He tucked a wisp of hair behind her ear. "I know a lot of things about you. I've been watching you for a very long time."

They spread their picnic out on the dock and lounged in the sun after they'd finished eating, dipping their toes in the still-cold water. They spent one of the most pleasant days together Iris had ever known, and by the time she left to drive back to Beaufort, she was once again confused about her feelings for him. Hence began the wildest emotional roller coaster of Iris's life. At night, as she tended to the needs of her six-month-old daughter, she'd vow to end her relationship with Wiley. But then the following morning, she'd read the notes he left for her at the shop professing his love, making her desperate to be in his arms again.

During the six months that followed, tormented by her feelings, Iris developed insomnia and had to see a doctor for sleeping pills. The days at the beach cottage with Wiley were like those out of a fairy tale. They shared all their hopes and dreams. And their secrets. The only physical contact they allowed themselves was the comfort of each other's arms. Their loyalty to their marriage vows and Iris's friendship with Lily prevented them from taking their relationship to the next level.

They wrote long love letters to each other. He scented his with the fragrance of gardenias, while hers included petals of whatever bloom fit her mood on any given day. Pink gerbera daisies when she felt playful and blue hydrangeas when she felt down. *P.S. Make sure you tear this up,* she wrote at the end of every letter. She ripped his letters into shreds and buried the tiny scraps of paper in the trash can at work along with discarded plant material.

Lily called Wiley daily, nagging him to consider a reconciliation, but instead of letting her come home, he drove to Atlanta once a month to see his son. He was standoffish toward Iris for days after returning from these trips. Missing out on his son's life was tearing him apart.

Iris felt as though she were living in a bubble, and she waited in dreaded anticipation for that bubble to burst.

Her relationship with Max had deteriorated to a new all-time low, and she found it difficult to make nice to him when all she could think about was being in Wiley's arms. Max was desperate to have a son, and she'd been putting him off for months. Iris wanted more children too. Just not with Max.

On a warm October evening, after a rare casual dinner with Edgar and Mrs. Forney on the veranda, Iris was in the bathroom performing her bedtime routine when Max approached her from behind, his hands pawing at her body as he rubbed himself against her.

"Stop it, Max." She elbowed him in the ribs, and he clamped his arms around her.

"I'm tired of waiting, Iris. You can't deprive me any longer. I want a son, and I aim to have one."

"I've told you a thousand times, Max. I'm not in a position to have another baby, not until I figure out my partnership situation at Lily's."

He breathed whiskey breath into her neck. "There's a simple solution for that—sell the damn shop and stay at home with your children where you belong. You tricked me into marrying you, Iris, by making me believe you'd be a good wife and mother."

"I didn't trick you into anything, Max. I've always been ambitious. You would've known that if you'd bothered to ask me what I want out of life. Instead, everything in our marriage has been about you. As for my parenting skills, I am a good mother. And I'd be a better wife if you'd be a better husband." She glared at him in the bathroom mirror. "I don't care what you say. I'm not selling the shop."

"You'll give me what I want, one way or another." Spinning her around, he bunched her nightgown up around her waist and yanked her panties off.

He overpowered her, and she forced her mind blank while he conducted his business. When he finished less than a minute later, he turned her loose and left the room. She slumped to the bathroom floor. *Is it possible for a husband to rape his own wife?* she wondered. *Because that certainly felt like rape.* Her only consolation was knowing that it was the wrong time of the month for her to get pregnant.

She was out of sorts when she met Wiley at the beach house the following day.

"I can tell something's bothering you," Wiley said. "Wanna talk about it?" They were curled up on the sofa after having his homemade chili for lunch.

"I can't do this anymore, Wiley," she said, shifting on the sofa to face him. "The guilt is killing me. But I can't stay married to Max either. I'm miserable with him." She didn't dare tell him what Max had done to her the night before.

Wiley took her in his arms. "Then let's get married."

"We need to get divorced first. And I'm terrified of how Max will react. The shame will destroy Mrs. Forney, and dear Edgar will hate me. I can't do that to them when they've been so good to me. And what about Lily? How am I supposed to live with myself knowing I stole my best friend's husband?"

She struggled to push him away, but he held her tight. "My marriage was in trouble long before I fell in love with you."

"I'm scared, Wiley. What if something happens and I lose Alex?"

"You're not going to lose Alex. We'll wait an acceptable period after our divorces are final before we start officially dating."

She looked up at him, her eyes wet with tears. "Dare we hope?"

"We'll do more than hope. We'll make our happily ever after happen for us." He kissed her lightly on the lips. "It's a lot to think about, and we don't have to decide today. We'll take our time. Plan it out right. Make sure that no one gets hurt."

"Everyone's going to get hurt, Wiley."

She kissed him back, a passionate kiss that left both of them longing for more. Stretched out on the sofa, they explored each other's bodies, venturing further than they'd ever dared.

She found Wiley's gentle hands and tender kisses reassuring after the rough way Max had treated her the night before. As they were approaching the point of no return, Iris jumped up from the couch, grabbed her clothes, and disappeared into the bathroom.

"I'm so sorry, Iris," Wiley said through the bathroom door. "I didn't mean for things to go so far. I can't help myself. I want you so badly."

Iris finished putting on her clothes and opened the door. "And I want you. But not like this." She grabbed her purse and coat from the living room and walked to the front door. "I can't meet you here anymore. Not until we figure things out. If we can figure things out."

She hurried to her car and sped away. She was ten miles outside of Beaufort when she spotted Max's Wagoneer behind her. Heart thumping against her rib cage, she drove straight to the shop and parallel parked on the street out front. When he drove past her, she waved and he waved back.

He was waiting for her in their bedroom when she arrived home three hours later. "Where were you coming from when I saw you this afternoon?"

"Cutting greenery at the Mathesons' farm." The lie came easily. She often went to the farm for greens. "What about you?" She tried to sound casual despite her pounding heart. "What were you doing on that side of town?"

"I was returning from a meeting with a client in Yemassee. But my whereabouts are not in question. Yours are. Who were you with at the Mathesons' farm? Since Lily's in Atlanta, I have to assume you were with Wiley."

"Don't be ridiculous, Max. I was cutting greens. Alone. Lily has given me permission to go there anytime I need."

Max grabbed a handful of her hair and jerked her head back. "I don't believe you. When I find out you're lying to me—and I *will* find out you're lying to me—you'll be sorry."

CHAPTER SEVENTEEN

Almost a year to the date, Lily returned to Beaufort as suddenly and unexpectedly as she'd disappeared. Wiley left Iris a note on the office desk. There was no fragrance or rose petals or salutation.

Lily's back. Meet me at the cottage as soon as possible. We need to talk.

Iris had spent the last three months on eggshells. She'd gone to Edisto to meet Wiley only once, and while she'd relished those few stolen moments in his arms, she'd been too much of a nervous wreck to risk seeing him again. However, they exchanged notes daily. As for Max, even though she hated every minute of it, she managed to be his dutiful wife. With the exception of sex. She kept that at bay by feigning a series of yeast infections.

Wiley's note had thrown her stomach in knots. "I'm going home. I'm not feeling well," she said to Felicia as she fled the shop.

She checked her rearview mirror frequently as she drove out of town, stopping only once for gas before she got on the highway. Iris had worked herself into a state of extreme agitation by the time she arrived at the beach cottage, her imagination tormented with visions of Lily's homecoming. Of Wiley giving his son a bath and tucking him into bed before joining his wife at a candlelit table. Of the elaborate feast Lily had prepared and the expensive red wine she'd brought with her from Atlanta. Of Lily seducing Wiley and Wiley agreeing to give their marriage another chance. Iris couldn't bear the thought of losing him.

Her car skidded to a halt in the gravel driveway in front of the cottage. She was so frantic to get to Wiley, she left her car door open and her purse on the passenger seat. It was the middle of winter. All the neighboring houses were boarded up, and no one was around for miles.

The front door banged open, and Wiley hurried out to greet her. When he tried to take her in his arms, she pushed him away and stepped back. "Tell me everything."

"She was served divorce papers two days ago. I was expecting her to call, not to reappear out of the blue. It was the strangest thing, Iris. When I got home last night, she was at the stove, barefoot, simmering marinara sauce as though she'd never left, as though everything was perfectly fine in our marriage."

Iris shivered, realizing she'd run out of the shop without her coat.

"You're freezing. Let's get you inside." Placing an arm around her waist, he walked her inside to the kitchen. "I'll make you some coffee."

"I don't want coffee, Wiley. I want an explanation. Are you going back to her?"

His jaw went slack. "Why would you say such a thing when you know I've started divorce proceedings? You're the one I want to be with."

Relief washed over her. "Did you tell her about us?"

He placed his hands on her shoulders. "I would never do that, Iris—not without discussing it with you first."

"What did you tell her?"

"The truth. That I'm not in love with her anymore. She threw a temper tantrum, of course. She says she'll never let me go."

"I'm so sorry, Wiley. I didn't know it was going to be this hard." She rested her head on his chest, and he pulled her close. Despite the reservations she'd harbored over the past three months, she knew in her heart they were meant to be together.

Wiley and Iris were so wrapped up in each other's arms that neither heard the front door open and close, followed by footsteps in the hallway. "Well now, isn't this cozy?" Max's loud voice startled them.

Iris shoved Wiley away. "Max, what're you doing here?"

Max crossed the room in three strides, grabbing her tightly by the arm. "You cheap little tramp, how dare you cheat on me."

"I didn't cheat on you, Max. At least not like you think. But I can't help my feelings for him. I love him." Iris readied herself for her husband's angry response, but the smack that landed across her face stunned her more than it hurt.

Max pointed at the door. "Go back to Beaufort, Iris. We'll talk about this tonight when I get home."

Her gaze shifted to Wiley, who nodded for her to leave.

She turned and fled the house. She trusted Wiley to handle it. He would convince Max that a divorce was the best thing for everyone. She started her engine, but she couldn't bring herself to put the car in gear. Her face burned where Max had hit her. She'd never seen him so angry. What if Wiley and Max got into a fistfight and one of them was badly injured? It would be her fault. She debated whether to go back inside, finally deciding to return to work and wait for word from Wiley. She traveled a mile down the road before turning around. She couldn't leave Edisto until she was certain that Wiley was safe.

The house was empty. Through the sliding glass doors, she spotted the men walking to the end of the dock with Wiley in front and Max closely behind. She tore through the sitting room, out onto the porch, and down the wooden stairs leading to the dock. When the sound of her feet pounding the boardwalk alerted him to her presence, Max grabbed hold of Wiley from behind and spun him around, pressing a revolver against his temple.

She gasped. "Don't hurt him! Please, Max! I'm begging you. This is between you and me. Leave him out of it."

Max tightened his grip on Wiley and aimed the gun at her. "Would you rather I shoot you instead, Iris?"

She stood motionless, terrified to move but willing her voice to sound calm. "There's no reason for you to shoot anyone. We can work this out."

"Wiley and I will work this out. You, Iris, are going to run along home. If you do as I say, no one will get hurt."

Wiley's brown eyes pleaded with her. "Think about your daughter, Iris."

Alex's sweet little face popped into her head. If Max killed Iris, he'd go to prison for murder and Alex would be left without parents. She would live with her grandparents, at least for a while. But they weren't getting any younger. After Edgar and Anna died, Alex would be an orphan. And she couldn't let that happen to her daughter.

"Why don't you come with me, Max? We can follow each other home. We'll have a nice long talk and work this out, just you and me."

He leveled the gun at her. "I'm warning you, Iris. Beat it."

She walked backward up the dock, holding her hands out in front. "Okay. I'm leaving. I'll go back to Beaufort and wait for you there. Walk away from this, Max. I realize you're upset, but it's not worth going to prison over."

She turned and sprinted up the dock, terrified she'd hear the crack of the revolver followed by the searing pain of a bullet ripping through her body. She skirted the house, jumped into her car, and sped toward Beaufort, praying the whole way. *Please don't let anything happen to Wiley. Please, God, oh please.*

Her heart rate had lowered slightly by the time she reached town, but she was too upset to go home. She returned to work, confident that Max would never come to the shop. Flowers were beneath him, frivolous women's business.

Iris opened the door, shocked to find Lily at the register, ringing up a transaction. "What're you doing here?" Lily asked when the customer had left the store. "Felicia said you went home sick."

"I'm better now. Must've been something I ate." Iris felt awkward, as though she should hug her friend, yet guilt prevented her from even looking Lily in the eye. She busied herself with tidying up the counter. "The bigger question is, what're you doing here, Lily? You disappeared suddenly, without so much as a word of goodbye. You never called once the whole time you were gone, and then you show up out of the blue as though nothing has happened."

"I didn't leave without a word, Iris. I left Wiley to take care of my share of the responsibilities in my absence. I wouldn't have gone if I didn't think you capable of handling the shop. I thought you'd be happy to see me." Lily reached out to her, and Iris gave her a stiff hug.

"Where's Felicia?"

"She took Gus for a walk in his stroller. That child has gotten to be a handful. The terrible twos, I guess." Lily moved to the front door, peering up and down the street as if looking for Felicia and Gus.

"Are you over your depression now?"

"I don't think of it as depression," she said, still staring out the window. "I felt like I was suffocating, and I needed to sort through my life."

"Sounds like depression to me. So, did you? Sort out your life?"

Lily turned around to face her. "I did some things in Atlanta I'm not exactly proud of, but those experiences taught me some valuable lessons and helped me find my way back here. I have a wonderful life in Beaufort and a marriage worth saving."

The color drained from Iris's face.

"Are you sure you're feeling okay, Iris? You look pale."

She shook her head. "I suddenly feel sick again. Excuse me for a minute." Iris burst through the swinging doors and locked herself in the tiny restroom in the back. She wet a paper towel and pressed it to her face and neck. Lowering the lid, she sat down on the toilet, propped her elbows on her knees, and buried her face in her hands. Lily had returned home to reclaim her life—her husband, her nanny, her place behind the counter at Lily's—everything Iris had helped herself to in her absence. And now her horrible mistake had put Wiley's life in danger.

Iris finally pulled herself together enough to exit the bathroom. Felicia had returned with Gus, his adorable face covered in chocolate from the ice cream cone Felicia had bought for him. He had his mother's red hair and clear green eyes. And his father's sweet smile and thoughtful expression.

For much of the afternoon, Felicia covered the front while Lily worked in the office and Iris cleaned out the cooler. Gus wandered around the shop, his eyes wide with wonderment at each new discovery. He helped Iris organize a large shipment of flowers, his lower lip sticking out in a pout when he accidentally broke the stem of a white tulip.

"It's okay, buddy," Iris said, taking him in her arms. "It happens all the time. Look"—she broke a stem in half to demonstrate—"I break them too." He giggled. She saw nothing of the terrible twos in him, only his father's gentle nature.

Despite having Gus as a distraction, she jumped every time the phone rang or the bell over the front door jangled, announcing the arrival of a customer. She hung around after closing on the off chance that Wiley might show up.

"You can go home, you know," Lily said at five thirty. "I'll take care of the deposit."

"Oh, right." The headache that had been threatening all afternoon began to throb. "I'm used to waiting for Wiley to go over the day's business."

"Well, you don't have to worry about that anymore now that I'm back. Wiley went to Edisto to make certain the pipes didn't freeze after this last cold spell." Lily retrieved Iris's purse and coat from the office. "Run along home now. You have your own family to tend to."

Iris gritted her teeth. *Run along home.* Max had said that same thing to her earlier. She was tired of everyone treating her like a child.

She took her things from Lily and headed toward the door.

"When you see Cora tonight, tell her to come to my house in the morning," Lily said. "You can drop Alex off on the way here. We'll share Cora until you can find your own nanny."

Iris left the shop without so much as a glance in Lily's direction. Iris and Wiley were simply pawns in Lily's Game of Life—puppets for her to manipulate to her liking.

CHAPTER EIGHTEEN

Dreading the inevitable confrontation with Max, Iris drove across the bridge to Lady's Island and back. When she finally summoned the nerve to go home, she found him in the upstairs sitting room, puffing on a cigar with the baby blowing bubbles and making razzing sounds in her playpen at his feet.

"Put that out, Max." She set an ashtray at the table beside his chair. "Cigar smoke is not good for the baby. Where's Cora?"

"I sent her home." As he stubbed the cigar out in the ashtray, she studied his demeanor. He appeared calm. Almost too calm.

"What'd you do to Wiley?" Her heart raced, and she worried it might explode.

Perspiration beaded along his brow. "I didn't shoot your lover, although I should've killed both of you on the spot."

"Quiet! You'll upset the baby."

"She doesn't understand what I'm saying." He lifted Alex out of her playpen and thrust her at Iris. "Put her in her crib. You and I need to talk."

As she changed the baby's diaper and settled her into her crib, Iris considered how to approach her husband about a divorce. *Confident and direct. Don't back down.*

She crossed the hall from the nursery and entered their bedroom, closing the door behind her. "Please believe me when I tell you Wiley and I never meant to hurt anyone. I want a divorce, Max. Our marriage is over."

He burst into maniacal laughter. "To give you a divorce, Iris, would be admitting I made a mistake in marrying you. And I can't do that."

She stared at her husband, seeing him for the sick man he truly was. "Because that would be the ultimate victory for your mother."

"You're a quick study," he said, tapping her cheek. "I also have my family's wealth to consider. Divorce is expensive. Especially when one is married to a gold digger like you."

She looked him square in the eye. "I don't want your money, Max. I want to be free of you."

Max's body tensed as his face grew dark. "Bad things happen to wives who disobey their husbands." In one swift motion, he grabbed the collar of her pleated shirtdress and tore it off her body, the buttons pinging as they hit the walls and hardwood floors. He threw her down on the bed, and with the weight of his body crushing her, he tugged off her panties. Fumbling with his pants, he kneed her legs apart. She screamed when he thrust himself into her, and he clamped his hand over her mouth. Panting loudly, he pounded his body on top of hers until he came. She squirmed beneath him, but he wouldn't budge. He pressed his forearm against her neck, crushing her windpipe. "If anything like this ever happens again, I'll strangle you with my bare hands. Do you understand?"

She nodded, her eyes wide with terror. What she understood was that her life was over. She would never again know happiness.

Iris took a long hot shower, scrubbing her skin until it was raw. Slipping on her flannel gown, she waited for Max to go downstairs for dinner before risking a phone call to Wiley. Her panic escalated when no one answered the phone at the beach cottage. She called Lily under the pretense of making arrangements for Cora to take care of the children the following day.

"I told you to bring Alex by here on your way to work," Lily said in a clipped tone.

"You sound preoccupied," Iris said, her knuckles white on the receiver. "Is something wrong?"

Lily let out a concerned sigh. "It's Wiley. I expected him home from Edisto hours ago."

"He probably got wrapped up in one of his home-improvement projects. I'm sure he'll be home soon," she said, managing to keep her voice even despite her fear he might never come home again.

After putting Alex down for the night, Iris curled up on the daybed in the nursery and pondered the future. Alex deserved a happy home with parents who loved one another. No matter how hard she tried, she couldn't imagine ever being happy as Max's wife.

The memory of his beefy paws bruising her skin, his mouth crushing hers, and his arm choking her prevented her from sleeping. She heard Max's heavy tread up the stairs, followed by the sound of the nursery door clicking open and then closed.

Around midnight, Iris tiptoed to the sitting room, where she'd left her purse when she'd come home. She searched by hand for the prescription bottle of sleeping pills she'd had filled earlier in the week before. When she didn't find them, she dumped the contents of her purse on the floor.

"What're you doing, Iris?"

Startled, she looked up to find Max looming over her. "I'm looking for my sleeping pills."

"I see." He leaned against the doorjamb, his arms crossing his ample girth and a smirk playing on his lips. "I thought maybe you were planning to run off with your lover."

She combed her items into a pile and transferred them back to her purse. When she stood to face him, Iris felt no fear, only pity. "You're a monster, Max Forney. If you ever treat me that way again, I will stab you in the heart in your sleep."

"Don't give me a reason to treat you that way, and we won't have a problem." He stomped off to bed, closing their bedroom door behind him.

By the time dawn broke on her sleepless night, Iris had resigned herself to a life of hell as Max's wife. He was a maniac. Leaving him would place not only her own safety but also her daughter's at risk.

She dressed early and was waiting with Alex in the kitchen when Cora arrived. "I can't wait to see that baby boy," Cora said when Iris told her Gus and Lily had returned from Atlanta.

"If it doesn't suit you to keep both children, I'll figure something else out," Iris said as she drove Cora and Alex to Lily's house.

"No, ma'am. This suits me just fine. My youngest, Lettie, is having a baby. She'll be out of work for a coupla months. She's gonna need all the financial help I can give her."

"All right, then," Iris said, planting her hands firmly on the steering wheel. "Lily and I'll see what we can do about getting a stroller fit for two."

Lily answered the door with Gus on one hip, the phone receiver tucked under her ear, and the long cord wrapped around her legs. Gus was slobbering over a set of keys gripped in his tiny fist.

"Thank goodness you're here," Lily said, placing the receiver in the phone's cradle. "Wiley hasn't come back from Edisto yet, and I'm worried sick. I'm going to drive up and check on him."

Iris leaned against the back of the sofa to prevent her legs from collapsing beneath her. "Do you want me to go with you?"

"I should probably go alone. You're needed at the shop anyway." Lily's green eyes darted about the room. "Can you help me find my car keys? I know they're here somewhere."

"Come to Cora," the nanny said, reaching for the toddler. "And give your mama her keys." She took the keys from the baby and handed them to Lily. "You be careful now, Miss Lily."

"Thanks, Cora. But I'll be fine." Lily removed her peacoat from the closet, retrieved her handbag from the kitchen, and hurried out the door.

Iris spent a few minutes helping Cora and the children get situated before heading off to the shop. *Keep busy,* she told herself repeatedly throughout the day as she prepared a special promotion for the upcoming Valentine's holiday. She'd had no word from Lily and was frantic by the time she returned to the Mathesons' after closing.

Lily had just arrived home from Edisto.

"Did you find him?" Iris asked, following her into the house.

"No. And I'm worried sick." Lily dropped her bag on the floor beside the door. "His car was parked in the driveway, and the house was unlocked, but there was no sign of him anywhere. I thought maybe he'd gone for a run, but after waiting for several hours, I finally called the sheriff and reported him missing. What do you know about his disappearance, Iris?" As she studied her face, Lily's questioning gaze left little doubt that she was suspicious of Iris.

"I . . . um . . ." The phone rang, saving Iris from having to answer.

Lily lifted the receiver. The color drained from her face, and her lip began to quiver as she listened to the caller.

"I'm on my way," she said and hung up the phone.

"What is it?" Iris asked. "What happened?"

"They just found Wiley's body three docks down from ours."

CHAPTER NINETEEN

Iris stayed by Lily's side for forty-eight hours after Wiley's body was discovered. She was ridden with guilt and anguish, and she felt like a fraud playing the role of supportive friend to the grieving widow.

Lily refused to discuss the details of the investigation except to say that Wiley had fallen, hit his head, knocked himself out, and drowned. "The coroner has ruled it an accident. At least preliminarily. They still have to do the autopsy."

Iris was surprised there was no mention of a gunshot wound. She suspected, she *knew*, there was more to Wiley's death than a simple accident. She was near hysterics when she finally had a chance to confront Max in their bedroom the evening of the third day.

"What'd you do to him?" She pounded her fists against Max's chest. "You killed him. You're a murderer and a rapist."

"Control yourself, Iris," he said, taking her by the arms and shaking her. "If you don't get yourself together, the wrong people might find out about your little affair."

"So what if they do?" She wrenched herself free of his grip. "I can't continue this charade for one more second. I'm going to the police and telling them everything I know about what happened at the cottage that day." She spun around and marched toward the door.

"I wouldn't do that if I were you. Unless, of course, you're prepared to go to jail."

She paused with one hand on the doorknob. "Why would I go to jail? I haven't done anything wrong."

"Maybe. Maybe not. But the police will think you killed Wiley when they find out you were sleeping with him."

She turned around to face him. "That's absurd. And for the millionth time, I wasn't sleeping with him."

"You were doing something with him. And I have the proof." Max opened the top drawer of his bureau and handed her a stack of five-by-seven black-and-white photographs.

Cold dread fell over her as she sifted through the photographs of Wiley and her in each other's arms. "Where'd you get these?"

"I hired a private investigator to follow you."

Iris held the photographs near his face and tore them in half.

Max laughed out loud. "You don't think I'm that stupid, do you? I have another set, along with the negatives, in my safe deposit box at the bank."

Iris jutted out her chin. "So it's your word against mine. The police will believe me over you when I convince them you killed Wiley in a jealous rage."

"I'm not the only one who had motive, my dear. Wiley's wife found out about your affair and demanded he break it off with you. In a fit of anger, you cracked him over the head, pushed him off the dock, and tried to cover it up by making it look like a suicide."

"Suicide? What suicide? The coroner ruled his death an accident."

"That'll change when they get the results from the toxicology tests. You see, Wiley had a lethal dose of sleeping pills in his system. Your sleeping pills. I dropped the empty bottle beside the boardwalk in plain view for the police to find. I'm expecting them to show up any minute to take you in for questioning."

Chill bumps broke out on her arms. "You framed me."

"What'd you expect? I'm certainly not going to prison for something you're responsible for. And you *are* responsible for this mess, Iris."

Iris bolted out of the bedroom and down the hall to the nursery, where she'd taken up residence since the night Max had raped her. She buried her face in her pillow, so as not to wake the baby, and screamed until she was exhausted and her voice was hoarse.

~

Iris waited on pins and needles for the police to come for her, feeling more relieved with each passing day and no sign of them. Any number of things could've happened to that empty pill bottle. The wind. The tide. An animal foraging for food.

With Wiley gone, Iris assumed Lily would move to Atlanta permanently. When Lily began working on floral designs for the upcoming wedding season, Iris broached the subject. "Are you planning to stay in Beaufort?"

"Where else would I go?" Lily asked, as though she'd never considered living elsewhere.

"To Atlanta, to be with your family. Or have you had a change of heart about our fair city? I seem to remember you saying this sleepy little town would never wake up."

"There's nothing left for me in Atlanta," Lily said in a snippy tone that ended the conversation.

I did some things in Atlanta that I'm not exactly proud of, Lily had confessed on her first day back in town. When Norma had come for Wiley's funeral, Iris noticed tension between Lily and her mother. She suspected whatever *things* Lily had done in Atlanta were responsible for that tension and were the reason Lily thought there was nothing left for her in Atlanta.

During the days and months following Wiley's death, Iris experienced a sadness she'd never known. She was too lost in her grief to notice she'd missed three periods until the middle of May, when the buttons on her jeans were strained. While she was excited about having another baby, the pregnancy served as a reminder of that horrible day in January.

She waited until the end of June, when she could no longer hide the pregnancy, to tell Lily as they walked home from work together.

Iris could see the wheels spinning in Lily's mind. "If the baby's due on October 22, that means you conceived at the end of January, around the time Wiley died."

"I guess so," Iris said with her best nonchalant shrug.

"There's something I've been meaning to talk to you about, Iris. You and Wiley worked together a lot while I was gone. I'm sure he told you about our marital problems. He'd grown so distant, and I wondered if maybe he was seeing someone." Lily stopped on the sidewalk and turned to face Iris. "Do you know if he was having an affair?"

Iris's heart skipped a beat, and her face warmed. She yearned to tell Lily the truth about her relationship with Wiley and the circumstances surrounding his death. Even though they'd never been intimate, she'd loved Wiley with all her heart, and in Iris's book, that was the greatest possible act of betrayal. To confess to Lily would mean the end of their friendship. She would lose the shop and her children. And depending on how things played out, there was a strong likelihood she would go to jail. "I know he had that big trial that kept him preoccupied. But another woman? I think you're mistaken."

Lily squinted her eyes and pressed her lips thin as she studied Iris. "I'm no angel, Iris. And neither are you. I promise we can get past this if you just tell me the truth."

"There's nothing to tell." Despite her best effort to keep a straight face, Iris knew that Lily knew she was lying.

She turned away and hurried off toward home before Lily could see the tears welling in her eyes.

Lily's suspicions and Iris's guilt added friction to their already-strained relationship, and their work suffered because of it. When the atmosphere became so tense that Felicia threatened to quit, Lily and Iris, with forced smiles, made an effort to get along.

On the second Tuesday in October, Iris was creating an arrangement of orange lilies for a client's dinner party when her water broke. Felicia was traveling with her boyfriend of the moment in Europe, and Lily had gone out to make a delivery.

Iris called Max at work. "I'm sorry, Mrs. Forney," his secretary said. "He's at lunch with a client."

Iris's eyes traveled to the wall clock. "But it's after three o'clock."

The secretary cleared her throat. "I'm aware of the time. I'll have him call you when he returns."

"But I need to reach him now," Iris said, the urgency in her voice increasing with the onset of a contraction. "It's an emergency. Did he say where he was going?"

"He did not say. Can I leave him a message?"

"Tell him his wife's in labor." She slammed the phone down and doubled over in pain. Ten minutes later Lily returned and found her on the floor behind the counter.

"Good Lord," Lily said, rushing to her side.

"I tried to call Max, but he's not in the office. I was going to drive myself to the hospital, but it hurts too bad to move. I feel the baby's head—" An intense contraction hit, and she let out a piercing scream.

Lily waited for the pain to subside before grabbing Iris by the arm. "I'm going to lift you up on a count of three. One. Two. Three." She helped Iris off the floor and out the front door to her car.

With the hazard lights blinking on her Pontiac station wagon, Lily blasted her horn and blew through red lights as they sped across town to the hospital. She never left Iris's side during the delivery, wiping sweat off her forehead and coaching her with encouraging words. After her baby's birth, Iris was too exhausted to care that Lily was the first to hold her.

Lily gazed down at the bundle in her arms. "She looks just like you, Iris," she said in a tone of relief. "I think you should name her Julia."

"Why Julia?"

"It's the name Wiley and I had picked out if Gus had been a girl."

She was touched that Lily would suggest such a thing. And she took the gesture as a sign that Lily had come to terms with the past and was ready to move on. Iris had not discussed names with Max, and she thought Julia had a certain romantic sound to it, so when Lily placed the baby in her arms, she said, "Julia it is."

Lily stayed with Iris until late that night. They experienced a closeness for the first time since before Gus was born. During the weeks that followed, Lily stopped by the house frequently during Iris's maternity leave under the pretense of discussing flower business, although Iris suspected she wanted to see Julia. Three-year-old Gus, equally enamored with the baby, fretted over her like a protective older brother in a manner that reminded Iris of his father.

Julia was a blessing in so many ways. She brought joy and peace to everyone with her bright smile and easygoing personality. It was because of her that Iris and Lily were finally able to heal.

CHAPTER TWENTY

Edgar Forney died unexpectedly in April 1982 after suffering a fatal heart attack at his yacht club. Mrs. Forney had a stroke in June and died in early August. When Max and Iris moved their family to the second floor of the house, they took separate bedrooms, a declaration that their sex life had ended. She'd pressed Max about his whereabouts on the day Julia was born, and he'd admitted to having taken a mistress. Although married to a husband who didn't love her, Iris had plenty else to be grateful for—daughters she adored, an elegant home in a picturesque town, and a career that brought her much joy.

On the second Tuesday in January of 1983, when Iris and Lily reopened the store after the holidays and their customary week of vacation, Lily announced she'd gotten engaged on New Year's Eve. She and Hector Jacobs had been dating for three months. He was recently retired from his job on Wall Street and was Lily's senior by twenty years.

"But don't you want more children?" Iris asked.

"Why would I want more children when I have Gus and Julia?"

Lily had come to think of Julia as her second child, but Iris didn't mind. Gus was without a father because of her, and sharing her daughter with them was the least she could do.

"Besides, I'll be too busy to have a baby. We're going to start looking for waterfront properties. I'd prefer to renovate a historic home, but if we can't find one, Hector says I can build as big a house as I want."

Lily and Hector were married in a small service at the Episcopal church in early February. Iris hosted the wedding reception, a catered sit-down luncheon for twenty, her first party as mistress of Live Oaks. She was proud to admit it went off without a hitch, and even Max complimented her.

Hector took Lily and Gus on a month's vacation to Europe. On the afternoon of her return, Lily invited Iris over after work for a glass of wine. "We have business to discuss. Can you arrange for Cora to stay late with your girls?"

"I'll call her right now," Iris said.

Lily was waiting for her at the front door of her little yellow house when Iris arrived at five thirty. She looked glamorous, her auburn hair had a healthy luster, and her emerald eyes sparkled.

"Married life really suits you," Iris said as she kissed the air beside her cheek.

"Hector spoils me rotten. He's upstairs giving Gus a bath as we speak. Come." She took Iris by the hand. "I can't wait to tell you my news." She led her through the house to the back porch, where she had a bottle of champagne chilling in an ice bucket.

"What're we celebrating?"

She pointed at the row of rocking chairs. "Sit down, and I'll tell you."

Once they were settled, Lily said, "We've made an offer on Riverview." She clapped her hands together like a child. "And they've accepted it. Hector spent the last week of our honeymoon on the phone negotiating with the owners. The house has over ten thousand square feet and needs extensive renovations."

"I'm so happy for you, Lily," Iris said, genuinely excited. "It's what you've always wanted."

"Here's the best part." Lily sat on the edge of her chair. "We're turning the house into an inn."

"But what about the shop?"

Her face grew serious, and she slid back in her seat. "I don't *have* to sell Lily's. I can remain an investor if you don't have the equity to buy me out. But renovating and running the inn will take all my time."

"The money's not the issue. You're the face of Lily's, the Flower Princess, not me. You're the one customers request for big events."

"Don't sell yourself short, Iris. You have great talent." Lily hopped up and paced around the porch. "I don't see any reason I couldn't continue helping with weddings. At least for a while. You could pay me an hourly rate. Heck, I'd do it for free for fun. I'll transition out slowly so people will get used to dealing with you." She stopped in front of her. "And don't forget—you managed just fine the whole year I was in Atlanta."

"That's true." She would need a loan. Iris, scared to death but never happier, stood to face Lily. "I'll do it! I'll buy you out. But only as long as you agree to help with big weddings."

"Deal." Lily held out her hand, and they shook on it. "Let's celebrate."

They drank the whole bottle of champagne while making plans for the future. Iris, more than a little tipsy when she left, skipped all the way home. She found Max in the study she still thought of as Edgar's.

"What d'you want?" he asked when he saw her in the doorway, his tone gruff and his speech slightly slurred.

"For you to loan me the money to buy Lily out of the business." She crossed the room to his desk but didn't sit down. She didn't plan to stay long enough to get comfortable.

"And why would I do that?"

"Because if you don't, I'll tell everyone in town about your extracurricular love life. As if they don't already know."

He brandished a silver-plated letter opener at her. "Fine. Anything to get you off my back."

Being sole proprietor gave Iris the boost of confidence she needed to make the changes she'd been wanting to make. She had good instincts. She knew her product and her clientele. And her changes paid off. Her reputation continued to grow, and within the year she was booking weddings up and down the South Carolina coast. By the end of the second year, she'd paid back Max's loan.

Lily immersed herself in renovating the inn, but she continued, as promised, to help with the big weddings. Spending less time together proved healthy for their friendship. Wiley's death had impacted them greatly and led to an unspoken agreement never to discuss the subject of the past.

~

Iris and Lily moved through the next three decades together as best friends. Regardless of how busy their lives, they spent every Sunday afternoon together. They shared the good times. When Gus was the star quarterback in high school, Iris never missed a game. Just as Lily was front and center when Julia graduated valedictorian. And they supported each other through the bad. When Alex was constantly stirring up trouble in high school. When, after five years of marriage, Hector died from lung cancer. When Julia dropped out of college and eloped with the man who'd gotten her pregnant. When the doctor diagnosed Lily with pancreatic cancer. Iris had been at her side then and nearly every waking moment since.

PART THREE

Iris and Julia

CHAPTER TWENTY-ONE

JULIA

Present Day

Julia packed up their clothes and Jackson's baby equipment and donated everything else in the house to the annual yard sale at Marty's fire station. None of the household items were worth anything. A collection of chipped pottery plates and mismatched furniture from Goodwill was all she had to show for fifteen years of marriage. She couldn't bring herself to go through Jack's things. She kept only his gold wedding band, his worn Bible, and the pewter urn containing his ashes. The firemen would find a home for the rest of his possessions.

After a tearful goodbye to first Sandy and then her friends at Duke's, she spent her last ten dollars on gas and coasted into Beaufort on fumes. She was surprised how much her hometown had grown since she was last there, that day in early May of 2002 when she'd gone to her parents for help and they'd turned their backs on her. The outskirts of the small town had expanded for miles with attractive-looking restaurants and shopping centers, but everything appeared the same in the historic downtown area.

As she drove down Port Republic Street toward home, she noticed new faces on the neighbors working in the yards of old houses that had been renovated. On both sides of the street, azaleas bloomed in vibrant shades of pink and red while trees and shrubs boasted the vivid green hue of new growth. Two cars were parked in the driveway at Live Oaks—her mother's Volvo wagon and a sleek black Cadillac that could only be her father's. The truck sputtered, and the engine died as she pulled in beside the Volvo.

Jackson had fallen asleep during the drive, and she eased him out of his car seat so as not to wake him up. She started for the side porch door leading to the kitchen and stopped when she was a few feet away. Family and friends used that door. She was neither. She walked around to the front of the house and rang the bell.

Her mother's jaw dropped when she saw Julia in her doorway.

"Hello, Mama. It's been a long time."

At the sound of her voice, Jackson whimpered and stirred in her arms.

Midway down the center hallway, Max emerged from his study in a cloud of cigar smoke with a tumbler of whiskey in his hand. "Who's at the door, Iris?" He tromped toward them, flashing a look of surprise when he saw Julia. "What on earth are you doing here? And where's your husband?"

Jackson's lip curled out in a pout at the sound of Max's gruff voice.

"My husband is dead," she said, jiggling the baby when he began to cry.

"I see," Max said, glaring at her through a haze of smoke. "I'm sorry to hear that for your sake, but that doesn't change anything between us."

Julia glared back at him. Middle age suited her mother. If anything, Iris was even lovelier than she'd been in her youth. But time had not treated her father well. Aside from a few wisps of hair, the top of his head was nearly bald. The wrinkles in his scowl had deepened, and he'd put on so much weight his belly sagged over his belt.

"I made a mistake in coming here." Julia took a step backward on the front stoop. "I'd rather sleep in my truck than ask a favor of you."

Iris opened the door wider. "Don't go, honey. This is your home. You're always welcome here."

"Really, Mama? Because that's not what you said when you kicked me out all those years ago," Julia said, hoping not to start an argument right out of the gate, even though the past weighed heavily between them. "I expected that of him." She aimed her thumb at Max. "But I was heartbroken when you took his side."

Iris lowered her gaze. "And I've regretted my actions every single day since then."

"Then why'd you do it?" Julia asked, her chin set firm.

"Because I thought you were making a mistake by dropping out of college."

Julia shifted the baby from one hip to the other. "I was pregnant, Mama. You wanted me to have an abortion."

"And where is that child now?" Max looked past her as though expecting to find a teenager standing in the yard behind her.

"I had a miscarriage. And three more after that. Jackson is the first baby I've been able to carry to term," she said, kissing the top of his head.

Iris touched her fingers to her lips. "How horrible for you. I'm so sorry."

An expression close to pity crossed her father's face when he said, "If you'd gotten pregnant with anyone else's child, I would've helped you. But that man was beneath you."

"How would you know? You never gave him a chance. Funny thing is, you would've really liked him. Jack Martin was the best person I've ever met. He died in a car accident rushing me to the hospital when I went into labor during a storm."

Unshed tears glistened in her mother's eyes. "Oh, sweetheart, you could've been killed."

"I wish I *had* died in the accident. My life is nothing without Jack." Tears slid down Julia's cheeks. "I was so distraught, I almost left the baby at the hospital. I should've put him up for adoption. I'm flat broke, but I love him too much to give him up. I can't lose the only piece of Jack I have left."

Iris reached out and cupped the baby's head. "He's your child, honey, your flesh and blood. He deserves to be with you. We'll help you get back on your feet."

"No matter how heartless you think I am, I can't turn an innocent child out on the street. You can either stay here until you get back on your feet, or"—Max clenched his cigar between his teeth as he tugged his alligator wallet out of his back pocket—"I'll give you what money I have on me." He opened the wallet and removed a wad of crisp fifty-dollar bills.

Julia's eyes grew wide. As tempted as she was to take it, a few hundred dollars would provide only a short-term fix for her situation.

Her mother jabbed an elbow into Max's side. "Put your wallet away, Max. That won't solve Julia's problem. That will only buy her a week's time. She's staying here with us, and that's final." She stepped out onto the stoop with Julia. "I'll help you get your things out of the car."

Julia locked eyes with Max. "This is not an ideal situation for me either. I promise it will only be for a little while."

He humphed and turned back toward his study.

Iris took her by the arm and led her across the lawn to the driveway. "You're welcome to stay in your old room, but if you don't mind the stairs, you can have the whole third floor to yourself."

"What about the guest cottage?" Julia asked, hoping to get as far away as possible from Max's cigar smoke.

"That won't work. Alex is currently occupying the guest cottage."

Julia raised an eyebrow. "What's she doing living at home?"

"A lot has changed around here. We'll fill you in over dinner. As it happens, I'm making shrimp and grits, your favorite, as I recall. I had a feeling something like this might happen today."

When they reached the truck, Julia held the baby out to her mother. "Do you want to hold him while I unload my things?"

Iris's face lit up as she took the baby in her arms. "Come to me, sweet boy. I finally got myself a grandchild."

He grinned, revealing his new bottom teeth, and threw his chubby arms around her neck.

Leaving her mother and son to get acquainted, Julia dragged her suitcase and Jackson's Pack 'n Play up three flights of stairs to the back-left corner bedroom with the cheerful pink striped wallpaper and green velvet draperies. The tension drained from her body as she stood in front of the window, staring over the tops of the oak trees to the Beaufort River. This room, with its natural light streaming through the four floor-to-ceiling windows, had been her secret hideout as a child, a safe haven where she'd kept her treasured books and toys away from her sister's destructive hands.

Her mother joined her moments later with Jackson on one hip and Julia's tote bag slung over the other shoulder.

"I remember I used to play here when I was little. Did this room ever belong to anyone?"

"Your father and I slept in this bedroom before your grandparents passed away and we moved down to the second floor. You were just a baby at the time. We used the other corner bedroom as a nursery." Julia followed her mother back into the hall to the smaller room next door. "Your crib is still up in the attic. We'll get it down tomorrow."

"That'd be awesome. Thanks, Mama."

"I'll go finish cooking dinner and leave you to get settled." Iris kissed the baby's cheek before handing him back to Julia. "He's a precious child, Julia, and I'm thrilled to have you home again. I hope we can put the past behind us. There's nothing I'd like more than to have you permanently in my life." She moved to the door. "Dinner's at seven thirty."

Julia smiled. "Glad to see some things haven't changed."

She spent the next ninety minutes unpacking their clothes, setting up the portable crib, and giving Jackson his nighttime feeding. After freshening up her face and hair, she took her paper grocery bag full of bottles and formula downstairs.

She'd failed to notice the changes on the main floor earlier. Someone other than her mother—the new decor was definitely not Iris's taste— had transformed the formal rooms from dark and gloomy to a stylish mix of tradition and contemporary. Walls washed in soft gray and sisal rugs complemented the priceless antiques that had been in the Forney family for four generations. The oil portraits of ancestors no one could name had been replaced by French mirrors and color-splashed canvases. But the fresh look could not erase the memories of loud arguing and angry voices. Alex had been the difficult child, testing their parents at every turn, while Julia had been the good girl, always abiding by her father's rules. Until she'd married a man he disapproved of.

She made her way through the dining room to the kitchen, where marble countertops had replaced Formica and stainless-steel commercial-grade had taken the place of the outdated appliances. A kilim rug in bold pinks and oranges adorned the floor, and a pine farm table occupied the side of the room along the bank of windows overlooking the porch and side yard.

Julia set the bag of baby bottles on the counter and joined her mother at the stove. "The house looks great, Mama. Did you hire a decorator?"

"Your father hired Alex to freshen up the place. Your sister has it in her mind to be featured in a design magazine," Iris said as she spooned grits and shrimp gravy onto four plates.

Julia tried to wrap her mind around how much the renovations were costing and how much her father was paying her sister. She'd been starving herself to feed her baby for the past eight months while her sister had been living off their parents, spending a fortune on decorating their house.

You could've had all this, Jules, she reminded herself. But she would not have traded her life with Jack for any of it.

"Dinner's ready," Iris announced, placing her spoon in the spoon rest. "The salad and bread are already on the table."

Julia took two of the plates and followed her mother into the dining room. The mahogany double-pedestal table had already been set for four with linen place mats and napkins and crystal wineglasses.

"I've been saving this rosé for a special occasion," Iris said as she poured the pink wine. "I'm sad to say I don't even know if you like rosé."

"I've never had any." Cheap chardonnay was the only wine Julia had ever been able to afford. And she hadn't bought any of that since the accident.

Voices from down the hall announced the arrival of Max and Alex. They stopped talking when they entered the room with smirks on their lips and tumblers of scotch in hand. Her sister, as striking as ever, wore gray fat-legged linen slacks beneath a cream-colored silk tunic with her dark hair cascading down her back. Her sharp facial features, chin and nose, were offset by her almond-shaped golden-brown eyes. She was a feminine, much more attractive version of their father.

Alex sauntered across the room and gave Julia a perfunctory hug. "I'm terribly sorry for your loss."

Julia held her breath to avoid inhaling her sister's overpowering floral perfume. She managed a mumbled thank-you.

They bowed their heads in prayer before claiming their seats, with Julia sitting next to her mother, opposite her father and sister. The mahogany table had been the dividing line for their family when Max and Alex teamed up against Iris and Julia in board games and family debates. And when one of the girls had gotten in trouble, their appointed parent was the one to support them. Julia tried to imagine what family dinners had been like in her absence for the past sixteen years. The vision of her mother sitting opposite Max and Alex like an innocent victim facing a firing squad came to mind.

In her youth, she'd preferred informal suppers in the kitchen on nights when her father was playing golf or out of town on business. When he was home for dinner, Max insisted they eat in the dining room. His strict enforcement of proper manners had brought many dinners to an abrupt ending with Alex and Julia in tears.

"So, where's the baby?" Alex asked.

"Upstairs, asleep," Julia said, savoring her first bite of her mother's shrimp and grits.

Alex looked about the room. "Where's your monitor thingamajig in case he cries?"

"I left his door open. My house was so small, I never needed a monitor."

"We'll go shopping for one tomorrow," Iris said. "You'll need a monitor, living all the way up on the third floor."

"Did you own or lease your house?" Alex asked, swirling her wine around in her glass. "I always envisioned you living in a double-wide."

Julia stiffened. "We owned a wonderful little waterfront cottage. It was all we ever needed. I couldn't make the mortgage payment without Jack's salary, hence the reason I'm here."

"That's the saddest thing I've ever heard," Alex said in an unsympathetic tone.

Julia set down her fork. "I've run into your friends on occasion at the beach. I heard you divorced. Twice."

"Right. And no children." She held her wineglass out to Julia as if to toast. "Never wanted any. Runny noses and regimented schedules aren't my thing."

Julia gritted her teeth. She hadn't missed their tit-for-tat insults one little bit.

Max was quiet while he ate, but Julia felt his eyes studying her. After everyone begged off dessert, Max and Alex returned to the veranda for post-dinner whiskey while Julia helped her mother with the dishes. It irritated her the way her father and sister expected her mother to wait on them. It irritated her even more the way her mother let them.

As they cleared the table, Julia asked, "Do they ever help you, Mama, with the cooking or cleanup?"

"Oh, I don't mind," Iris said, nonchalantly, as she stacked the dinner plates. "I'm used to it."

Julia gathered up the wineglasses and went with her mother to the kitchen. "It's not my place to say this, since I'm not part of the family anymore, but they should help out around here. Jack and I always shared all the household responsibilities."

Iris set the plates on the counter and turned to face Julia. "You're still very much a part of this family, Jules. Your presence might very well be the positive influence we need to change some things in this family." She turned on the faucet and began rinsing plates while Julia took them from her and placed them in the dishwasher.

"Maybe we could eat in here or out on the veranda. The relaxed atmosphere might encourage everyone to be more pleasant."

A flash of hope crossed Iris's face but quickly fell away. "Your father wouldn't go for it. You know how he likes things a certain way."

"You have a right to have your way every now and then, too, you know." When Iris scowled, Julia knew she'd gone too far. "Sorry, Mama. I didn't mean to stir the pot on my first night home."

"Not at all. You've given me something to think about," she said, attacking her iron skillet with a stiff brush.

Julia finished helping with the dishes before excusing herself for bed. She was checking in on Jackson after her shower thirty minutes later when she realized she'd forgotten to fix a bottle. He usually slept through until early morning, but she liked to have a little formula on hand for the rare occasions when he woke up during the night.

The sound of muffled voices greeted her at the bottom of the stairs. She tiptoed down the hall to her father's study. Pressing her ear against the closed door, she heard her mother say, "Yes, Max, I've told you a thousand times—she's your daughter. I've offered to get a DNA test to prove it."

Julia sprang back from the door as if she'd been scalded. The baby's bottle forgotten, she hurried back to her room upstairs and slipped beneath the crisp bed linens, pulling the covers up tight under her chin. Her mind raced as she considered the implications of what she'd overheard. Was it possible her mother had slept with another man? To think of Iris as an adulteress was outrageous, yet it made perfect sense. The hair coloring was all wrong, but the shoe fit. Her father had always treated Julia like his redheaded stepchild—because she was.

CHAPTER TWENTY-TWO

IRIS

Iris's first thought when she blinked her eyes open at daybreak on Thursday morning was of Julia. Her darling daughter had come home with her precious grandson, a little boy with all his snips and snails and puppy dog tails for Iris to spoil. She slipped out of bed, changed into her gardening clothes, and went to the kitchen for coffee. As she did every morning, rain or shine, winter or summer, she took her coffee outside to the veranda. The sunrise brought with it the promise of a new day. As the sky transitioned from lavender to pink to yellow, the first rays of golden light streamed through the canopy of live oaks onto her manicured lawn.

Her daughter's return and the subsequent argument with her husband had stirred in Iris a mixture of emotions, the primary one being guilt. Why had she gone along with Max, allowing him to banish their youngest from their lives when Julia had needed them the most? To think she'd suggested her daughter abort her own grandchild.

Iris would never forget the night in May of 2002 when Julia showed up from college out of the blue. Alex had finished her senior exams at the University of Georgia and had come home with a load of her things to await graduation the following weekend. She'd enlisted Estelle to make her favorite lamb chops and insisted they dine alfresco to celebrate the end of her academic career. Max, Alex, and Iris had been seated at the marble-topped table on the veranda when Julia's Toyota Camry pulled into the driveway. The moment she saw her daughter's puffy face and red-rimmed eyes, Iris knew something was terribly wrong.

She excused herself from the table and went to the driveway to greet Julia. "Sweetheart, this is a surprise. Are you taking a break from exams? Let me fix you a plate."

"Thanks, Mama, but I'm not hungry. I need to talk to you. I'm in a bit of a bind."

"Sure, sweetheart." She cast a nervous glance toward the veranda, where Alex and Max were watching them with interest. "Shall I call your father?"

"In a minute. I need to talk to you first. Let's go in the kitchen," Julia said and started toward the back door.

When they were alone in the kitchen, Julia blurted, "I'm in love, Mama. And I'm pregnant with his baby." Tears streamed down her cheeks, and her nose began to run. "Daddy's gonna be so mad."

"Oh, honey." Iris took her daughter in her arms and held her tight. "There, now. Everything will be all right."

But everything was far from all right. Max was irate when he found out about the pregnancy. Iris had sent Alex to her room and summoned Max to his study, the location for all serious family discussions. His hands shook as he lit a cigar. "Who's the father, damn it?" he bellowed at Julia from behind his desk. "And why didn't the coward come with you tonight?"

"He has to work tomorrow, Daddy. He's nobody you know. He's from Edisto."

Iris cringed at the mention of Edisto.

"Humph. What does he do for a living? Is he a lifeguard?"

Staring down at her feet, Julia answered, "He's a boat mechanic."

Max coughed, and cigar smoke spewed out of his nostrils. "No daughter of mine is going to marry a boat mechanic." He settled back in his chair, arms crossed over his ample belly and cigar clenched between his teeth. "You'll get an abortion. I'll pay for it, of course. I'm sure your boat mechanic can't afford it. And I'll send you backpacking in Europe this summer. By the time you get back, you'll have forgotten all about this bum."

Julia shook her head. "I love Jack too much to ever forget about him, and I'm not going to abort his baby. Will you at least meet him? He's really a nice guy."

"Never!" Max's roar echoed throughout the room. "He's not allowed in this house. And as long as you continue to see him, neither are you. Get out." He jabbed his fat finger toward the door.

Julia jumped to her feet, her face flushed with anger. "Are you seriously kicking me out of the house?"

"And the family until you come to your senses."

"I've already come to my senses," Julia said and stormed out of the room.

When Iris tried to go after her, Max blocked the door. A horrible argument ensued, the same argument they'd been having for years and would continue to have for the rest of their married life. The argument full of empty threats. She threatened to leave him, and he threatened to go to the police about her involvement in Wiley's death.

"We only have one chance at life, Max. Why not get a divorce so we can be happy?"

His answer was the same as always. "I've told you a thousand times. I'm not willing to part with half of everything I own. Besides, I like things just the way they are."

"You mean you like having me as your servant to cook and clean and do your laundry."

His twisted grin revealed teeth yellowed from cigar smoke. "If the shoe fits."

So, for the next sixteen years, they'd coexisted in their unhappy marriage, living under the same roof but sleeping in separate bedrooms. For appearances' sake, they attended certain social functions together, while leading separate lives for the most part.

~

Out of the corner of her eye, Iris detected movement in her garden. Alex never showed herself before nine, and even then, Iris avoided having a conversation with her until Alex had consumed three cups of coffee. She set down her empty mug and left the porch. As she approached the garden, she saw Julia moving from plant to plant in a dreamlike state as she sniffed the blossoms.

When Julia noticed her watching her, Iris asked, "Do you still love flowers the way you used to?"

"I guess. Although my experience has been limited to the wildflowers I used to grow around my patio."

"How would you like to work for me at Lily's? I've been interviewing for someone to take Felicia's place. She finally found the love of her life. She's getting married at the end of the month and moving to California."

A glimmer of hope crossed Julia's face and then disappeared. "I'd earn the same amount of money working for you as I would waitressing. I'm hoping to go back to school to study nursing or something tangible that would provide real career opportunities."

They walked together down the gravel path to the edge of the marsh. "This *would* be a career for you, Jules. I'll work with you for a couple of years until you learn the trade, but eventually I would turn the business over to you. We can make the finances work so that you can get a place of your own. The business is prosperous. There's plenty of income for both of us."

They sat down together on the teak garden bench. Julia said, "I was just thinking about the good times we used to have, getting up at the crack of dawn and foraging for greens with Lily as our getaway driver. She knew where to find all the good stuff. How is Lily?"

"Not well, I'm sad to say. She has end-stage pancreatic cancer. The doctor has called in hospice."

Julia's hand flew to her mouth. "Oh no! That's horrible. Where is she?"

"She insisted on staying at Riverview until the end."

"Can I see her?"

"I don't know, honey. She's in an awful lot of pain. Other than Gus and me, she hasn't seen anyone in weeks. But I will certainly ask her. She might make an exception for you."

"How is Gus handling it?"

"He's hanging in there. He's as steady as they come, just like his father."

Jackson squirmed in his mother's arms, and Iris took him from her. Placing him on her knee, she played Humpty Dumpty with him while he giggled with delight. When she glanced up, Julia was staring at her with a strange look on her face.

"I saw you at Duke's the other day. Why'd you run away when I called you?"

A moment passed before Iris responded. "I've been keeping tabs on you all these years. The other day was as close as I've ever dared come, but I got scared. Don't ask me why. Maybe because I was afraid you hated me." Jackson rested his head on her shoulder, and she held him tight. "I've missed you terribly, Jules, and for my own sanity, I needed to know you were safe."

"I wrote to you once, right after Jack and I got married. Why'd you never write back?"

Iris appeared confused. "I never got a letter, sweetheart. I most certainly would've written back."

"I'm sure Max probably intercepted it."

For the next few minutes, they sat in silence, each lost in thought, as they stared out over the marsh.

"So, Mama," Julia said, wiping her eyes as a tear escaped her lid. "About that job offer . . . I accept."

Iris grinned. Jackson had fallen asleep, and she didn't want to wake him. "That's the best news I've heard in a long time."

"I'd like to start right away, though, if that's okay. I spent my last ten bucks on gas. The tank is empty, and I need a new battery. I doubt the engine will even start."

"Oh, honey," Iris said, cupping her daughter's cheek. "I wish you hadn't waited so long to come home."

"I'm here now. That's all that matters. I may have to ask for an advance to pay for childcare for Jackson."

"I want you to stop worrying about money and let me handle everything. Cora's daughter, Lettie, has been cleaning for me one day a week. Let's go inside and call her." Sleeping baby in arms, Iris slowly rose to her feet. "I know she's looking for more work. I would think a full-time nannying job would be of interest to her."

Julia stood to face her. "Thank you, Mama. Your willingness to help me means so much."

"I should've been there for you years ago, Julia, when you came to me for help. I've got a lot of making up to do."

They headed up to the house. "Is Cora still alive?" Julia asked. "She must be ninety."

Iris smiled. "Ninety-two. But she's alive and kicking. She has all the men in her nursing home chasing after her."

"That sounds like the Cora I remember."

CHAPTER TWENTY-THREE

JULIA

Julia fed Jackson his baby bananas and cereal while her mother placed her phone call. Much to her relief, Lettie jumped at the opportunity and agreed to start as Jackson's nanny the next day.

As soon as her parents left for work, Julia put Jackson down for his nap and went to her mother's bedroom. Iris's words echoed in her mind as she rummaged through the drawers and closet. *Yes, Max, I've told you a thousand times, she's your daughter. I've offered to get a DNA test to prove it.* She couldn't imagine Iris with another man. Then again, she knew very little about her parents' marriage, other than they slept in separate bedrooms and appeared not to like each other very much. She'd never seen a photograph of them as bride and groom, never heard them mention their wedding or honeymoon.

At the back of her mother's lingerie drawer, Julia discovered a tattered photograph of a man, woman, and child. She retrieved her mother's readers from the nightstand and slipped them on. Through the cracks, she could identify the little girl as Iris at about eight years of age. Julia found her resemblance to her mother at that age uncanny.

She lowered herself to the edge of Iris's four-poster bed and studied the picture carefully. She'd often quizzed her mother about her past, only to get vague answers. Iris had grown up in Columbia, and her parents had passed away before Julia was born. As to her mother's education or whether she'd had a career prior to becoming a florist, Julia knew nothing.

Now I have two missions, Julia thought. Maybe they were related, maybe not. Finding out more about her mother's past and her parents' marriage might explain what drove Iris to have an affair. And, perhaps, who that man could possibly be.

The phone on the nightstand rang and startled Julia out of her trance. She stared at it, debating whether to answer. Julia hadn't lived in the house for some time and wasn't ready to explain to the person on the other end—no doubt one of her mother's friends—where she'd been and why she'd suddenly returned home.

She heard Jackson crying and glanced at the clock. An hour had passed since she'd put him down. She returned the photograph to the lingerie drawer and dashed up the stairs to the nursery. She changed his diaper, grabbed his blanket and some toys, and took him down to the family room. Spreading the blanket out on the carpet, she placed the baby on his tummy with his toys. She opened the cabinet that housed the family albums and took them out one at a time, looking specifically for photographs of her parents at their wedding or from their premarital lives. She came up empty on both counts.

She moved Jackson to the floor in her father's study and ventured behind the massive leather-top desk positioned in front of the windows. Seated in Max's high-back chair, she scrutinized the handsome wood-paneled room with his book-lined shelves and masculine furnishings. His study was the one room on the main floor that had not changed in her absence. He was paying her sister a fortune to redecorate the house, yet he'd kept Alex from waving her decorator's wand in his lair. The room would be an inviting place to curl up and read a book on a rainy day if not for the permanent stench of cigars and the memory of stern lectures her father had given her when she fell out of line.

She ignored the phone when it rang on the desk beside her. She would have to hurry. It was only a matter of time before Jackson grew hungry for his lunch. She went to work on the desk drawers, quickly combing through the contents of each. The bottom right-hand drawer was locked. She spent twenty minutes looking for the key, which she finally discovered at the bottom of her father's neatly stacked Cuban cigars in his wooden humidor. She knew she'd hit the jackpot when she slid the drawer open and saw the hanging folder marked PERSONAL.

"What're you doing in here?" Alex asked from the doorway.

Julia's head shot up in surprise. "Looking for something," she said, returning her attention to the file drawer.

"Clearly." Alex strode across the room to the desk, stepping over the baby. "What exactly are you looking for?"

"Answers."

"What sort of answers? Dad would be pissed if he knew you were snooping around in his desk."

"If he didn't keep secrets, I wouldn't have to snoop." Julia removed the files from the hanging folder and placed them on the desk. In the first file folder, she found the letter, unopened, she'd written to her mother all those years ago.

"That figures," she mumbled and stuffed the letter into the back pocket of her jeans. "What do you know about Mom and Dad's wedding?"

"Only that . . ." Alex started but stopped herself.

"So you do know something." Julia opened the folder on the desk and flipped through the files. "As I said a minute ago, if people didn't keep secrets, I wouldn't have to snoop." She found her parents' marriage license in the bottom file and scanned the document. "I don't believe it. Mom and Dad got married by the justice of the peace in Asheville, North Carolina. Does that mean they—"

"Eloped? Yep. That's exactly what they did," Alex said with a smug smile.

"But why? I don't understand." Julia glanced down at the date. May of 1977. Alex had been born in September 1979, so the timing was wrong for her mother to have been pregnant with Alex.

"Because Mom was an orphan who had no money and no family except a mean old spinster aunt who raised her from the time she was eight."

"How do you know all this?"

"Dad told me," Alex said as she examined her manicured fingernails.

"I see." It suddenly made sense why her family had always been divided. Alex was Max's legitimate child, and Julia was the product of her mother's love affair.

"Not to change this riveting subject," Alex said, "but where'd you get that god-awful truck?"

"It's Jack's truck. Mine was totaled in the accident." Julia returned the file to the drawer and slammed it shut.

"Do you think maybe you could park it down the street? It's an eyesore in our driveway."

Julia rolled her eyes. Her sister had not changed one bit. "No can do. There's not enough gas to move it anywhere."

Alex cocked a pencil-thin eyebrow. "Are you seriously that broke?"

Julia got to her feet and went around to the front of the desk to face her sister. "Yes, Alex, I'm seriously that broke. But I was doing just fine before Jack died. I had a job, my own home, and a happy marriage of fifteen years. Which is more than I can say for you." She narrowed her eyes as she glared at her sister. "Why are you so mean?"

"I'm not mean, Julia. I'm tough, because Daddy has made me that way. 'Suck it up, Alex,' he always says. 'Be formidable. Never show your fear. You're a Forney. Act like it.'"

Her sister's words were a kick in the gut. Max had never said those things to Julia. Because the Forney blood didn't run through her veins. "We're sisters, Alex. We grew up together. We both know you were born mean."

"Maybe so. But I'd rather be mean than spineless."

Julia clenched her jaw. "Are you calling me spineless?"

"Shoe fits," Alex said. "You're the one who ran away."

"And you wanna know why? I'll tell you why." Julia scooped up her baby. "This is Jackson, your nephew. His father is the reason I *ran* away. And I'd do it all over again if given the chance."

Alex gave the baby a quick once-over. "Cute. But I'm not into babies."

As she watched her sister saunter out of the room, the all-too-familiar hurt came crashing down on Julia. She'd always run away, from the time she was a little girl retreating from her sister's pranks and insults to the corner bedroom on the third floor where she was now staying. Did that make her a spineless coward? *No, Jules, it makes you a survivor.*

She stomped down the hall to the kitchen, where she paced in circles and took deep breaths until her heart rate slowed. As she shoveled sweet potatoes into her son's birdlike mouth, she forced her sister from her mind and contemplated what she'd discovered in her father's study desk.

Everything made sense, yet nothing made sense at all. There were no photo albums because there'd been no wedding. Her paternal grandparents had died when Julia was a baby, but their reputation for being devout Catholics and outstanding citizens outlived them. Anna and Edgar Forney had insisted on proper etiquette. They would never have condoned their son's marriage to a woman inferior to their family's social stature. Julia could only imagine the fireworks display when Max returned home to Live Oaks with his new bride on his arm. But Max had loved Iris so much he'd eloped with her despite their wishes. He knew what it felt like for his parents to disapprove of the woman he loved, yet he'd treated Julia the same way when she wanted to marry Jack. Max Forney was a hypocrite of the worst order. She was glad his blood did not pump through her veins. But if not his blood, then whose? Her discovery about her parents' elopement had brought her no closer to finding out who her father was. There was only one way to get answers. She'd have to ask her mother.

CHAPTER TWENTY-FOUR
IRIS

Iris was organizing a flower order prior to opening the shop when she received an urgent text from Gus. Come quick. Mom's asking for you. Diana said the end is near.

"I need to get to Lily. You'll have to manage without me today," Iris said to Felicia as she dashed out the back door. When she reached her car, parked in the small lot they shared with neighboring businesses, she realized she'd forgotten her purse. *Never mind,* she thought. *I can get to Riverview faster on foot.*

Gus was waiting for her at the end of the driveway, slumped against the split-rail fence with his head lowered. Even after all these years, the sight of him took her breath. He looked so much like his father.

"Come here, sweetheart," she said, wrapping her arms around him. "I know this is hard."

He sniffled, his breath tickling her neck. "I wasn't prepared for just how hard it would be."

"Your mama is one of a kind, a truly special lady."

He drew away from Iris. "She's waiting for you. We've already said our goodbyes."

The idea of Gus and Lily saying their final words to each other caused Iris to stumble backward a few steps. Gus caught her, and taking her by the arm, he walked her toward the house.

"Is she in much pain?" Iris asked, lengthening her stride to keep up with his pace.

He shook his head. "Diana's giving her high doses of morphine. She's been slipping in and out of consciousness since midnight."

Lily had continued to accommodate her guests throughout her treatments, but at the beginning of March, when her team of doctors ascertained the chemo wasn't working, Gus had insisted she cancel all future bookings.

"You need to take some time for yourself," he'd argued with his mother.

She'd reluctantly agreed. Sadly, she'd been blessed with only a handful of good days before she'd taken to her bed.

Gus walked Iris up two flights of stairs to his mother's room. "I'll be right out here in the hallway if you need me."

Lily's corner bedroom offered a magnificent view overlooking the marsh to the river. Lily often joked, "This is not a bad place to be sick, if you gotta have cancer."

But on that morning, the drapes were drawn tight against the bright sunshine. The hospice nurse who'd been by Lily's side for the past few weeks rose to greet her. Iris had grown to appreciate Diana for her quiet effectiveness and truthful answers to their many questions.

"She's asleep now, but she'll wake up in a minute," Diana said. "She asked me to back off the morphine so she could be clearheaded when she talks to you. I'll be out in the hall if you need me."

Iris took a seat beside the bed. Translucent skin was drawn tight across Lily's bony face, and a mint-colored beanie covered her bald head. She'd always been thin, but she'd lost an enormous amount of weight to the point of emaciation.

Five minutes passed before she blinked her eyes open. She smiled when she saw Iris. "You're glowing. Something's happened."

"You know me so well." She'd never been able to hide her emotions from Lily. She was as happy about Julia being back in her life as she was distraught over her best friend dying. "Julia's finally come home, and she brought my grandson with her."

"That's wonderful news. But what about her husband?"

Iris moved the chair closer to the bed. "Oh, Lily, the saddest thing happened. He was killed in a car accident the night their baby was born."

A wounded expression crossed Lily's gaunt face. "How tragic for that poor girl. Please give her my love."

"You know I will. She asked if she could see you. I told her I'd talk to you about it."

"There's nothing I'd like more, Iris, but my time is up." She touched her fingers to her turbaned head. "I wouldn't want her to see me like this anyway. This way, I'll be forever youthful in her memories."

Iris's face softened. "Just this morning, Julia was remembering all the good times we had together."

The two old friends shared a smile as their minds wandered back over the years.

Lily squeezed her eyes tight as she grimaced. "I won't be able to stand the pain much longer. We need to clear the air before I die."

Iris drew in an unsteady breath, bracing herself for what she knew was coming.

"Tell me the truth about you and Wiley."

Iris bit back tears. "We never meant to hurt you, Lily."

"I know that, which is why I was able to forgive you. You're the second-best person I've ever known. Wiley was the first."

"But—"

"Please, hear me out," Lily said, lifting her right index finger to silence her. "I was mad as hell at first, but after the haze from Wiley's death lifted, I could see how perfect the two of you were for each other. Don't get me wrong, I loved him dearly, but we were all wrong together. It's my fault anyway. I took our child and ran off to Atlanta at the first sign of trouble in our marriage." Lily licked her cracked lips. "Can I have some water?"

Iris dipped a sterile lollipop sponge in a Styrofoam cup of water and handed it to Lily. She sucked on it a minute before handing it back.

Lily continued, "I couldn't very well condemn you and Wiley when I was unfaithful myself. During my time in Atlanta, I had an affair with my mother's best friend's husband. Not only did I break up their marriage, I brought shame on my family and strained my relationship with my parents. I lost their respect, which was almost as bad as losing my husband. What I don't understand is why you never trusted me with the truth. We've been as close as sisters all these years. I point-blank asked you that day on the way home from work when you told me you were pregnant with Julia. You had the perfect opportunity to confess. I even promised you we would get past it. But you lied to me. And I need to know why."

"There's a lot you don't know about his death. I was terrified of losing you, even more so of losing my children."

Lily unclenched her left fist, revealing an empty pill bottle. "Did it have something to do with this?"

Iris stared down at the pill bottle in her hand. The label was weathered, but her name was still legible in tiny type across the top. "Where'd you get that?"

"That morning I drove to Edisto looking for him, I found it lying in the sand beside the boardwalk leading out to the dock. As you can see, it's a prescription for sleeping pills, and it has your name on it. The medical examiner determined that drowning was the official cause of death, but the toxicology report showed a large amount of this drug in his system. Wiley was not one to take pills, even vitamins. As you know, he had a serious laceration on his head. The sheriff speculated that

Wiley passed out from the sleeping pills, hit his head, fell off the dock, and drowned. He ruled the case a suicide and closed the investigation. I've kept this to myself all these years. But you and I both know Wiley was not the type of person who would've killed himself. Tell me, Iris, how did your sleeping pills get in my husband's system? I need to know what happened to him."

Iris debated how much to tell Lily about his death but decided she couldn't lie to her best friend on her deathbed. "When I went to see Wiley that day, I left my purse on the passenger seat of the car. A full bottle of pills was in my purse. I'd just had the prescription refilled. I didn't realize the pills were missing until that night, when I couldn't sleep."

"Are you saying Wiley willingly took them?"

"Not at all. My carelessness cost Wiley his life, Lily." Iris removed a tissue from the box on the nightstand and dabbed at her eyes. "Without my knowledge, Max had followed me to the cottage. He was outraged when he found Wiley and me together. He ordered me to go home and wait for him. I left the cottage, but I only made it a mile down the road before turning back. They were out on the dock when I got there. Max had a gun aimed at Wiley's head. He threatened to kill us both. He promised he wouldn't hurt Wiley if I left. I had Alex to think about. I knew what it was like being an orphan, and I couldn't let that happen to my daughter. So I drove home to Beaufort and went back to work as if nothing had happened. And I prayed. God, how I prayed that Wiley would come home to you that night."

Lily nodded, as if accepting her explanation. "I've always had a special place for Julia in my heart. Is she Wiley's daughter?"

Iris took hold of Lily's hand and looked her in the eyes. "I can say with absolute certainty that Julia is not Wiley's daughter. We were in love. We planned to ask you and Max for divorces so we could marry. But we never slept together."

She shook her head. "Why? I don't understand."

"Because we loved *you* too much."

"But if you were so in love with Wiley, why were you still having sex with your husband?" When Iris looked away, Lily added, "I'm sorry. That's none of my business."

"All of this *is* your business. I'm only sorry we didn't talk about it a long time ago. I confronted Max that night, begging him to tell me what he'd done to Wiley. And he forced himself on me. That's the last time we ever had sex."

Tears welled in Lily's eyes and streamed down her cheeks. "Oh, Iris. He's a murderer, an adulterer, and a rapist. Why'd you stay with him all these years?"

"My list of reasons is long. Max refused to give me a divorce for fear of parting with one dime of his family's money. And he threatened to go to the police about my involvement in Wiley's death. He has proof of our relationship, pictures taken by the private investigator he hired to follow me. But the main reason is, I hold myself responsible for Wiley's death. If only I'd been more careful. If I hadn't fallen in love with him. I can think of a thousand ifs, all of them pointing the finger at me." Iris stood and went to stand in front of the window, peeking out between the crack in the drapes. "Beaufort's a small town, and Wiley was one of her favorite sons. Our townsfolk would've crucified me if word had gotten out that I had something to do with his death. And the gossip would've ruined the business. After Julia left, the business was the only shred of happiness I had left. And my friendship with you. I couldn't stand to lose either."

"Come, sit back down." Lily patted the bed beside her. "The pain is getting bad, and I'm gonna need Diana soon."

Iris returned to the bed and sat down gently on the edge of the mattress.

"I want you to know, I don't hold you responsible for what happened with Wiley. None of us is without blame. I have to say I'm disappointed, though. As screwed up as this sounds, I've always hoped that

Julia was Wiley's daughter, that she and Gus shared the sibling bond. I need you to make me two promises."

Iris, unable to stifle a sob, muttered, "Name them."

"Take care of my boy. Gus is going to need you."

"That's easy," Iris said as she cried into her tissue. "I love him like my own."

"And leave that rotten, son-of-a-bitch husband of yours. Please ask Diana and Gus to come in now."

Iris opened the door for Gus and the nurse. When she started to leave the room, Lily said, "Please don't go, Iris. We need you here."

Iris understood Lily's silent appeal. She didn't want Gus to be alone.

Gus and Iris went to opposite sides of the bed. They stroked her arms and spoke encouraging words while Diana administered the morphine. Lily closed her eyes, and within a few minutes, her breathing changed and eventually subsided as her life slipped away.

CHAPTER TWENTY-FIVE

JULIA

Julia strapped Jackson into his stroller and spent the afternoon reacquainting herself with the neighborhoods and businesses of historic downtown Beaufort. She stood in front of a row of adorable Victorian houses on Craven Street, daydreaming that she might be able to afford a home like these for Jackson one day. She wouldn't be able to live under the same roof with her father for long. If he even was her father.

When she returned home, Julia found her mother at the kitchen table, shoulders hunched and head bowed as she stared into a cup of hot tea. Julia's answers would have to wait.

"What's wrong?" Julia asked, sliding into the seat beside her mother.

"Oh, sweetheart," Iris said, cupping the baby's head as she kissed Julia's cheek. "I'm sorry to have to tell you this, but Lily passed away this morning."

Julia's expression morphed from surprise to sadness. "I'm so sorry. I didn't even get a chance to see her."

"I told her you'd come home and that you'd asked about her. She sent you her love." When Jackson started to squirm, Iris got up and took him from her, dancing him around the room. "I tried to call the house several times to tell you about Lily. I didn't think to ask you for your cell number this morning."

"I don't have a cell phone, Mama. Jack and I never saw the need, and I couldn't have afforded one these last few months anyway."

"We'll take care of that right now," Iris said, lifting her purse off the table.

"Now? Seriously, Mama. Lily just died. I think we can wait for a more convenient time to buy a cell phone."

"That's the point, though. I could use the distraction. Staying busy will keep my mind off Lily." She shifted Jackson to the opposite hip as she held the door open for Julia. "It won't take long. The transaction should be easy enough. I'll add your line to my business account. If you're going to be working for me, I need to be able to reach you at all hours." Iris locked the door behind them. "We have an empty gas can in the garage. We'll fill it up on the way back. If your truck starts, we'll take it to a place I know on Lady's Island and get the battery replaced."

"When's the funeral?" Julia asked ten minutes later as they drove through town in her mother's old Volvo with Jackson strapped in his car seat in the back.

"On Sunday. Lily left very specific instructions for the arrangements."

"Sunday was our special day." Julia stared out the car window, thinking about her youth and the Sunday afternoons and evenings mothers and children spent together. When the weather was nice, they'd have picnics or go boating or sailing. On rainy days and during the winter, they'd work puzzles or play games or have movie marathons. A casual supper—a bowl of chili or hot dogs on the grill—always ended the day. "Poor Gus. I imagine he's a wreck. He loved his mother so much."

"He's putting on a good front, but I can tell he's hurting. He's been devoted to her these past few months. He even took a leave of absence from his job."

Julia had often wondered about Gus after she left. Growing up, he'd been like a brother to her, and she'd missed him. More than she'd ever missed Alex. "I don't know anything about his life. What does he do? Who'd he marry? Anyone I know?"

"He's a partner in his father's law firm. He never married, believe it or not. He came close a couple of times, though." Iris adjusted her rearview mirror and smiled when Jackson came into view. "He asked me to go to the funeral home with him tomorrow. We'll need someone to stay at the inn, to accept flower and food deliveries. I was hoping you'd be willing."

So much for easing back into her old life. The town's biggest busy-bodies would grill her about her whereabouts for the past sixteen years. "What about Alex? Can't she do it? She and Gus are tight."

Iris shook her head. "Not anymore. They had some sort of falling out."

"What happened?"

"I'm not sure, to tell you the truth. Neither of them will talk about it." Iris waited for traffic to clear before veering left onto Robert Smalls Parkway. "They were close when you children were young because we were together so much. And they're closer in age than you and Gus. But they were never really friends outside of our little family."

"We were like our own little family, weren't we?" Julia's lips parted in a smile as images of the good old days popped again into her mind's eye. "I'm happy to stay at the inn while y'all go to the funeral home, but I thought you wanted me to start work at the shop tomorrow."

Iris turned into the parking lot of their cellular provider. "With the funeral and all, we might as well wait until next week."

"Do you keep the same hours at the shop as you used to? Tuesdays through Saturdays, ten to five."

"Same days, but we stay open until six now." She pulled into an empty parking space and turned off the engine. "I want to do a spec-tacular spray for Lily's casket, something fitting for the South's Flower

Princess. We'll have to put it together on Saturday. I've already called Lettie and booked her through the weekend to stay with Jackson."

Julia recognized the coping mechanism—stay busy to avoid grieving. Then again, her mother had always possessed the most efficient organizational skills. Good old Iris, always coordinating everyone's lives. In addition to having a full-time career, she'd been the Girl Scout troop leader for Julia and the cheerleading parent rep for Alex. She was always the mom driving a carload of their friends to the movies or ball games. Their home was always tidy, their laundry done, and dinner on the table at seven thirty every night. She worked tirelessly without complaining. Her best friend had passed away that very afternoon, yet Iris was worried about buying Julia a cell phone and getting her truck fixed. She rarely saw her mother flustered, and she'd never seen her cry. Could it be that her composure masked her frustrations?

~

The following days passed in a frenzy of activity. A multitude of friends and colleagues passed through the Riverview Inn to pay their respects to Gus. Julia greeted visitors, logged flower and food deliveries in the guest book, and answered the endless stream of phone calls. Her heart was warmed by stories of Lily touching the lives of so many.

At first glance, nothing appeared to have changed at Riverview, but on closer inspection as she wandered around, Julia noticed the Oriental rugs were threadbare, the upholstery on the furniture had worn thin, and the trees and shrubs had tripled in size. Being back at Riverview reminded her of how she'd always felt more at home here than she ever did at Live Oaks.

A traditional service was held at the Anglican church where Lily had been a faithful member for years. Her mahogany casket was adorned with a glorious spray of hydrangeas, peonies, roses, and lilies, of course. The minister delivered the opening remarks, Iris read passages from Lily's favorite Bible verses, and the congregation sang her favorite hymns. Everyone laughed and cried when Gus delivered his heartfelt eulogy, his abounding love for his mother evident in every single word.

Julia never got a chance to exchange more than a few words with Gus until the reception following the service on Sunday afternoon. During the years since she'd last seen him, he'd shed his ginger cuteness—orange hair and a face full of freckles—and grown every bit as handsome as his mother had been beautiful. The smile lines around his sparkling green eyes belied the serious expression he wore most of the time.

The sun shone brightly on the large crowd gathered on the front lawn at Riverview. A bartender was serving sweet tea and soft drinks on the veranda, and down on the lawn, tables draped in white linens showcased the widest assortment of food Julia had ever seen, from casserole dishes of creamy macaroni and cheese to platters of fried chicken to crystal bowls of pickled shrimp.

Worn out from small talk, Julia was standing at a distance from the crowd, sipping a glass of tea, when Gus sought her out. "I've been looking for you everywhere. I wanted to thank you for all your help these past few days. It's been so crazy, I haven't even gotten the chance to properly welcome you home."

"Thank you, Gus. I'm glad I was here for her funeral. I only wish I'd come home in time to see her."

"She missed you a lot, you know. She was always anxious for reports from your mother's spying missions."

Julia lowered her chin and peered at him from under her brow. "Her *spying missions?*"

"That's what Mom called them," he said with a chuckle. "As much as they hated being out of touch with you, Lily and Iris were relieved that you'd found happiness. Tell me about Jack. What was he like?"

A lot like you. The thought took Julia by surprise. She'd never considered it before, but her oldest friend had much the same temperament as her late husband. "He was a gentle soul who loved spending time on the water. We lived an easy life that suited us both."

"How do you go on with your life without the person who matters the most to you?" Gus asked with a sad, faraway look in his eyes.

"One second, moment, hour at a time. Tomorrow will be the hardest. All of this"—Julia spread her arms wide—"will go away. Time has paused this weekend for your friends to help you celebrate your mama's life. But tomorrow, they will go about their business as usual, and you will feel lost. Simple things like making a slice of toast will require a huge effort. Nothing will feel normal for a long time. That's how it was for me anyway."

She didn't realize she'd started to tear up until Gus pressed his linen handkerchief into her hand. Taking her by the arm, he led her to the edge of the marsh for privacy. A majestic egret with snowy-white feathers stood stock-still in the marsh twenty feet away. The bird reminded Julia of Lily, so graceful and serene.

"I'm sorry, Gus. I didn't mean to be so melodramatic," Julia said, drying her eyes. "One minute I'm sure I'm over the worst, and then something happens that brings it all back."

"No need to apologize. What happened to Jack was tragic. I was able to prepare myself for Mom's death, to say goodbye to her. You never got that."

"No, but every time I look into my son's little face, I'm reminded of his daddy. Jackson is my reason for living." Julia sniffled as she inhaled a calming breath. "Anyway, enough of the morbid talk. Mama told me you'd taken a leave of absence from your law firm. Are you planning to go back to work?"

"Not yet." Gus turned around to face the inn. "Mom let the place go these past few years. I need to spruce things up before we reopen in May."

"Lily was the heart and soul of Riverview," Julia said, staring up at the nineteenth-century Lowcountry-style home, three stories of maintenance nightmare. "Who's gonna take her place?"

"We have a full-time staff of three—cook, maid, and reservationist—all currently on paid leave."

"But you need someone in charge, the innkeeper, that person the guests expect to greet them upon arrival. Have you ever considered running it yourself?"

"I've thought about it a lot, actually." He placed his hand at the small of her back, nudging her onward. They strolled along the edge of the marsh to the tire swing, dangling from a live oak, that'd been there since they were young.

"I used to love this swing," Julia said, giving the tire a twirl.

"Climb up and I'll give you a push," Gus said with a mischievous grin.

She laughed. "And show your guests my panties? I don't think so."

"Next time you come over, wear jeans."

Julia smiled at the idea of next time. "Deal." She leaned back against the tree, crossing her feet. "So, what's holding you back? Why not quit your job and run the inn?"

Gus fell back against the tree beside her. "I wish it were that simple. All my life, all I ever wanted was to follow in my father's and grandfather's footsteps, to be the man I thought they'd want me to be. But I don't love the law the way they did, and I'm only a mediocre lawyer. I've never been married. I have no children. And my mother was my best friend. I'll turn forty in September and I'm still trying to figure out my life."

"Maybe you should move to Charlotte or Atlanta where you'd have more opportunities."

"I could never leave Beaufort. I love it here. This is my home." Gus pointed at the ground. "Riverview is my home."

Julia nudged him with her elbow. "Sounds to me like you've got your life all figured out. What's so great about having a professional career if you don't enjoy it?"

He shrugged. "I wish it were that simple. I need to be certain I'm making the right move before I give up on my law career to become an innkeeper. I've notified the firm that I won't be coming back right away. I need that time to myself."

"There you are!" Alex hollered as she marched across the yard toward them. "What're the two of you doing out here all alone? Is something going on between you that I should know about?"

Julia inched away from Gus. "What do you want, Alex?"

"I'm leaving. Mom wanted me to see if you needed a ride home."

Avoiding Alex's stare, she kicked at the dirt beneath the tree. "No thanks. I'll walk."

"Whatever," Alex said and stomped off in a huff.

Julia waited until her sister was out of earshot. "Mama mentioned there's some tension between you and Alex. What happened?"

"It's a long story." He pushed off the tree and headed back toward the house.

"I've got time," she said when she caught up with him. She tugged on his shirtsleeve. "Come on, Gus, tell me. I've been gone for a long time. I'm trying to get the lay of the land. My sister has never been an easy person, but she's become downright hateful in my absence."

"I can't argue with that." They reached the sidewalk and turned left toward Lily's rose garden at the side of the house. "Okay, I'll tell you. But I warn you, it's not a pretty story."

"I've yet to hear a story involving my sister that is."

When they reached the rose garden, they sat down side by side on one of two iron benches. "So, a few years back, after the breakup of Alex's first marriage, I ran into her at a party one night. She tried to hit on me, but I blew her off. I was dating someone seriously at the time— a woman named Cynthia, who was in Ohio visiting her parents that particular weekend. But the following Friday night, Cynthia was with me when I ran into Alex again at Saltus Grill."

Julia furrowed her brow, and he explained, "It's a newish waterfront restaurant in town, a popular hangout with our peers. Anyway, Alex sat down next to us at the bar and started chatting up Cynthia. A bit later, she followed Cynthia to the restroom and told her we'd slept together the weekend before. Of course I denied it, because it wasn't true, but Cynthia didn't believe me. Turns out Alex did me a favor."

"If she didn't trust you any more than that, Cynthia isn't the right girl for you."

He nodded. "Precisely."

"Alex and I are so different, I've often wondered how we could have the same parents." Julia pressed her fingertips to her lips as the enormity of her statement hit her.

"I know one thing for sure—your mama is certainly glad to have you back." Gus sat back on the bench and surveyed his mother's rose-bushes. "I'm glad my mom's not here to see her overgrown garden. What do I know about taking care of roses?"

Julia fingered the branch of a dormant bush beside her. "I helped Lily plant a lot of these bushes. I used to know all the names by heart. Gentle Giant. Paradise. Apricot Candy. They just need a healthy pruning."

He gave her a sheepish grin. "Would you be willing to offer some guidance?"

"Sure! What're you doing tomorrow?"

CHAPTER TWENTY-SIX

IRIS

Iris hated to see the last guests leave the reception. She'd been surrounded by friends and acquaintances who, for three days, had comforted her with their presence as they told tales of Lily's antics and good deeds. To have that come to an end felt as though she were severing her last remaining bond with her best friend.

She lingered at the inn long after everyone had gone. She helped store the leftovers in the refrigerator and put away the tables, linens, and serving platters. When there was nothing left to do, Gus walked her to her car. "Are you sure you'll be all right?" she asked, taking her shopping bag of leftovers from him.

"I'll be fine. I need some time alone to sort out my life." He opened her car door for her. "Besides, I know where to find you if I need you."

"And I'll come running, anytime day or night."

Iris turned her Volvo around in the driveway, but instead of going home, she drove to the small cemetery in the church's side lot where, only hours ago, Lily had been laid to rest. Her casket had already been lowered into the ground, and the spray of pink and white flowers was draped across the fresh mound of dirt that covered her grave. Iris stretched out in the grass alongside the grave and stared up at the live oak trees. The church workers had gone home, and the cemetery was peaceful aside from the occasional car passing by on the street.

"What's it like up there, my friend?" Iris called out. "I imagine blue skies, bright sunshine, and flowers in full bloom all around. Any fear you had is gone, and only love fills your heart. I know Hector and Wiley were waiting at the pearly gates to greet you, dressed in white suits with golden wings perched atop their shoulders."

Iris rolled over on her side, facing the grave. "Why'd you have to leave me now? I was so looking forward to growing old with you. What about our plans to visit the world's gardens? I hope you realize what an impact you made on my life. You taught me about true unconditional love. I tried to follow in your footsteps. But I was never a match for you. How am I supposed to go on without you?"

"When I left Gus just now, I couldn't bring myself to go home to that hostile environment." She held her hand out to the grave, as if to silence Lily. "I know, I know. I have Julia now. And my adorable grandson. God has blessed me with another chance. I hope I don't let her down again. Compared to Julia's goodness, Max's nastiness and Alex's self-absorption are more pronounced than ever. It's not right for me to compare my daughters. They are two very different people. I'm so proud of the woman and mother Julia has become, but it's like a knife in the heart knowing I had nothing to do with how she turned out.

"I can almost hear you telling me to get my butt in gear and whip my family into shape. But I'm not you, Lily. I lack your fortitude. I'm too weak to stand up to my own family."

Iris waited until the evening breeze produced chill bumps on her arms before saying goodbye to Lily. "These flowers will be toast tomorrow. I'll come back with some fresh blue hydrangeas when our shipment comes later in the week. Maybe I'll talk to Gus about planting a rosebush at your feet."

Iris tried to perk herself up on her drive home, but as she was unpacking the leftovers into the refrigerator and contemplating what she would fix for dinner, a wave of exhaustion hit her, making her knees go weak. She removed a full bottle of pinot grigio from the refrigerator, poured herself a glass, and took the bottle with her to the second-floor veranda. She relaxed in a lounge chair with her feet propped on an ottoman and forced her mind to go blank. She listened to the birds chirp and felt the soft breeze on her face while she sipped her wine. Two glasses later, she was in a state of intoxicated bliss. She'd closed her eyes and was just dozing off when the click of a doorknob followed by Alex's and Max's voices on the porch below awakened her.

"I'm starving," Max said. "Wonder what your mother's making for dinner."

"She's not cooking anything. At least she wasn't when I came through the kitchen a minute ago."

"She probably went to the grocery store to pick up some meat."

Am I that predictable? Iris wondered. Julia was right. With four grown people living in this house, they needed to share the responsibilities of shopping for groceries and cooking meals.

"Where's Julia?" Max asked.

"Who knows? She probably went with Mom to the store."

Iris heard a squeaking noise as one, or both, of them sat down on the bench swing.

"You should know, Dad, that I caught Julia going through your desk the other day. With Lily's funeral and all, I haven't had a chance to tell you about it yet."

Tattletale, Iris thought.

"Damn it!" A thump vibrated the porch floor, undoubtedly Max pounding the railing with his fist. "My study is strictly off-limits to everyone in this house except me. Did she say what she was looking for?"

"No. But she was asking a lot of questions about your wedding. I had to tell her the two of you eloped. I hope you're not mad."

Iris sat up straight in her chair. Max had forbidden Iris to ever tell a soul about their elopement. *Wonder what else he's told her.*

"Why would I be mad?" Max said. "She was going to find out sooner or later anyway."

"She wants answers, Daddy. Are you prepared to give them to her?"

"Answers about what?"

Are you really that stupid? Iris thought.

"About why it was okay for you to elope with Mom but you kicked Julia out of the family when she wanted to marry Jack."

"And I have an answer for her. I was trying to prevent her from making the same mistake I made by marrying someone beneath me."

Heat flushed through Iris's body. She may have come from nothing, but she'd made something of herself, something most men would've been proud of.

"That's not very nice, Daddy." Iris heard the sound of hand smacking skin, and she envisioned her daughter playfully backhanding her father in the arm.

"But it's true. I let my sexual attraction for your mother cloud my judgment."

"Ew," Alex said in a high-pitched tone. "That's way too much information."

Iris's muscles quivered in fury. How often did her husband and daughter have these little chats about her behind her back? And what else had Max told Alex about their past? Did she know about Iris's relationship with Wiley? And Wiley's death?

"I'm starving." Max's gruff voice rumbled from the porch below. "It's seven forty-five, way past dinnertime. Go see what's taking your mother so long."

Iris rose out of her chair and left the veranda without making a sound. She went to her bedroom and crawled fully clothed beneath the covers of her bed. When Alex knocked loudly on the door a minute later, she called out in a weak voice, "Come in."

Alex's heels clicked against the hardwood floors as she crossed the room. "Are you in bed already? It's not even dark out. Dad wants to know what's for dinner."

"I don't feel well," she said without lifting her head off the pillow. "I think I may be coming down with the flu."

"You're just tired," Alex said in a dismissive tone. "I'm sure you'll feel better tomorrow. Is there anything to eat in this house?"

"There are plenty of leftovers in the refrigerator."

"I'm tired of funeral food," Alex said. "But we'll figure something out. Night, Mom. Get some sleep."

Alex closed the drapes and turned off the bedside lamp before exiting the room.

The sound of Jackson crying came from a distant part of the house. A good grandmother would get out of bed and see if she could help her daughter with the baby. But she was too tired to even brush her teeth or put on her nightgown. She'd been on autopilot ever since Wiley's death thirty-seven years ago, tending to everybody's needs without taking time for herself. She would probably never get another chance at love, but she was determined to find happiness.

If only I knew where to start.

CHAPTER TWENTY-SEVEN

JULIA

After an early breakfast on Monday morning, Julia grabbed the tools she needed from her mother's gardening shed and tossed them, along with Jackson's stroller, in the back of her truck.

There was no sign of life at the inn when they arrived. "We won't bother Gus," she said to Jackson as she fastened him into his stroller. "He deserves to sleep late after what he's been through." She wheeled the stroller to the shade of a tree inside the rose garden where Jackson could see her while she worked. "There now." She attached the activity arch to the arms of the stroller. "That'll keep you busy for a while."

Everything Lily had taught her about roses came back to Julia as she attacked the bushes with her clippers. The mindless activity provided an escape she didn't know she needed, and she was so engrossed in her work, she didn't hear Gus approach until his shadow crossed her line of vision.

"Why didn't you tell me you were here? I would've come out to help."

"I thought maybe you needed to catch up on your rest," she said, and tossed a cane of dead rose wood onto the pile beside her.

"I've been up for hours, working on our website. For better or worse, we're officially open for reservations starting on May first."

Julia shielded her eyes as she stared up at him. "It's good to have a deadline to work toward."

He chuckled. "But only if the goal is attainable. There's so much to do around here. I don't see how I can get it all done." Gus caught sight of the baby behind her. "Who is this handsome fella?" He brushed past Julia and knelt down in front of the stroller.

"This is Jackson."

"Hey there, Jackson." He squeezed the baby's chubby leg. "You've got the makings of a linebacker."

"Not if he's anything like his daddy. Jack was only five eight on a good day. He was strong, though, so you never know. Jackson certainly has a football player's appetite."

Gus talked to the baby in a goo-goo voice for another minute before straightening. "Whoa," he said, looking around the rose garden. "You're almost finished. I didn't mean for you to do it all yourself."

"Here." She handed him her clippers. "There's still plenty of work left."

Julia stood over him, pointing out the dead and diseased wood and showing him where to make his cuts as he worked his way through the remaining bushes. "I'm surprised Lily never showed you how to prune roses."

He made a fresh cut and threw the cane in the pile. "She tried. But there was always so much else that needed fixing around here, leaky faucets and broken ice makers."

"I never knew you were so handy."

"You can learn how to do anything on YouTube, Jules."

"I'm not much with computers." She pinched off one of the leaves of the last bush, turned it over, and held it up close to his face. "See those little green bugs? They're called aphids."

Gus squinted as he studied the tiny bugs. "How do we get rid of them?"

"It's been so long, I don't really remember. Dishwashing liquid, maybe. We're better off asking someone at a garden center. I'm sure there's a new and improved method anyway."

"Do you have time to go with me now? I could use your advice on which plants to buy for Mom's containers."

She glanced over at Jackson, who'd begun to squirm. "Sure, I just need to change Jackson first. I have some snacks I can give him in the car on the way over."

She laid the baby on a blanket in the grass and changed his diaper. "It'll be easier if I drive so we won't have to move the car seat," Julia said as they walked together to the driveway. "If you don't mind riding in my truck, that is."

"Why would I mind?" he asked, opening the rear car door for her.

She raised an eyebrow. "Because it's an eyesore. Alex called it an embarrassment. She asked me to move it out of our driveway and park it down the street."

"You shouldn't listen to Alex. I think your truck has serious swag."

"It has swag. Just not the good kind," she said, looking back at him as she fastened Jackson into his car seat.

"I'm being serious. She has character." Gus ran his hand down the side of the dented rear fender.

"*She's* ready for the junkyard." As if to prove her point, the door moaned and creaked when she slammed it shut. "See what I mean?" she said, and they both laughed.

As they headed down the gravel driveway, she said, "Seriously, though, having a pickup is handy. All innkeepers should have one."

He cocked an eyebrow at her. "Who says I've made up my mind to become an innkeeper?"

"You have," she said with a confident nod of her head. "You just don't realize it yet. This place suits you. I've never seen you at your law firm, but you're definitely in your element here."

The lines deepened in his forehead. "Maybe you're right." After a brief silence, he added, "And just so you know, I already have a pickup truck. Mom drove a white Chevrolet Silverado with the Riverview Inn logo painted on the side. It's parked in the garage."

The thought of Lily driving through town in a pickup truck brought a smile to Julia's lips. "Do you have a recent picture of her? I'd really like to see it."

Gus tugged his phone out of his back pocket, and when they stopped at red lights on the way to the garden center, he flashed photographs of Lily at her.

"She was always so pretty. From what I can tell, she aged well."

"That she did," Gus said with a sad smile as he returned his phone to his pocket.

Jackson had fallen sound asleep by the time they pulled into the garden shop on Lady's Island. "This is his usual nap time," Julia said, placing him in his stroller. "He's pretty good about sleeping on the go."

Julia and Gus spent the next ninety minutes picking out plants. They loaded the back of her pickup with hanging baskets of Boston fern for the porch, flats of annuals and potting soil for the containers, and bags of gravel to freshen up the paths in the rose garden.

Jackson didn't stir until they were arriving back at the inn a few minutes after noon.

"Somebody's hungry," Gus said when the baby began to fuss. "I'd offer him some leftover chicken salad, but I'm not sure his tiny teeth can chew it."

Julia killed the engine. "No, but I can feed him baby food, and you can offer his mama chicken salad."

"Deal," Gus said. "I'm impressed you remembered to bring along baby food. You came prepared."

"Out of habit," Julia said. "I'm used to packing his bag for day care."

They took their picnic out to the porch. Gus offered to hold Jackson while she fed him. "I've never held a baby before, but how hard can it be?" He was stiff and awkward at first, but he soon relaxed. He didn't even mind when Jackson smeared green peas all over his favorite Atlanta Braves T-shirt.

Once the baby was fed, they placed him on a yoga mat at their feet while they ate their chicken salad sandwiches.

"You were so much younger than me, growing up," Gus said. "I always felt like I needed to protect you, like I was your big brother."

"I needed protecting, all right. From my sister."

He chuckled. "Now that you mention it, I remember saving you a time or two from Alex's vicious attacks." He popped his last bite of sandwich in his mouth and gulped it down with lemonade. "Anyway, I'd already gone off to college when you reached high school. And you'd left town by the time I graduated from law school and came back to Beaufort. My point is, I never knew you as an adult. I enjoy your company, and I hope we can be friends. I could really use one right now."

"Trust me, so could I," Julia said with a sad smile.

While Jackson napped on the yoga mat, Julia and Gus hung the fern baskets around the perimeter of the porch and planted annuals in the assortment of terra-cotta, ceramic, and concrete containers positioned in key places around the property.

It was late in the day before Julia packed up Jackson's things. "I sense you're hesitant about going home," Gus said. "I'd love for you to stay for dinner."

"You have no idea how tempted I am, but I'm out of baby food, and Jackson needs a bath." Julia slung the diaper bag over her arm and hoisted the baby to her hip. "You know, there was something else about that time in my life I'd forgotten, or that my mind had suppressed, until I came home. My family is dysfunctional, Gus. My father's a hypocritical male chauvinist pig. My sister is plain mean. And my mother is content to let the two of them walk all over her. The environment at Live Oaks is toxic. If I had anywhere else to go, I would leave tonight and not look back."

Julia considered telling him about the conversation she'd overheard between her parents the night of her homecoming. But this new adult version of their friendship was too new for family secrets.

"I'm so sorry, Jules. You're always welcome to stay here. You've been through so much already, and now you're having to deal with this. I only wish my mom were here to advise you." He took the baby from her as they walked toward her truck.

"You're doing a fine job in Lily's absence, Gus. As you said earlier, what I really need right now is a friend."

~

Julia found her sister pacing in circles in the kitchen.

"What're you doing?" Julia asked. "You're wearing out Mom's new rug."

Alex stopped pacing and stared at her as if she had no brain. "This isn't a new rug, Jules. It's hundreds of years old. And I'm trying to decide what to do about dinner."

"I can see where that would be a difficult decision for someone like you."

"Ha ha. Aren't you the funny one? For your information, I know how to cook. I just don't like to."

"Here, hold him a sec." Julia handed the baby over to her sister without giving her a chance to object.

Alex sniffed the baby. "He smells bad."

"That's the way babies smell, Alex. Besides, he needs a bath and a change of clothes." Julia unloaded the empty bottles from the diaper bag into the dishwasher. "Where's Mom?"

"She's sick." Alex held the baby at arm's length, examining him with an upturned lip.

"Mom? Sick? What's wrong with her?" Julia asked, her eyes on Alex as she retrieved two clean bottles from the cabinet beside the sink and filled them with formula.

"How would I know? She has the flu or something."

Julia loaded her diaper bag with the bottles of formula and several jars of baby food and turned to face her sister. "But flu season's over."

"I'm just telling you what she said, Julia. She's been in bed all day." Alex eyed her dirty T-shirt and jeans suspiciously. "Where have you been, by the way?"

"At the inn. Helping Gus in the garden." Before her sister could make any snide remarks about her relationship with Gus, she grabbed her diaper bag and her baby and darted up two flights of stairs to the third floor. She laid Jackson in his crib and stuck a pacifier in his mouth. "I'll be back in a minute, sweet boy. I need to check on your grandmama, and I don't want you catching her germs."

The drapes were drawn tight against the afternoon sun in her mother's bedroom. Julia followed the pathway of light streaming in from the hallway to the bed. She placed a hand on the mound that was her mother's body. "What's wrong, Mama? Alex says you're sick."

Iris's voice was muffled by the covers. "I have the flu."

"It's a little late in the season to be getting the flu." She peeled back the covers enough to feel her mother's forehead. "I don't think you have a fever. Should I call your doctor?"

"It's probably just a cold. Nothing for you to worry about. I'll be better in a couple of days."

When her mother rolled over on her side, Julia caught a glimpse of the black fabric of the dress Iris had worn to Lily's funeral. Alarm bells sounded in her head. Growing up, she'd never known her mother to get sick, aside from the occasional cold that had barely slowed her down. But Iris was in her midsixties. Maybe her health wasn't what it'd once been.

"You can't be comfortable in that dress, Mama. Why don't you put on your nightgown? I'll get one for you." She felt her way over to the dresser, turned on the lamp, and began opening and closing drawers.

"Please, Julia! Turn off the light. It's so bright." Iris pressed the back of her hand against her eyes. "Just leave me be for now. I'll change into my gown in a minute."

Julia removed a pale-blue cotton nightshirt from the drawer and placed it at the end of the bed. "Here's your gown when you're ready for it. Have you eaten anything today?"

Iris shook her head. "I'm not hungry."

"You need to eat. I'll bring you something after I put Jackson to bed."

She turned off the lamp and tiptoed out of the room. Back upstairs in the nursery, Julia strapped Jackson into his bouncy seat and fed him a jar of squash mixed with baby cereal. She gave him a long bath and played with him on the floor until he was ready for his bottle. Her stomach was rumbling by the time she'd tucked him in for the night.

She was descending the stairs to the kitchen when she heard her father's and sister's voices coming from the veranda. In the kitchen, she found empty Chinese food cartons littering the counter, alongside a nearly empty bottle of wine. How rude. Max and Alex had ordered takeout without bothering to ask Julia or Iris if they wanted any.

You have no choice, Julia reminded herself. *You have nowhere else to go.*

Rummaging through the refrigerator, she located a container of fruit and a bowl of pasta salad. Too angry to think about eating, she scooped some of each onto a plate and dropped it off in her mother's room on her way back upstairs. She peeked in on Jackson to make certain he was asleep before continuing on up to the attic. For the next hour, she rifled through three generations of her family's castoffs.

She found the hand-painted crib where all Forney babies from those three generations had slept, a round pine table, and the mahogany rocker with the intricately carved arms from her childhood bedroom. Although she remembered very little of it, she wanted to believe she'd had a happy childhood, oblivious to the dysfunction around her.

Dragging all three items down the steep flight of steps, she left the crib and rocker in the hallway outside of Jackson's room and placed the pine table in the sitting area. There was enough room on the third floor—including a second bathroom she would use as a makeshift kitchen—for them to seclude themselves. If she was careful, she could avoid any and all interaction with her father and Alex.

She slept soundly that night, comforted by the knowledge she would be starting a new job the following morning. Earning a salary would enable her to find an apartment and get out from under her father's roof.

CHAPTER TWENTY-EIGHT

IRIS

Julia's voice, soft and near her ear, lured Iris from the depths of sleep. "How're you feeling, Mama?"

Iris raised a heavy eyelid. "Tired."

"You didn't eat a bite of the food I left you last night. And you still haven't changed into your gown." Julia pressed her hand against Iris's cool forehead. "No fever. Do you hurt anywhere?"

Iris felt guilty for making her daughter worry about her. She should be indulging Julia, not the other way around. Her daughter was the one who'd lost her husband and her home. She struggled to sit up. "I'm just exhausted, honey. That's all."

Julia went to the windows and opened the drapes. "I'm supposed to start work today. Lettie's already here. Should I go ahead to the shop?"

"Of course," Iris said, rubbing the sleep from her eyes. "I'll try to make it in later. You grew up helping me at Lily's. You already know the ins and outs of the business. Felicia will give you a refresher course."

"Okay then." Julia kissed her forehead. "You'll feel better if you get up, take a shower, and eat something."

"I'm sure you're right." Iris forced a smile on her face, but the minute Julia left the room, she removed her bottle of sleeping pills from the drawer of her night table and popped one into her mouth.

What's today? she asked herself. *It must be Tuesday if Julia's starting work.*

She'd been sleeping for more than thirty-six hours. Every time she'd opened her eyes, she'd taken another sleeping pill. She craved the dark abyss of dreamless sleep like a junkie craved heroin. With enormous effort, she swung her feet over the side of the bed, holding on to the night table as she stood. She shuffled across the room to the windows and drew the drapes tight. She changed into her nightgown before crawling back into bed and falling immediately asleep.

When she woke again hours later, she sensed someone's presence near the foot of the bed. "Who's there?" she called out.

"It's me." Lettie inched forward into Iris's view. "Miss Julia called from the shop and asked me to check on you. She's worried about you."

"Where's Jackson?"

"Taking his afternoon nap." Lettie turned on the bedside table lamp. "I brought you some ripe tomatoes from my garden this morning. Can I make you a sandwich?"

"I'm not hungry, Lettie, but thank you." She slid farther beneath the sheets. "I think I'll sleep awhile longer."

Lettie cocked a hip and crossed her arms over her small chest. "Are you sick, Mrs. Forney, or are you playing hooky from your life? If you're sick, I'm gonna call Miss Julia home to take you to the doctor. If you're feeling poorly about Miss Lily's death, then own up to it. There's not a thing in the world wrong with mourning your best friend. Mama always said she'd never known women, white or black, who loved each other as much as you and Miss Lily."

A dam burst inside of Iris and sent out a torrent of tears. "Oh, Lettie, I don't know how to go on without her. She was my reason for living."

Lettie sat down on the edge of the mattress. "But what about your family?"

"Max and Alex don't need me," Iris said, dismissing her daughter and husband with a flick of her wrist. "They don't even know I'm alive."

Lettie covered her mouth to screen her smile. "I don't mean any disrespect, Miss Iris, but that's because they're too busy worrying about themselves."

Iris smiled through her tears. "You're not being disrespectful. You're speaking the truth."

"But Miss Julia's home now, and she's a sweet lady. Just like you, Miss Iris."

"Thank you for saying that. Having her home is a dream come true for me. But her homecoming happened at a really bad time."

"I suspect she wouldn't be here if she didn't need you. Miss Julia's trying really hard to keep it together, but I can tell she's struggling." Lettie squeezed Iris's knee beneath the cover. "Love on her and that precious baby. And let them love you back. I'm not suggesting they take Miss Lily's place, but I know you have room in your heart for Miss Julia and Jackson."

"You're right, Lettie. Focusing my attention on my daughter and grandson is exactly what I should be doing right now." She glanced over at her alarm clock. Three o'clock. "I'm going to take a long hot bath and then make myself a tomato and mayonnaise sandwich." Iris felt dizzy when she got up and had to sit back down for a minute.

Lettie furrowed her brow. "Are you all right, Miss Iris?"

"I'm a little dizzy. Probably from not eating." When the sound of Jackson crying echoed down the hall from upstairs, Iris waved Lettie on. "Go see about him. I'll be fine."

"All right, then." Lettie rose from the bed. "Call me if you need me. I'll be right upstairs."

Iris looked longingly at the mountain of pillows on her bed. She was tempted to take another pill and sleep away the rest of the day, but

Lettie was right. Julia needed her. Using the bedpost and dresser and chaise longue for support, she slowly made her way to the en suite bathroom, where she filled the tub with warm water and lavender bubbles. She stripped off her clothes, slipped into the velvety water, and rested her head against the back of the tub. She was asleep again within minutes. The water was tepid when she woke sometime later. She dried off with a towel, put on her terry cloth robe, and returned to her bed. After a short rest, she would get dressed, go to the grocery store, and make a nice meal for her family.

At five o'clock, Lettie entered her room and shook her awake. "Time for you to get out of that bed, Miss Iris." She loomed over her with Jackson dangling from her arm. "Fire me if you will, but you need a push, and I'm gonna give it to you. I've got a tomato sandwich and a glass of sweet tea waiting for you at the kitchen table." She went to the closet, using her free hand to flip through Iris's clothes. "What would you like to wear?"

"I'll just throw on some jeans and a blouse," Iris said, making no move to get up.

Lettie eyeballed her. "Fine. But I'm warning you, if you're not downstairs in ten minutes, I'm coming back up here after you."

Iris could tell by Lettie's insistent tone that she meant business. "I'll be down in a few minutes. I promise."

Iris slowly dressed and dragged herself like a slug down the stairs to the kitchen. With the baby on her lap, Lettie sat across the table from Iris and watched until she'd taken every bite of her sandwich, leaving only crumbs on her plate. Handing Iris the baby, Lettie took the plate and said, "Miss Julia will be home soon. I'm going to leave a few minutes early. I want to stop in and see Mama at the nursing home on my way home."

"I know what you're doing, Lettie. You're using that as an excuse to leave me with the baby." Iris hugged Jackson to her. "But that's fine by me. It's time we got better acquainted. Be sure and give Cora my love."

She'd been gone less than five minutes when Jackson let off an explosion in his diaper. "You little booger. You did that on purpose."

She glanced at the clock. If Julia left the shop at closing, she would be home in twenty minutes, but it could be longer if she made a stop along the way. She'd hate for her grandson to get diaper rash on account of her. Besides, the smell was rancid.

She got up and walked with him through the dining room to the hallway. Eyeing the grand staircase, she questioned whether she had the energy to carry this heavy baby up to the third floor. "You can do this, Iris." She grabbed on to the railing, tightened her grip on Jackson, and trudged up to the nursery. Laying him on a waterproof pad on the bed, she peeled off his diaper, jumping back in surprise when he peed on her. "If only Lily were here, she'd know how to change a little boy's diaper." She held her nose as she wiped his fanny. "I'm pretty sure my girls never had BMs that smelled like this."

Iris ruined two diapers before she finally managed to fasten one on the squirmy baby. He started to whimper on their way downstairs and was crying in earnest by the time they reached the kitchen. Alex was uncorking a bottle of wine, and Julia was coming in the door from work.

"Please make him be quiet," Alex said as she struggled with the bottle opener. "All that crying is making me a nervous wreck."

"Give him to me." Julia clapped her hands together as she held them out to Jackson. "He's probably hungry." She smiled at Iris. "I'm glad to see you're feeling better."

Julia moved to the counter beside the sink, opening the cabinet over Alex's head where she stored the baby's food.

Out of the corner of her eye, Alex gave Julia the once-over, taking in her green polo shirt with the Lily's logo on the left breast. "Where have you been all day?"

"At work," Julia said, removing two jars of baby food from the cabinet.

Alex froze. "At work where?"

"At Lily's," Iris interjected. "I hired her to take Felicia's place. I'll eventually turn the business over to her, sooner rather than later if I keep feeling like this."

"You can't do that!" Alex slammed the wine bottle down on the counter.

"Of course I can. It's my business. I can do anything I want with it." She was too tired to care if she made her oldest daughter mad. Didn't Alex make Iris angry on a daily basis?

Alex crossed the room in three easy strides. "But what about me?" she said, inches from Iris's face.

"What about you? You've never expressed any interest in the flower business."

"Because you never wanted me there." Alex held her fists balled by her side. "Julia has always been your favorite child."

"Oh, for Pete's sake. That's ridiculous." Iris started to walk away, but Alex grabbed her by the arm.

"No, it's not ridiculous, Mother. It's the truth, and you know it." Alex tightened her grip on Iris's arm. "Admit it. You've always loved Julia more."

"That's simply not true, Alex," she said in a calm voice, despite her overwhelming feelings of anger and sorrow. And guilt, because it was true. She had always loved Julia more.

Alex began spouting off accusations of all the ways Iris had failed her over the years, and Julia came to Iris's defense. Their angry voices upset Jackson, and his crying escalated to a wail.

"Shut up, all of you!" Iris stomped her feet, and when that didn't quiet them, she began jumping up and down. "Stop it! I can't take it anymore."

Taking her by the arms, Alex shook her hard. "Get a hold of yourself, Mother."

Iris shoved Alex away and sank to the floor. She pounded the hardwood with her fists as decades of pent-up emotions erupted like a volcano.

Max appeared in the doorway. "What on earth's going on in here?"

"What does it look like," Alex said. "Mom's having a nervous breakdown."

CHAPTER TWENTY-NINE

JULIA

While Max and Alex stood watching her mother's meltdown and discussing what to do about it, Julia, with screaming baby in arms, raced upstairs for her diaper bag and purse. She returned to the kitchen and knelt down beside her mother. "Come on, Mama. We're going to get you some help."

"Where are you taking her?" Alex asked.

"To the emergency room," Julia said, struggling to help her mother to her feet.

"Are you taking the baby with you?" Alex asked.

Julia paused to consider her options. Leaving Jackson in her sister's care was not one of them. "Unless you want to take Mom to the hospital?"

"No can do," Alex said. "I don't do hospitals."

Julia shifted her gaze to Max, who had a cigar in one hand and a whiskey on the rocks in the other. "What about you? Will you take Mama to the hospital?"

"Why don't we call an ambulance?" Max said. "Then none of us has to go."

Julia shook her head in disgust. "Never mind. I'll take her. I wouldn't want anything interfering with your cocktail hour." She started walking her mother toward the door.

"Wait! Don't forget this." Alex shoved Iris's purse at Julia. "Her insurance card should be in her wallet."

Julia threw the purse over her shoulder with the other two bags and kept walking.

"Let us know what the doctor says," Alex called after her.

Julia helped her mother into the front seat of her truck before buckling the baby into his car seat. As she was closing the back door, she caught a glimpse of herself in the window. She was a mess with hair glued to her perspiring face and her polo shirt soaked through with Jackson's tears and nasal mucus.

Jackson conked out by the time they got to the end of the block, and shortly thereafter, Iris stopped wailing. Julia didn't say a word on the drive to the hospital for fear of setting her mother off again.

The emergency room was crowded with people of all ages and ethnicities. They were directed to registration, where the check-in agent, a young pregnant woman named Sally, queried her mother about her reason for seeking medical attention. Iris's eyes were glazed over as if in some kind of trance, and her words came out as incoherent babble that made Julia worry she'd suffered a stroke.

"She's been under a lot of stress lately," Julia said, and left it at that. She would wait and tell the doctor about Lily's death.

"You can have a seat in the waiting room," Sally said as she attached a hospital wristband to Iris's arm. "The doctor will be with you soon."

Jackson had slept through registration, but as they were searching for vacant seats, he woke and began to cry again. When Julia offered him a bottle, he greedily latched on to it. They had just gotten situated in the last two empty chairs when she heard a dinging sound in her pocketbook. She removed her new phone and read the text from Gus.

How was your first day at work? Fumbling with the phone, she attempted to return his text but accidentally placed a call to him instead.

"I'm sorry, Gus. I was trying to text you back. I'm still figuring out how to use this phone."

"No worries. You sound exasperated. Is everything okay?"

"I'm with Mom at the emergency room." Julia angled her body away from her mother. "She's having some kind of emotional breakdown."

"Do you need me to come?" Gus asked in a concerned voice.

"Do you mind? I hate to inconvenience you, but I've got Jackson with me, and I'm not sure I can juggle it all by myself."

"I'm on my way."

Dropping her phone back into her bag, Julia turned toward her mother. "Are you okay, Mama? Can I get you anything?"

"You can get me outta here!" Iris cried, wrapping her arms around herself and rocking back and forth. "I don't wanna be here! I don't wanna be anywhere! I just want to die!" Her sobs grew louder and louder until all eyes in the waiting room were staring at them.

Julia stood up and collected their belongings. "Come on, Mama." Taking her mother by the hand, she hauled Iris to her feet and dragged her back over to Sally's desk. "I need some help. My mother is extremely agitated."

Iris bawled and trembled and uttered noises that sounded like a wounded animal.

"I can see that." Sally picked up the phone and punched in a number. Seconds later, two orderlies appeared with a wheelchair.

"My friend will be here in a minute," Julia told Sally. "His name is Gus Matheson. Can you have someone bring him to me?"

With a sympathetic smile, Sally nodded. "Sure thing, hon."

When they whisked her mother away, Julia followed on their heels. With lightning speed, they wheeled Iris to a private examining room and lifted her onto the bed. A doctor and two nurses arrived. While the doctor typed away on a laptop computer, one of the nurses inserted an IV into her mother's arm, and the other hooked up monitoring devices.

After barking a string of orders to his nurses, the doctor turned to Julia. "The first step is to sedate her. Then we'll talk, and you can tell me what's going on."

"Yes, sir. Thank you." Julia noticed Gus standing outside the room and excused herself. "I'll wait out in the hallway."

The baby's face lit up when he saw Gus, and he pushed the bottle away. Gus held out his arms, and Julia gladly handed Jackson over. "You'll need this." Julia dug in her diaper bag for a burp cloth and draped it over Gus's shoulder. "Pat him gently on the back until he burps."

"I'm confused here, Jules. Why are you here alone with your mom and the baby? Where are Max and Alex?"

"They're at home. I don't trust them to keep Jackson, and they refused to bring Mom to the emergency room. Alex doesn't *do* hospitals, and Max offered to call an ambulance instead of driving her here himself."

"What the—" Gus stopped himself. "Never mind." He nodded at the examining room. "What's going on with Iris?"

Julia sighed as she slumped against the wall. "I think she's having an emotional breakdown. She took to her bed Sunday night after the funeral and stayed there all day yesterday and today. She'd finally gotten up and was in the kitchen with Jackson when I came home from work. When Mom told Alex that she was turning the business over to me, Alex picked a fight with her that set her off like a nuclear missile. Bottom line, she's having a difficult time coping with Lily's death."

"Poor Iris. She loved my mom so much." Jackson let out a loud burp, and Gus congratulated him. "Why don't I take this little guy home with me so you can focus on your mom?"

"What do you know about babies?"

"I'm sure we can wing it." Gus held the baby out in front of him. "What say, little man? The Braves are playing tonight. We'll pop some popcorn and drink a few brews."

"Not with my baby, you're not." Julia fished out her phone. "I'll call Lettie and see if she can stay with him." She glanced through the window at her mother, who appeared to be sleeping. "We could be here all night, and I have no intention of leaving her here alone."

She stepped away from Gus and placed the call to Lettie, who offered to pick Jackson up at the hospital and keep him as long as needed. "It's all my fault, Miss Julia. I pushed your mama hard today. I didn't realize she was so fragile."

"Please don't blame yourself, Lettie. None of us saw this coming."

~

Julia told Dr. Long everything she knew about her mother's situation, which really wasn't all that much. At eleven o'clock, the doctor informed Julia and Gus that he was transferring her mother by ambulance to one of the state's leading psychiatric hospitals in Charleston.

Julia found it difficult to breathe at the thought of her mother in a psych ward. "You mean, tonight?"

"They have a bed available now," the doctor explained. "But they'll only hold it for so long."

"I don't want her to be alone. Can I go with her in the ambulance?"

"As long as you can find a ride back," the doctor said. "I imagine her team in Charleston will prohibit visitation for the first few days."

Julia's mind raced. "She's going to need some of her things. Do I have time to run home and pack her bag?"

Dr. Long glanced at his watch. "You have at least an hour. We're still filling out the paperwork." He excused himself and stepped away to the nurses' desk.

"Let's go get your mom's things." Gus placed a hand at the small of Julia's back as they walked toward the exit. "I'll follow the ambulance to Charleston and bring you back."

Julia pushed through the double doors to the waiting room. "That's asking too much of you, Gus. I can't let you do it."

"I'm not just doing it for you, Julia," he said as they continued through the waiting room to the parking lot. "Iris is like my second mother. I trust that the hospital in Charleston is the best place for her, but we'll both feel better once we talk to the staff."

They arrived at Julia's truck, and she unlocked the door. "If you're sure. I'd rather not be alone anyway."

Gus followed Julia home and parked in the driveway alongside the back porch. So far, neither Max nor Alex had called or texted to check on Iris, and the house was quiet when she sneaked upstairs to her mother's room. How could they sleep with her mother in crisis? Did they not care about Iris any more than that?

Locating a small rolling suitcase in the hall closet, she quickly threw in several nightgowns and matching robes, two pairs of slippers, three changes of clothes, and all Iris's toiletries.

Gus was waiting for her by the back door when she emerged from the house. He took her mother's suitcase and purse and stored them in the back of his SUV. There was no traffic at that time of night, and they cruised back through town to the hospital without stopping. Two paramedics were loading her mother in the ambulance when they arrived.

Her mother never opened her eyes during the hour-and-a-half drive to Charleston. Alice, the paramedic who rode in the back with them, assured Julia her mother would receive top-notch care from the staff at the hospital in Charleston.

"Prepare yourself," Alice said. "She'll probably have to stay a few days. Maybe even a week."

Christine, the night charge nurse, greeted them on the fourth floor of the psychiatric hospital and took Iris to her room. "Don't you worry," she said in response to Julia's concern. "We'll get to the heart of your mother's troubles and set her on the road to recovery. But you'll need to be patient. Breakdowns don't happen overnight. Hers has probably been in the works for a while, if not years. And her recovery will take a great deal of patience and hard work on her part and a lot of love and support from her family."

"Can she have visitors?"

"We have regular visiting hours, but it's up to your mother whether she wants to see you. Honestly, in her condition, it might be best to give her a couple of days to stabilize."

Christine searched Iris's suitcase. "It's our policy. For safety purposes." She allowed Iris to keep two changes of clothes, a nightgown, a robe, one pair of slippers, and her toiletries. She sent everything else—including her purse and cell phone—home with Julia.

"Please call me anytime night or day," Julia said when she gave Christine her contact information. "When should we expect to hear from the doctor?"

"Sometime tomorrow. Someone from the team will call you as soon as they've completed their assessment. They'll be able to tell you more about her treatment plan at that time."

Julia went to her mother's side. "I hate to leave her. Are you sure I can't stay?"

Christine joined her bedside. "I promise you, she's in good hands. We'll take excellent care of her." She removed an orange card from her uniform pocket. "You can call this number if you'd like to check on her. Your mother's patient identification number is here." She pointed at the card. "I caution you about overusing it, as it takes the nurses' time away from the patients. We pride ourselves on efficient communication with families."

"I understand," Julia said, slipping the card in her bag.

"I know this is difficult." Christine placed a hand on Julia's arm. "The process is often harder on the family than on the patient. Your mother needs this time to herself, to focus on the problems that landed her here."

~

"Do you think Mama will be afraid when she wakes up in a strange place?" Julia asked Gus after they'd stopped for coffee and were speeding down Highway 17 toward Beaufort.

"I don't think so," Gus said, his tired, bloodshot eyes focused on the road. "She'll be dazed and confused from all the drugs. And the nurses will be there with her to explain the situation. You heard Christine. This process is harder on the families than the patient."

"She also said Mama's going to need support from her family. But there is no love in our home." With head in hand, Julia planted her elbow on the car door. "I made a mistake in coming back to Beaufort."

"Don't say that." He took his hand off the steering wheel and brushed a stray lock of blonde hair out of her face. "Your mom needs you right now. No telling what might've happened if you hadn't been here tonight. Thanks to you, she's getting the right kind of help."

"Do you think I'm one of the reasons for her breakdown?"

Gus jerked his head toward her. "Not at all. I see how she looks at you. She's beyond thrilled to have you back. You just came at a bad time."

Julia exhaled loudly. "Tell me about it."

Gus took a sip of coffee and returned his cup to the cup holder. "I've often wondered about Iris's home life. She does a good job of covering it up, but I've seen the sadness in her eyes. As well as I know your mother, I hardly know your father at all. He was never around when we were young. I used to envy your nuclear family—mother, father, siblings. I thought you were exaggerating the other day when you said the environment at Live Oaks is toxic. But tonight . . ." He shook his head. "I still can't believe they didn't offer to either keep Jackson for you or take your mother to the hospital."

Julia stared out the window into the black night. "Time has a way of dimming bad memories. I thought I could handle living at Live Oaks, at least for a while until I got back on my feet. But I can't do it. I can't go back to that house, Gus. I just can't." She burst into tears. "I'm sorry. The stress of the night has gotten to me."

"It's not safe for me to pull over here in the middle of nowhere. Otherwise, I would," Gus said, opening his center console and handing her a pack of tissues. "Why don't you and Jackson come stay with me at the inn? I have plenty of empty rooms. We even have a crib. Mom insisted we keep one for guests traveling with small children."

She wiped her eyes and took a deep breath. "But what about your renovations? Wouldn't we be in the way?"

"Not at all. The reopening is not for another month. And I don't have to go full occupancy right away. I can easily hold back a couple of rooms. I probably will, anyway, until we work out the kinks." Gus reached for her hand and squeezed it. "Please! You'd be doing me a favor. Truth is, I'm missing my mama something fierce. I could really use the company."

Julia found the warmth of his hand comforting and the idea of living at the inn with him appealing. Was it possible she was falling for him? "I can't afford to pay you."

"I wouldn't accept your money if you could. We're friends, Jules. Friends help each other."

"I don't travel light, you know. I'm packing a baby and a nanny."

"We have plenty of room for all your luggage," Gus said. "If it makes you feel any better, I'll put you to work in the garden on your days off."

Julia smiled. "Then we have a deal. As long as you promise to tell me if we start to get on your nerves."

They didn't speak for the rest of the drive, just rode along, lost in their thoughts, with Van Morrison playing softly from his playlist. Gus continued to hold her hand until he had to return his to the steering wheel on the outskirts of Beaufort. Julia felt oddly dejected, and she reprimanded herself. *Your mother had a nervous breakdown tonight, Jules. Now is not the time for romance.* Jack would want her to move on, and she knew he would approve of Gus, but was it too soon? She would be thirty-seven in October. She wasn't getting any younger.

CHAPTER THIRTY

JULIA

Julia's stomach twisted into knots as she unlocked the kitchen door. She dreaded spending even one more minute in the same house with her father and sister. As she walked through the hallway and up the stairs, all the hurtful things they'd ever said to her came flying back. Alex calling her a loser and picking petty fights to prove she had the upper hand. "You'll get an abortion," Max had said on the night he'd kicked her out of the house. "No daughter of mine is going to marry a boat mechanic."

Fueled by caffeine and the events of the night, Julia tried not to disturb Lettie, who was asleep on the sofa in the living room. It was past four o'clock in the morning when she removed her suitcase from the closet and packed up her things. She even managed to shower and dress for the day before she heard Lettie stir.

"How's your mama?" Lettie asked when they met in the hallway outside the nursery.

"I'm not sure, honestly. They took her to the psychiatric hospital in Charleston. I rode with her in the ambulance, but they wouldn't let me stay at the hospital. I hope to hear from the doctor today."

Lettie gripped the fabric of her uniform top. "Oh, Lord. This is all my fault."

"Don't start that again. The nurse said that whatever caused her breakdown has been a long time in the making. The best thing we can do for Mama is be strong." Julia peeked in the nursery at Jackson, who was rocking back and forth on all fours in his playpen. "Listen, Lettie, I'm going to stay with Gus for a while at the inn. It's difficult to explain, but I . . . well, I simply can't live in this house."

"You don't need to explain what goes on under this roof, Miss Julia."

Julia's eyes grew wide. Her family's secrets weren't so secret after all. "Are you okay with keeping Jackson at the inn?"

"I can't think of anywhere I'd rather work. That place is as pretty as a picture. And full of positive vibes. Let me help you pack the baby's things," Lettie said, reaching for the doorknob.

"I've got this," Julia said, brushing Lettie's hand away from the knob. "You go home and get ready for the day. Meet me at the inn whenever you can get there."

"Yes'm," she said and hurried down the stairs.

Within the hour, Julia had fed and changed the baby, gathered up all his belongings, and loaded everything into her truck. And just as she'd done when she ran off with Jack, she drove out of the driveway without so much as a glance in the rearview mirror. On the way to the inn, she parked along a side street and finished the text she'd started in the car on the way home from Charleston. Mom has been transferred to the psychiatric hospital in Charleston. I rode with her to make sure she got settled. That's all I know for now. She didn't tell Alex and Max she'd moved out. What Julia did with her life was none of their business.

Gus rushed out to the driveway to greet her when she arrived. "I have two of my favorite adjoining rooms ready for you on the second floor," he said, grabbing an armful from the back of the truck. "And I already set the crib up in the smaller of the two."

With Jackson on one hip, Julia followed Gus as he wheeled her suitcase up the curved staircase to the second floor. Despite the musty smell that was not uncommon for a waterfront home of considerable age, her rooms were cozy with handstitched quilts on the beds and blue shag carpet on the floors. She parked the suitcase near the foot of the mahogany rice bed and crossed the room to the window. The view was stunning across the lush green lawn to the river and the Woods Bridge beyond. "I feel better already just being here."

Gus came to stand beside her. "This place has special healing powers," he said, and in a melancholic tone added, "For everyone but Lily."

"Lily experienced those healing powers for many years. She lived a happy life here, despite having lost two husbands at a young age."

He nodded. "That's very true."

Julia turned to face Gus. "I can't thank you enough for everything you've done for us. With Mama in the hospital and Felicia's last day on Saturday, I need to focus on work. And I can do that knowing Jackson is safe here with you and Lettie." She glanced anxiously at her watch. "Speaking of Lettie, she should've been here by now."

"You go ahead to work. I'll keep Jackson." When Gus held out his hands to the baby, he leaped into his arms.

"She should be here soon, but if he gets cranky, there's a bottle in the diaper bag," she said, kissing the top of her baby's head.

"We'll be fine." Gus shooed her out of the room and called after her, "And leave the car seat in the driveway. We may go on an outing."

Lettie was coming in the front door as Julia was leaving. "Jackson is upstairs with Gus. I'm sorry, but I didn't have time to unpack. I left you with a big mess. Do the best you can, and I'll get settled tonight."

"We'll be fine, Miss Julia. You have enough to worry about at the shop."

On the drive over, Julia contemplated the long list of decisions she faced at Lily's. She knew a little about flowers but nothing about running a business.

Mama is counting on me, she told herself. *I can do this. Regardless of who my father is, I'm my mama's daughter. Hold your head high and act like you know what you're doing.*

Felicia was already at the shop, creating an elaborate arrangement of spring flowers for a funeral, when Julia arrived. She was not surprised to hear of her mother's hospitalization.

"I've seen it coming for a long time," Felicia said, shaking her head as she poked a yellow lily in her arrangement. "Iris is always too busy worrying about the business and taking care of everyone else to nurture her own soul."

"She's going to be nurturing her soul for the foreseeable future. Meanwhile, your last day is on Saturday, and I have a lot to learn about running this business between now and then."

"Not the least of which is the wedding we've booked for Saturday."

Julia slumped against the counter. "Ugh. You're kidding me. I haven't done wedding flowers in years. It could ruin our business if word gets out that Mama's in a mental hospital."

"That's why we're not going to tell anyone. Your mama is the queen of organization. You'll find everything you need to know about the wedding in a file on the desk in the office."

Julia disappeared into the back and returned with the file. She flipped through the elaborate sketches and detailed lists. *Thank you, Mama.* "Does she have files for all her weddings?" she asked, thinking ahead to the summer months when they'd booked either a wedding or a rehearsal dinner or both most weekends.

Felicia looked up from her arrangement. "Most of them, yes."

Julia closed the file and waved it in the air. "Even with this, I can't handle the wedding alone. Can you?"

"I could in a bind, but I'd rather not. Iris always does the weddings." Felicia inserted a stem of purple freesia and stood back to admire her work.

216

Julia dropped the file on the counter. "Then we'll either need to hire someone this week or close the shop on Saturday."

"I already know of someone interested in taking my place," Felicia said. "I told Iris about her last week, but in all the confusion over Lily's funeral, I'm sure she forgot."

Julia shifted her gaze from her flowers to Felicia. "Who is it?"

"A friend's daughter who's taking some time off from college. She's a great kid, just not a very good student. The downside is, she may only be looking for something temporary."

"I can live with that. As long as we have someone now, we can take our time figuring out a permanent arrangement. Can you get her in here today?"

"I'll call her right now," Felicia said, removing her cell phone from her apron pocket.

Julia took the file back to the office, where she spent the next two hours on the phone with her mother's accountant, adding herself to the payroll at a salary they agreed seemed reasonable and discussing the particulars of the business side of Lily's.

Danielle Jordan, a fresh-faced girl of about twenty with strawberry-blonde hair and a trail of freckles across the bridge of her nose, arrived promptly at noon for her interview. "Please, call me Dani."

She admitted she knew nothing about flowers. "But I consider myself the creative type, and I have good computer skills. I'm hard working, and I don't mind staying after hours."

Julia, admiring her honesty and eagerness to please, saw no reason to interview other applicants. "When can you start?"

Dani beamed. "Is now too soon?"

"Now is perfect." Julia pushed back from the desk. "Let's go find you an apron."

By the end of the day, Julia had gained confidence in her ability to run the shop. While she already had extensive knowledge of flowers, she still had much to learn. But she was more enthusiastic about her future in the business than she'd ever been about anything relating to a career. While she'd taken a lengthy detour by dropping out of college and marrying Jack, she'd ended up where she was always meant to be. Her mother had shown faith in her by giving her this chance, and she was determined to make Iris proud.

Julia was locking up the shop that evening when she received the awaited call from her mother's doctor.

"I'm Dr. McBride, the head doctor in charge of your mother's case."

She tightened the grip on her phone and took a deep breath. "Yes, sir. I've been waiting to hear from you. How is she?"

"She had a tough day, truthfully. But that's not uncommon at the beginning of treatment when we're adjusting her meds and she's learning to trust us. I don't have much to report at the moment. I just wanted to touch base with you."

"Is she going to be okay, Doctor?"

"I can't say for sure until I know what we're dealing with, but I believe so, yes. She's a very sweet lady."

"Is there anything I can do to help?"

"Family therapy is a vital part of your mother's recovery, but we're not there yet. We'll let you know when we need you. In the meantime, either I or someone else from my team will communicate her progress with you daily. And you can always call the central number for updates from the nursing staff. Do you have that number?"

Julia patted her purse where she'd placed the orange card. "Yes, sir, I do. Thank you."

After hanging up, she drove to the inn with a heavy heart. She felt like everything was falling into place for her, and she wanted to share her new life with her mother.

When she entered through the front door, she heard voices in the kitchen. She walked to the back of the house and stood in the doorway watching the happy threesome—Lettie cooking at the stove and Gus feeding Jackson, who was strapped in what appeared to be a new high chair. A baby Exersaucer stood on the floor near them, and paper shopping bags were strewn about the room.

Jackson was the first to notice her, his pea-smeared face breaking into a wide grin that revealed two baby teeth on his bottom gum.

"Look at you sitting up in your high chair like a big boy." Julia kissed the top of his sweaty head. "Where did all this come from?" She gestured at the Exersaucer.

"The three of us went to Walmart on a shopping spree. Didn't we, little man?" Gus said as he spooned in more peas.

"Gus bought one of every baby gadget at the store," Lettie said, her eyes on the stove.

Gus looked up at her with a smile every bit as innocent and sweet as Jackson's. "I may have gotten a little carried away. I had a hard time saying no to Jackson. He wanted one of everything."

Julia laughed. "Right."

She kissed Gus's cheek and went to stand with Lettie at the stove, hugging her from behind. "The two of you have no idea how wonderful it is to come home to this happy scene."

Lettie waved a long stainless-steel fork at her. "You deserve this happiness and more."

"What're you cooking?" Julia stood beside her at the stove, staring down at the sizzling meat in the iron skillet. "Is that fried chicken?"

"Yes, ma'am. My mama's buttermilk recipe."

Julia placed a hand on her rumbling tummy. "Well now. This truly is a happy homecoming."

Just like family life would've been with Jack.

CHAPTER THIRTY-ONE

IRIS

Iris embraced the bliss, the drug-induced fog protecting her from the demons of the outside world. When the fog burned off and the demons threatened to attack, she begged the people in blue uniforms for more drugs. Over time—how much of it she had no way of knowing—the haze slowly began to clear, and she discovered she was no longer afraid.

She opened her eyes one morning to bright sunshine filling her room. The fog had lifted, and her spirits had as well. "Where am I?" she asked the nurse, who was taking her blood pressure.

"At the psychiatric hospital in Charleston." The nurse removed the blood pressure cuff and keyed the results into her computer. "How're you feeling this morning?"

"Hungry. What day is it, and how long have I been here?"

"Today is Thursday. You were brought in Tuesday night around midnight." The nurse handed her a menu. "You don't have any dietary restrictions. If you'll decide what you'd like to eat, I'll place the order for you."

Iris perused the menu. "Oatmeal, sausage, and hot tea," she said, dropping the menu onto the bed table.

A distinguished-looking man with gray hair and horn-rimmed glasses appeared in her doorway. "Welcome back." He entered the room and offered her his hand. "I'm Dr. McBride. How're you feeling?"

"Still a little groggy but much better." Iris pressed the arrow-up button on the control panel and raised the head of the bed. "Why am I here, Doctor?"

"You've been through a lot with the death of your close friend. Your mind decided it needed a little vacation."

"But—"

He silenced her with a raised hand. "We'll discuss your condition in due time. First, I want you to get your physical strength back. After you finish your breakfast, I'd like for you to get yourself cleaned up and take a stroll around the ward. We'll meet for our first session at eleven."

Iris did as instructed. She ate, showered, dressed, and exercised. And she felt back to her old self and ready to go home when she met with Dr. McBride in the consultation room down the hall three hours later.

The doctor greeted her at the door and motioned her to the sitting area. "Please sit wherever you feel comfortable."

Four lounge chairs formed a circle in the center of the sun-filled room with an assortment of potted plants lining the windowsill.

Iris sat down on the edge of the nearest chair. "There's been some sort of mistake, Doctor. I don't belong here. As you can see, I'm perfectly fine. I have a business to run at home in Beaufort. How did I get to Charleston anyway? I don't remember anyone driving me here."

"You were brought here by ambulance. And I'm afraid you're not ready to go home quite yet. I want you to sit back and relax"—he patted her on the shoulder as he took the seat next to her—"while we get better acquainted."

Iris settled back in her chair.

"Now then, why don't you tell me why you're here," McBride said, opening the cover on his iPad.

Iris stared at him as if he were the one who needed counseling. "That's what I just said. I don't know why I'm here. The last thing I remember was coming home from my best friend's funeral. I was a little upset, but that's understandable."

"You were more than a little upset." He set his iPad on his lap and removed his glasses. "Losing a loved one can be traumatic. You're feeling better today because of the medications we have you on, but your grief didn't just go away. It will eventually rear its ugly head again, and I want to make certain you have the skills to cope with it when it does. I sense there's something else troubling you. In the coming days, we'll need to identify what that thing is and address it."

The lines in Iris's forehead and around her eyes deepened when she frowned. "Days? Are you saying I have to stay here for a while?"

He nodded. "At least until we can determine which of your meds work best and eliminate the rest."

"But what about my family? Do they even know I'm here?"

"Your daughter"—he consulted his iPad—"Julia, came with you in the ambulance the night you were admitted. I spoke with her late yesterday afternoon. She is concerned about your health and ready to aid in your recovery. You may call her whenever you're ready."

Iris held out her hands. "But I don't have my cell phone."

"We don't allow cell phones on this hall. The nurses will show you how to dial out from the phone in your room."

Iris got up and went to the window, staring down at the people lined up at the food trucks in front of the building. A perfect spring day to enjoy lunch outdoors. "I feel like I'm in prison."

"This is not a prison, and you're free to leave at any time." He joined her at the window. "You have a choice. You can leave now and return to your troubled life, or you can stay and tough it out. I won't lie to you. Therapy is never easy. But the process will work if you let it. My goal is to set you on the road to recovery, to a brighter future. Only you can do this, Iris. And the more cooperative you are, the sooner you'll go home."

Outside the window, the cloudless deep-blue sky allowed Iris to see all the way across the church steeples and buildings of downtown Charleston to the harbor. Was she ready to own up to the mistakes she'd made? She was ready to make amends to her loved ones, but was she prepared to go to prison?

She turned to face the doctor. "In that case, let's get started."

The doctor smiled. "You're making the right decision."

"You might not think so when you hear what I have to say."

He chuckled. "I can assure you, I've heard it all." Her face remained serious, and his lips grew thin. "I'll remind you that I'm bound by a code of ethics and the law to keep everything you tell me during our sessions confidential."

Iris let out a deep breath. "That makes me feel a little better."

"Tell me about your childhood," Dr. McBride said once they'd returned to their seats.

"My parents were killed in a car accident when I was eight. I was raised by my aunt Ethel, who reminded me every day how much of an inconvenience and burden I was to her."

McBride leaned forward in his chair. "Now we're getting somewhere."

~

Iris's first therapy session lasted more than two hours. She met with McBride three more times over the course of the next thirty hours. She ate, slept, swallowed pills, and confessed her deepest secrets. She cried more tears than she thought it possible for a body to produce. But she didn't call home. She wasn't ready to talk to her family.

During these four sessions, Iris told him about falling in love with Max, their elopement, and his parents' disapproval of their marriage. She spoke at length about her friendship with Lily and their success with the flower shop. When he asked about her daughters, she said,

"One's a peach, and the other one's rotten. I let them both down in different ways. I spoiled Alex by giving her everything she wanted, and I turned my back on Julia when she needed me the most."

"Why did you spoil Alex?" McBride asked.

Iris shrugged. "Because she's strong willed and I'm a coward. It was easier to let her have her way. I'm afraid of my own daughter. How pathetic is that, Doctor?"

"And Julia? Why'd you turn your back on her?"

"Because I wanted her to have a life of her own, away from our dysfunctional family."

She told him about the girls' marriages, Alex's divorces, and Julia's husband's tragic death.

"So, let me get this straight," McBride said, rubbing his clean-shaven chin. "Your husband eloped with you because his parents didn't approve of you, yet he banished his daughter from your lives when she wanted to marry a man he deemed unsuitable."

Iris stared into her lap, her vision blurred by tears. "A bit of a double standard, isn't it?"

"Where are the girls now?"

"They're both living at home at the moment. The environment is hostile on a good day," she said, and recounted how the argument over ownership of the flower shop had led to her breakdown. The medications had helped her mind become more lucid, permitting her to remember the events of the days following Lily's funeral.

Iris felt, in one sense, like a witness for the prosecution being cross-examined by the defense attorney. With every statement she made, McBride pushed for more, eliciting her deep-seated anger and sadness and guilt. He communicated with kindness in his voice and warmth in his brown eyes, and he accepted what she told him as fact without passing judgment.

It took Iris until the next day to gain the courage to tell him about Wiley.

"We never meant to hurt anyone. It just happened. My marriage was in trouble, and his was over. At least that's what he thought. Before Wiley, I'd never experienced that kind of happiness. Or that kind of heartache when he died."

They spoke of her relationship with Wiley until her brain felt rattled from exhaustion. "Please, Dr. McBride, can't we talk about this tomorrow?"

"I'm off tomorrow and Sunday. I don't want to quit now when I sense we're nearing a breakthrough. What is it you're not telling me, Iris? I sense that whatever it is, it's somehow related to Lily's death."

She sat perfectly still in silence, her face set in stone.

He set his iPad on the coffee table in front of him and leaned in close to her. "Why have you stayed married to Max all these years when you're so obviously miserable?"

"Because Max killed Wiley, and I helped him cover it up."

CHAPTER THIRTY-TWO

JULIA

Late Friday afternoon, when Julia was in the back room at the shop organizing her plant material for the Nuckolses' wedding the following morning, she heard a pounding on the door. She turned the lock and opened the door a crack. There stood Alex, wearing a black, tailored dress that clung tightly to her slim figure and shoes that undoubtedly cost more than the mortgage on Julia's former house on Edisto.

Alex tugged on the door handle, but Julia held firm. "I'd invite you in, but as you can see, I'm in the middle of something," she said, gesturing at the buckets of flowers and conditioned greens crowding the back room.

"What the heck's going on, Julia? Why'd you move out of the house without telling anyone?"

"What's it to you, Alex? You missed me so much it took you two days to notice I was even gone."

Alex planted a manicured hand on her boyish hip. "You're broke, so I know you're not staying in a hotel. Who are you mooching off now, Jules?"

Heat flushed through Julia's body. "Where I'm living is none of your business."

"But I'm your sister. You could've at least told me where you were going."

"Why, Alex? So you could forward my mail? Sisters don't treat sisters the way you've treated me all my life. You bullied me to no end when we were little, and you've made it clear you don't want me in your life as adults."

Alex flipped her hair over her shoulder with an exaggerated *huh*. "I have no clue what you're talking about."

"All those years I was gone, you never once tried to get in touch with me."

With a modicum of sadness, Alex said, "It works both ways, Jules. You never tried to get in touch with me either. When you left, a part of Mom went with you. And I was stuck here to pick up the pieces. You've been off living your life while I've been taking care of our parents."

"And what a bang-up job you've been doing of it. You couldn't be bothered to take Mom to the hospital the other night, and you haven't called or texted once to find out how she is."

"Duh, Jules. That's why I'm here now. Dad wants to know if you've heard anything from her. He misses her."

"Yeah, right. He misses her home-cooked meals. Is he getting low on clean underwear?"

"Have you heard from the doctor or not?" Alex said, her tone now bored.

"If he misses her so much, why hasn't Dad called the doctor himself?" Julia didn't wait for a response. "Yes, I've heard from the doctor. Mom's had a couple of difficult days, but she's making slow progress. I have no idea when she'll be coming home."

"This is all your fault, Julia. We were doing just fine until you came back to town."

"Bad timing is the only thing you can blame on me. Lily's death was hard on her, but your little temper tantrum about ownership of the flower shop is what sent her over the edge."

Alex bared her teeth through red-painted lips. "You won't get away with it, Julia. I won't let you take what's rightfully mine."

"I'm not taking anything, Alex. Mom's giving it to me."

"Watch out, little sister. You don't know who you're messing with." The hate in Alex's eyes sent shivers down Julia's spine.

She watched her sister teeter on four-inch heels across the small parking lot. Just as Alex turned the corner and disappeared out of sight, Julia's cell rang in her apron pocket with a call from Dr. McBride.

"Your mother experienced a breakthrough today," McBride said. "She's exhausted and needs the weekend to recover, but she'd like to see you Monday morning. Can you be here around eleven?"

"Yes, of course. What about the rest of my family? Should I bring my father and sister with me?"

"Not this time," the doctor said. "She's not ready to see them just yet."

Julia was encouraged by her mother's progress, but Monday seemed so far away. "Is it possible for me to call her now?"

McBride hesitated. "I would hold off. If she reaches out to you over the weekend, then fine. But she really needs this time to herself."

"I understand. I'll see you on Monday," she said and ended the call.

Julia's thoughts focused on her mother as she finished organizing flowers and gathering supplies for the next morning's job. She wondered again if Iris's breakdown or breakthrough had anything to do with the mystery man, the man who might be Julia's father.

"I guess I'll take Jackson to Charleston with me on Monday," Julia said to Gus over dinner that night. She'd stopped in at the Lowcountry Produce Market for takeout on the way home. They had already put the baby to bed and were perched on barstools at the kitchen counter eating shrimp and grits. "I hate to ask Lettie to stay with him on her day off."

"Well, I was just thinking, why don't I go with you to Charleston? Jackson and I can find something to do while you're with your mom.

You're liable to be upset after seeing her and might need someone to drive you home."

"You're too good to me, Gus."

He touched his wineglass to hers. "What're friends for?"

~

The temperatures dipped into the low fifties Friday night, and Saturday dawned with plenty of sunshine and cloudless skies—perfect weather for an outdoor wedding ceremony and reception. Julia offered a prayer of gratitude. *Now please let everything else go okay.*

Julia met Dani at the shop at seven to load up the van with flowers and supplies.

"It's freezing out here," Dani said with a shiver.

"You can wear my jacket," Julia said, tossing her fleece to her new employee. "The cooler weather will help keep the flowers fresh."

Once the van was loaded, they made the fifteen-minute drive to Millie and Brett Nuckols's waterfront home outside of town. The bride and her mother greeted them at the door in terry cloth robes with fat curlers in their hair. They were none too pleased that Julia showed up in Iris's place to do the flowers. But they softened when she explained her mother was sick.

"Oh dear," Millie said, her pointy face pinched in concern. "I hope it's nothing serious."

"She should be better in a few days." Julia felt obligated to protect her mother's privacy. It was up to Iris to decide what she wanted people to know about her illness.

While Dani quizzed the bride about the wedding, Millie pulled Julia to the side. "I hate to be rude," she whispered, "but do you know what you're doing? Meredith is my only daughter. We've been planning this wedding for more than a year. Everything must be perfect."

"Don't you worry about a thing." Julia held up a manila file folder. "We have Iris's detailed drawings and notes about the arrangements. She placed the order for the flowers herself from her top supplier." Which was true. Iris the Efficient had called in the order to the wholesaler last week before Lily died. "And they are gorgeous."

Millie gave her a wary look. "All right, then. Make yourself at home. And let me know if you need anything."

The sprawling green lawn, mossy oak trees, and sparkling waters of the Beaufort River provided a spectacular venue for the outdoor wedding. For the rest of the morning and much of the afternoon, with Dani's assistance, Julia created floral arrangements in citrusy colors—hot-pink peonies, green hydrangeas, yellow ranunculus, and roses in a multitude of colors—for the makeshift altar and food tables. They formed a pathway of pink rose petals between the rows of white Chiavari chairs and draped the wooden arbor, built specifically for the occasion, with gauzy white fabric and flowers in the same citrusy colors.

The members of the band were tuning their instruments, and the caterer was setting up food tables when Millie came out to check on their progress around three o'clock. "It's stunning," she said with a tear in her eye and face aglow. "Just what I envisioned. I'm going to tell all my friends about you, young lady. You may be more talented than your mother, if that's even possible."

"Thank you," Julia said with a satisfied smile. "That means a lot."

The first guests had begun to arrive when Julia and Dani left the house a few minutes before five. By the time they'd unloaded the van, Julia was dead on her feet.

"Mama will be disappointed that she missed the chance to say goodbye," Julia said as she gave Felicia a farewell hug.

"You tell your sweet mama I love her dearly, and I'll be in touch." Felicia patted Julia's cheek. "I'm so relieved you're here to take my place at Lily's. Iris needs you, and you need her. Y'all take care of each other now, you hear?"

Tears pooled in Julia's eyes as she watched Felicia drive away. She'd worked for her mother so long she was like a member of the family. Scratch that. She was *better* than a member of the Forney family.

Lettie had already gone home and Gus was giving Jackson a bath when she arrived at the inn. "What a pleasant surprise to come home to," she said, kissing the tops of both their heads and plopping down on the floor beside Gus.

"We aim to please. Don't we, little man?" Gus said, pinching Jackson's cheek. "How'd the flowers turn out?"

"Oh, Gus! I couldn't be happier with the outcome. I took a ton of pictures."

"Great! Show them to me during dinner. I'm cooking steaks on the grill." He lifted the slippery baby out of the tub and wrapped him in a towel. "I know you're exhausted. Why don't you go shower. I'll give Jackson his bottle and put him to bed."

She hadn't seen her baby all day, but as much as she wanted to spend time with him, the thought of a hot shower won out. She would make it up to him the next day. She had all of Sunday to relax and enjoy being at the inn.

"Let me just give my baby a hug." She took Jackson from him and held him tight, burying her nose into the damp folds of skin on his neck and inhaling his sweet baby scent. Reluctantly, she returned him to Gus's arms. "Thank you, Gus. I won't be long in the shower."

True to her word, her shower lasted only a few minutes, but she took time to blow-dry her hair and put on some makeup. She pulled on a pair of white jeans with a long-sleeved pale-blue cotton sweater and slipped her feet into her favorite pair of worn-out espadrilles.

She found Gus on the terrace scraping the grill with a wire brush. He'd changed into a blue-checked button-down shirt and khaki pants.

The woodsy cologne he wore sent tingles to her nether regions. Lit candles in hurricane lanterns illuminated the seating area behind him. In the center of the coffee table sat an open bottle of red wine, two glasses, a plate of cheese and crackers, and the baby monitor he'd purchased at Walmart.

"What can I do to help?" she asked.

"Pour us a glass of wine. I'll put the steaks on in a minute. Everything else is ready."

Julia filled two glasses with pinot noir and handed one to him. Hanging his brush on the side of the grill, he lifted his glass to her. "To your first wedding."

She clinked his glass, sipped, and held hers out to him again. "To our friendship. I wouldn't have survived these past few days without you."

"It's been my pleasure." His voice was soft and husky, and Julia found herself wanting to kiss him. "I always questioned whether I was the fatherly type, but being around Jackson has stirred some paternal emotions in me I didn't know I possessed."

"You'd make a wonderful father, Gus. You're a natural."

Turning her back on him, she walked to the edge of the terrace and savored her wine as the orange sky faded to black. A gentle breeze ruffled the calm surface of the river and rustled the leaves in the trees. All of this—quiet evenings at home, the children tucked in for the night, red wine dinners, and moonlight lovemaking—resurrected thoughts of how it would've been if Jack were still alive. Her heart still ached when she thought of him, but she missed him less and less every day. She found her new life in Beaufort full of challenges and excitement, and she was discovering a confidence she'd never known. She gazed up at the stars. Jack was up there somewhere, watching over her. He would want her to be happy. Was it too early to be contemplating another relationship? Maybe so. But Jack's sudden and tragic death was a reminder of the fragility of life. She was determined not to waste one single minute, to live her life to the fullest.

She sensed Gus's presence behind her. "You're a million miles away," he said, his breath near her ear.

"Mm-hmm." She leaned back against him. "These past few days have felt so right to me. I never dreamed I'd one day have a career I enjoy so much. And living here has been a godsend. I don't have to worry where my next meal is coming from, and you've spared me the family drama at Live Oaks. I just wonder what'll happen when Mama comes home." She turned to face him. "I have something I need to tell you."

"Shall we wait until dinner?" he asked, the light from the candles glistening off his emerald eyes.

"I'm worried I will lose my nerve if I don't tell you now."

The lines on his brow deepened. "Sounds serious."

"It is." She pulled in a deep salt-infused breath. "I have reason to believe Max may not be my father," she said and told him about the conversation she'd overheard the night of her homecoming.

"Whoa," Gus said, raking his hands through his auburn hair. "I have a hard time imagining Iris having an affair."

"Which is why I didn't tell you sooner. I know how close the two of you are. I didn't want to damage your opinion of her."

"I love your mother too much for anything to change the way I feel about her." Taking her by the hand, he led her over to the sofa. "Sit. And I'll pour you more wine." He refilled their glasses and sat down next to her. "So, you were born in what year, 1981?"

"That's correct. October thirteenth," Julia said, taking a sip of wine.

"Which means you were conceived in"—he counted the months backward on his fingers—"January. Interesting coincidence. My father died in January of 1981." The color drained from his face. "Or maybe it's not a coincidence."

Julia touched his hand. "What do you mean?"

"Mom and I had just come back from spending a year with my grandparents in Atlanta when my father died in a drowning accident. I was too young to remember it, only two years old or so, I think. But Mom has told me bits and pieces over the years. She never admitted it outright, but I got the impression they were on the verge of getting a divorce. I've often wondered if he was having an affair. Do you think it's possible . . ." His voice trailed off as the implication set in.

An affair between his father and her mother would make them half siblings. The prospect both excited and disappointed Julia. Every girl dreamed of having an older brother as kind and considerate as Gus. And every girl dreamed of having a husband as handsome and loving as Gus.

"Let's not get ahead of ourselves, Gus. Max may very well be my biological father. Mama sounded confident of the outcome when she suggested the DNA test." Julia set her wineglass down on the coffee table. "For as long as I remember, my parents have always had separate bedrooms. I never gave it much thought growing up, because for me it was the norm. After I overheard their conversation, I got to thinking about their marriage and realized I'd never seen a single photograph from their wedding. The next day, I tore their house apart searching for albums or photographs, anything that might give me a better perspective about their marriage. When Alex caught me going through Max's desk, I told her what I was looking for, and she was all too eager to inform me that our parents eloped because his parents didn't approve of their marriage. Sound familiar?"

Shaking his head, Gus muttered, "Sounds hypocritical to me."

"Exactly. There is so much I don't know or understand about my mother, and I have this feeling her mysterious past is somehow related to her breakdown."

"One can harbor secrets for only so long. One way or another, they eventually catch up with you." He stood and pulled her to her feet. "I have feelings for you, Julia, that aren't of a brotherly nature." He cupped her cheek. "I haven't acted on them because you're still mourning your husband. Is there any chance you might have feelings for me?"

Butterflies batted around in her belly. "I'm starting to, Gus, but I need to take things slowly."

"Which is totally understandable. And I'm willing to give you all the time you need, but if there's any way we could possibly be half brother and sister, I need to know now before my feelings for you deepen."

CHAPTER THIRTY-THREE

JULIA

Julia and Jackson tagged along with Gus to church on Sunday. She was worried about leaving her baby in the nursery, but Jackson was fascinated by the other children. They picked him up after the service, and he fell asleep in the stroller before they reached the end of the sidewalk in front of the church.

They opted to stroll the long way home to take advantage of the springlike weather. The birds chirped merrily, and the fragrances of honeysuckle and jasmine perfumed the air. They were on Carteret Street when Julia noticed an old warehouse building for sale.

"Do you know if it's been on the market long?" Julia asked Gus as she paced back and forth in front of the building.

Gus shrugged. "At least a couple of months. Maybe more."

"This would be an ideal spot for Lily's."

"Since when is Lily's moving?" Gus asked, pushing the stroller behind her as she rounded the building to the back.

"Our lease is up in October," she said over her shoulder. They stood together on the loading dock and peered through the glass door at the exposed brick walls, worn oak floors, and floor-to-ceiling windows. "What do you think?"

"The place has potential."

"It's charming," Julia said, her excitement growing. "I'd love to expand our business. We could offer garden-related gifts as well as a self-serve display of bundled flowers and single stems for customers to create their own bouquets."

Gus nudged her. "I can see you've given this a lot of thought."

She nodded enthusiastically. "Our building is so run down. I don't think anything's been updated since our moms started the business. Besides, I think we have the potential to be more than just a florist."

"I definitely think there's a need for it in Beaufort."

A horn blew behind them, startling them and waking Jackson.

A handsome gentleman wearing a sport coat and tie climbed out of a navy Jeep Grand Cherokee. "Afternoon, folks. Can I help you with something?"

"Are you the owner?" Julia asked.

His warm smile met his sparkling blue eyes as he dangled a set of keys in front of her. "I'm the listing agent. Are you interested in taking a look?"

"Sure! Why not?" Julia said.

He unlocked the door and let them enter first with the stroller. "What kind of business are you in?" he asked as Julia marveled at the tall ceilings and abundance of natural light streaming through the windows.

"Flowers. My mother owns Lily's." She extended her hand to the man. "I'm Julia Martin. I've just moved back to town."

"Of course. I know Iris. I'm Arnold Scott." He shook her hand and turned to Gus. "You look familiar. Have we met?"

"I'm Gus Matheson. I did a closing for one of your clients a while back."

"That's right. Good to see you, Gus." He handed Julia an information flyer about the building. "Are you looking to relocate Lily's?"

"I haven't talked to Mom about it yet. She's . . . um, out of town. But when she gets back, I'd like to show it to her. Do you think the owner would be interested in leasing?"

"Unfortunately, no. He's fallen on financial hard times and needs to sell." When Arnold's phone rang in his pocket, he glanced at the screen and said, "If you'll excuse me, I need to take this. Make yourselves at home and have a look around."

Julia stood in the center of the empty room, envisioning how she would utilize the space. She gestured toward the south end of the building. "We could wall off that whole side for an office, a workroom, and a cooler." She opened her arms wide. "Which would leave all this for the showroom." She walked to the north end of the warehouse. "We could widen this doorway and have an outdoor section with annuals and perennials in the spring and summer, mums and pansies in the fall, trees and wreaths at Christmas." She noticed Gus smiling at her. "What? Am I getting carried away?"

He patted her head. "Not at all. I admire your enthusiasm."

"Do you think Mom will go for it?"

"There's only one way to find out."

When the Realtor came back inside, Julia thanked him for his time and promised to schedule an appointment for Iris to tour the facility in the coming week. On their short walk back to the inn, she rambled on about ways to upscale the business by incorporating a variety of new products.

They ate spinach omelets for lunch, put Jackson down for his nap, and tackled their afternoon chores. Julia prepared the ground and planted vegetables and herbs in the garden behind the kitchen while Gus began the somber task of going through his mother's belongings. She was patting the earth around the last tomato plant when Gus appeared at the kitchen door with a dismal expression on his face.

"What's wrong?"

"I found these stashed away in a shoebox at the back of Mom's closet," he said, holding out a thick bundle of envelopes.

She got to her feet and walked toward him. When she neared him, she could see the envelopes were note card–size and tied together with a red satin ribbon. "What are those?"

"Letters from your mother to my father."

Julia drew in a quick, sharp breath and grabbed on to the iron stair railing. "Was he Iris's mystery man?"

"I'm not sure. Here." He handed her the bundle. "Read them for yourself and let me know what you think." He turned and went back inside the house.

Julia took the baby monitor and the envelopes around the house to the front porch. She sat down on the bench swing and began to read the letters. Forty-five minutes later, Gus found her in tears.

He sat down beside her. "Well?"

"I don't know what to think," she said, stuffing her mother's last letter to Gus's father into the yellowed envelope. "Their relationship started off innocent enough. They were both unhappy in their marriages. Your mother had taken you to Atlanta, and they didn't think she was coming back. They clearly had strong feelings for each other, but their love for Lily prevented them from acting on them. I wouldn't bet my life on it, but from what I read, they never slept together."

"Let's think about this," Gus said, rubbing his chin. "Dad died on January thirtieth. At least that's when they discovered his body. Again, from what Mom told me, we'd just come back to Beaufort from Atlanta."

"In this last letter"—Julia lifted the envelope off the stack in her lap—"Mom talks about missing your father over the holidays, as though the holidays had just ended. Which leaves several weeks unaccounted for between this letter and when your father died."

"Several weeks when anything could've happened. We need answers, Jules."

"Agreed. I just hope Mom's in the right state of mind tomorrow to give them to me." They sat for a few minutes in silence. "I wonder how your mother came to be in possession of the letters."

"I guess she must have found them among Dad's things after he died."

"Why leave them for you to find instead of destroying them?"

Gus shook his head. "We may never know the answer to that. What I'd like to know is how our moms continued to be best friends considering the situation. *And* . . . Mom always led me to believe that Dad's drowning was an accident. Now I'm not so sure."

Julia's head jerked around. "Are you suggesting that someone murdered him?"

"Or that he took his own life."

~

Iris appeared withdrawn and distracted when Julia entered the consultation room at the psychiatric hospital where she'd left her mother five days before. The sunny decor was too cheerful for the somber mood inside the room, but Dr. McBride's gentle manner set her at ease. During their brief exchange of chitchat, Iris appeared relieved to hear business at Lily's had run smoothly in her absence.

"I guess we should begin," Iris said, and looked at Dr. McBride, who nodded in encouragement. "There's a lot you don't know about my life, Julia. I've done some things I'm not proud of, and after Lily died, it all came crashing down on me. I can't move into the future until I face the past. It's time for me to own up to my mistakes. With Dr. McBride's support, I've taken the first steps toward doing that." She angled her body toward Julia. "It's unfair of me to ask this of you when you're still recovering from your own tragic loss, but I need to know if I can count on your support as well."

"Don't worry about me, Mama. I'm feeling stronger every day. Of course you can count on me. I'm happy to help you in any way. But what about Max and Alex?"

Iris shook her head with vehemence. "Your father is part of the problem, not the solution. And you know Alex. She takes his side every time. Dr. McBride is prepared to release me today, on the condition I find somewhere else to live. I can't go back to that house—"

Julia held up a hand to silence her mother. "Say no more, Mama. I get it. I moved out of Live Oaks myself last Wednesday after your . . . uh . . . break . . ."

"It's okay, sweetheart. You can say the word. We have to face the truth. I had an emotional breakdown." Iris reached for the cup of water on the table in front of her. She took several gulps, licked her lips, and set the cup back down. "If you don't mind me asking, where're you living? It's really none of my business, but—"

"I'm staying at the inn. Gus and I talked about it last night. He's offered for you to stay there as well. He's not reopening until the first of May, which gives us three weeks to find somewhere else."

Julia watched the tension drain from her mother's body. "Wonderful," Iris said, clasping her hands together. "That will give me time to sort out my affairs."

Julia nearly choked on the word *affair*.

McBride leaned forward in his seat. "I've left it up to your mother's discretion as to how she sorts through these 'affairs,'" he said, using air quotes. "If you ever need anything, Julia, do not hesitate to call. You have my number."

Sensing the session was ending, Julia took a deep now-or-never breath. She'd discussed the situation with Gus well into the night, and they'd agreed that Julia should raise the issue of her paternity in McBride's presence so that he could deal with the fallout. Regardless of her mother's emotional instability, Julia refused to go another day without knowing who her father was.

"There is one *affair* we need to sort through now." She focused her gaze on her mother. "On the night of my homecoming, I overheard you and Max arguing in his study. He has reason to question whether he's my biological father." Julia removed the stack of letters from her purse and handed them to Iris. "And I'd like to know if Wiley Matheson is that reason."

CHAPTER THIRTY-FOUR

IRIS

Iris's mouth dropped open. "Where'd you get these?"

"Gus found them in Lily's room when he was cleaning out her things."

An awkward silence settled over the room. Wiley had sworn to her that he'd destroyed the letters. Her face warmed at the idea of her best friend and her daughter reading her private words to Wiley.

Iris felt her daughter's eyes on her, but she couldn't meet them. She'd hoped to explain everything to Julia in due time.

"You don't have to do this now, Iris," McBride said in a warning tone.

"Yes, I do," Iris said, staring at the letters in her lap. "Do we have time?"

He patted her hand. "Take all the time you need."

"So, Gus knows?" Iris asked.

"Yes, Mama. Gus knows. But he's not angry at you or anything like that. He cares about you. We both just want answers."

"Then the short answer, Julia, is *yes*. Max is your biological father. There is absolutely no question about his paternity. But the longer answer isn't as clear cut." Iris paused to gather her thoughts. "Shortly after Gus's first birthday, Lily took him to Atlanta to visit her family. She was gone for a year. She was suffering from depression and needed time to sort through her feelings. She asked Wiley to help out at the shop in her absence. We saw each other nearly every day. Both of our marriages were in trouble, and we found our way to each other. We were very much in love at the time. At least I thought we were. It was truly a confusing time. In hindsight, I may have mistaken comfort for love. But we never slept together out of respect for Lily because we loved her so much."

Julia sat rigid in her chair, her expression unreadable. "How did Max find out about your relationship?"

Iris cast an uncertain glance at McBride, who offered a sympathetic smile in return. She breathed in deeply. "That's where the story gets dicey." Snatching two tissues from the box on the coffee table, Iris left her chair and went to the window. She couldn't bear to see her daughter's reaction when she told her about Wiley's death. With her forehead pressed to the glass and tears on her cheeks, she walked Julia through the events of that horrible winter day on Edisto. And what Max did to her that night.

Iris finished talking, and silence fell over the room. She continued to stare out the window, terrified to see her daughter's face. After a few minutes, Julia spoke in a faint voice. "Not only am I the product of a rape, I have a murderer's blood pumping through my veins."

Julia was as pale as a ghost when Iris turned to face her. She left the window and knelt beside her daughter's chair. "No matter how you were conceived, you were a blessing to me. You saved me from the depths of depression. You still are the best thing that's ever happened to me. It nearly killed me when Max sent you away, but I went along with it because I knew it was your chance at a normal life. I didn't want him to ruin you the way he's ruined Alex. My frequent trips to Edisto to check on you were my way of staying close."

"Why did you stay with him, Mother? You had your own business. You didn't need his money."

Iris winced. She couldn't remember her youngest ever calling her *Mother*. "Wiley's death was ruled an accident, but Max had proof of our relationship and the ability to frame me for his murder. I couldn't risk losing you girls. And Lily."

"He's every bit the monster I thought he was," Julia said, staring straight ahead at nothing.

Iris needed to tell her daughter so much more, but she felt her tank running low, and the doctors had warned her about pacing herself.

"I think that's enough for today," McBride said. "I know you still have a lot of unanswered questions, Julia, but you're going to have to let your mother explain things to you in her own time."

"Oh, right. Of course." She stood and helped Iris to her feet. "I'm sorry for all you've been through, Mama. If you'll let me, I'd like to help you through this."

Iris collapsed in her daughter's arms. "There's nothing I'd like better," she sobbed. "I still have a lot to figure out, but I hope you and I will be able to share our lives, running the store together and raising your precious boy."

Julia, with tears glistening in her eyes, held her mother at arm's length. "I'd like that very much. Let's get your things and go home. I think you'll find peace at the inn. I know I have."

~

On the way down in the elevator, Julia said, "I'm sure Gus would prefer to hear from you about your relationship with Wiley. I won't be able to put him off for long. We are here for you, Mama, but we deserve to know the whole truth."

"Understood," Iris said with a nod.

Gus greeted Iris with a warm embrace in front of the building. With Julia pushing the stroller, they walked to the parking deck together. Gus stowed Iris's bag in the trunk and helped her into the passenger side while Julia climbed into the back seat with Jackson.

"I don't know about you, ladies, but I'm starving," Gus said as they exited the parking lot. "I've got a hankering for fried chicken. What say we stop for lunch on the way out of town?" Iris's new meds had zapped her appetite, and the thought of food made her nauseated, but she was in no position to complain.

It was almost two o'clock when they parked down the street from Leon's, a trendy oyster bar that offered a variety of craft beers. On a normal day, Iris would've enjoyed the relaxed and cheerful atmosphere, but the seriousness of what awaited her at home dampened her spirits.

The lunch crowd was thinning, and they were shown to a table right away. The harried young waitress quickly recited the specials, and Gus ordered the fried chicken platter with hush puppies and black-eyed pea salad for the table.

While waiting for their food, they talked about renovations at the inn and the goings-on at Lily's. Iris was relieved to hear the Nuckolses' wedding had been a success and that they'd hired someone capable to take Felicia's place.

When the food arrived, Iris took tiny bites of her avocado toast, pretending to eat while watching the threesome across the table. The ease with which Gus and Julia interacted suggested they'd spent a lot of time together and hinted their friendship had developed into something more serious. Iris's heart warmed. Her daughter deserved to be happy. Gus was honest and good, so much like his father, and Iris loved him dearly. There was no one she'd rather have as a son-in-law.

No wonder they're so concerned about the letters, Iris thought. *They're worried Wiley is Julia's father, which would make them half brother and sister.*

When they arrived at the inn, while Julia took the baby upstairs to change his diaper, Iris asked Gus to walk with her down to the water. They stood at the edge of the marsh watching the sky darken as a line of thunderstorms rolled in.

"I want to thank you for taking such good care of Julia and Jackson. Thanks to you, she seems to be adjusting well to Beaufort." The air was humid ahead of the front. She slipped off her cotton cardigan and tied it around her neck. "There are some things I need to tell you that won't be easy for you to hear."

Emotions crossed his face—bewilderment followed by dismay followed by anger—as Iris repeated not only what she'd told Julia that morning but also the things Lily had said to Iris the day she died.

After she finished talking, she gave Gus a few minutes to process this new information before adding, "I never meant for anyone to get hurt, Gus, least of all your father. He was a wonderful man, and I robbed you of the chance to know him. I plan to do what I should've done when he died. I'm going to the police with my knowledge of the circumstances surrounding his death."

Gus's eyes grew wide. "Does Julia know this?"

Iris shook her head. "I haven't decided whether to tell her or not. She has a right to know, but she'll try to talk me out of it, and this is something I have to do."

"When will you do it?"

"In a couple of days. I need to put some things into place at work first."

Gus grabbed her hand. "Iris, please. Don't do anything rash. At least take some time to think about it. You've been under so much stress these past few weeks with Mom's illness."

"I've had years to think about it, Gus. Keeping all this inside for all that time landed me in a psychiatric hospital."

"Considering the circumstances, I'm surprised you didn't have a breakdown sooner."

"I'm the queen of denial, Gus. Since your father died, I've gone through the motions of life without allowing myself to think or feel. I can't go on this way. In light of what I just told you, I'd understand if you'd rather I stay somewhere else."

"Oh no you won't. You'll stay right here with us. I have every intention of standing by you, Iris, just as Mom stood by you all these years. She forgave you your relationship with my father because she loved you. I've gathered from things she told me over the years that they didn't have the best marriage. I know you, Iris, certainly well enough to know you would never intentionally hurt anyone. As for you robbing me of the chance to know my father, I had a wonderful father in Hector. While he wasn't my biological father, he instilled in me the principles that formed the man I've become. Do I wish Wiley had lived longer? Of course. But life happens, and I in no way blame you. Understood?"

She smiled. "Understood."

"Now, let's go back to what you said earlier. If you ultimately decide to go to the police with this, I'm happy to counsel you as a friend and help you choose an attorney should you find you need one."

"I may take you up on that offer. Do you think I should warn Max that I'm going to the police?"

Gus hesitated before answering. "He's a murderer. With a move like that, you could be placing your life in danger. And Julia's and Jackson's as well."

CHAPTER THIRTY-FIVE

JULIA

Iris insisted on going to work on Tuesday, despite her daughter's pleas that she take some time for herself.

"Then why don't we walk to the shop, Mom. The exercise and fresh air will do you good."

But when they reached Carteret Street and Julia started off in the direction opposite the shop, Iris said, "Where are we going?"

"You'll see." Julia looped her arm through Iris's and dragged her along.

As they walked the four blocks to the warehouse, Julia mentioned some of the changes she'd like to make at Lily's. To her delight, her mother seemed receptive to all of her ideas.

"And speaking of changes," she said when they were standing in front of her dream warehouse, "our lease is up this fall. Now might be a good time to think about expanding. And it just so happens this warehouse is for sale."

They walked around to the back and peeked inside through the door. "Gus and I ran into the listing agent on Sunday when we spotted the **FOR SALE** sign on the way home from church. He was more than happy to give us the tour. The place has real potential. Sectioning off one end of the building would allow us to double the size of our workroom. And we can build a covered area off the other end for outdoor plants and maybe trees and wreaths at Christmas. I can see it now—a florist, gift boutique, and garden center, a one-stop shop for all flower needs." She stepped away from the window and faced her mother. "So, what do you think?"

"I love the idea. Your fresh concepts are just what our business needs," Iris said, her voice full of enthusiasm.

Julia experienced a rush of adrenaline. "I have an appointment with the Realtor to see it again after work today. Will you come with me?"

"I'd be delighted. Who's the listing agent?"

"Arnold Scott. He mentioned that he knows you."

Iris nodded. "I did the flowers for his wife's funeral a few years ago. Poor woman died after a long battle with breast cancer."

"That's too bad. He seems like such a nice man," Julia said distractedly.

As they walked toward Bay Street, her mind was not on Arnold or his wife but on the endless possibilities for the new Lily's. She wanted to pinch herself to make sure her new life was real. She was falling for a man she'd once loved like a brother, and she was working side by side with her mother in the career she'd always dreamed of.

~

Iris spent most of the day in the office with the door closed. She left the shop without explanation around three that afternoon and returned an hour later.

"You've been acting mysterious today, Mama. What's going on?" Julia asked while they waited for Arnold on the warehouse loading dock a few minutes past six.

"Well, I—" When Arnold turned into the parking lot in his Jeep, she said hurriedly, "I'm making a few necessary changes to the business. I'll explain over dinner."

Iris and Arnold exchanged pleasantries for a few minutes before he led them around the warehouse, pointing out the many advantages the building offered.

"The natural light is lovely," Iris said. "Cozy touches like rugs and built-in shelves would make the space warm and inviting."

Arnold nodded. "I'll give you ladies a few minutes alone to talk." He stepped outside, pressing his cell phone to his ear.

"I love your idea for a create-your-own-bouquet section," Iris said, circling the room. "We can sell terrariums, high-end paper products, and seasonal decorations for the various holidays."

A wide smile spread across Julia's face. "And cachepots and vases and unique gardening tools."

They discussed the possibilities awhile longer before joining Arnold outside.

"I have my computer in my car," Arnold said with a twinkle in his pale-blue eyes. "Say the word, and we can make an offer right now."

Iris laughed. "My daughter and I need to discuss it some more. How long has it been on the market, and have you had much interest?"

After a brief discussion about price and logistics, they thanked Arnold and promised to be in touch.

"I'm an insomniac," Arnold said. "Feel free to call me anytime day or night."

On the way back to the inn, Julia said, "Perhaps I jumped the gun by taking you to see the warehouse before I asked if you can afford to buy it. Obviously, I don't have the money . . ."

"Your father has no idea how successful my little flower business has been. Because he's always paid our household expenses, I've been able to invest nearly everything I've made. And I've built up equity in the business itself. So yes, I can afford a healthy down payment on the warehouse that will make our mortgage payment equal to what we pay in rent now. Of course, we'll need money for the renovations, which shouldn't be a problem. If we're going to expand, I say we do it right by redesigning our logo and hiring a publicity firm for a marketing campaign."

Julia stopped in the middle of the street and gave her mother a tight hug. "We're going to have so much fun working together. Arnold said to call him anytime. Maybe we can make the offer later on tonight."

"Perhaps. But first I have something important I need to discuss with you over dinner."

~

Julia spent longer than usual with Jackson at bedtime, and when she came downstairs for dinner, she found her mother and Gus at the grill, talking in hushed tones with their heads close together. They didn't hear her approach them, and both their heads shot up when she said, "You two look serious. Is something wrong?"

Gus appeared flustered. "Your mother has something she wants to talk to you about over dinner."

"She mentioned that earlier," Julia said, eyeing them suspiciously. They were obviously cooking up something other than tuna steaks. "I have to admit my curiosity is piqued. Can I do anything to get dinner on the table sooner?"

"You can check on the corn bread," Iris said. "It should be about ready to come out of the oven."

Julia walked around the porch to the kitchen, where she found the table already set and a bottle of pinot noir breathing on the counter. She removed the corn bread from the oven, cut it into squares, and tossed the salad. Everything was waiting on the table when Gus and Iris brought the tuna steaks in five minutes later.

"Spill it," Julia said as she buttered her corn bread. "What's this important matter we need to discuss? I hope nothing is wrong."

Iris and Gus exchanged a knowing look.

"Can we wait until dessert?" Iris asked. "I'd hate to ruin this splendid dinner."

Her skin prickled. "So there *is* something wrong?"

"Depends on how you look at it." Iris took a sip of wine and dabbed her lips with her cotton napkin. "I'll start with the good news. I transferred ownership of Lily's to you today. Congratulations, you're now the sole proprietor."

Julia's jaw hit the table, and she set down her corn bread. She knew her mother would one day turn the business over to her, but not before she was ready to retire. "Why now?"

Iris looked at her squarely. "Because tomorrow morning I'm going to the police with the information I have about Wiley's death."

Julia narrowed her eyes. "You mean you're turning Max in?"

"There's no way to sugarcoat it, honey. Yes, I'm turning your father in for the murder of Wiley Matheson."

Julia's chest tightened, and a bead of perspiration dribbled down her back. "Is this really necessary?"

"I believe it is, sweetheart, in order for me to live a normal life. Lily's death slapped me awake from a very deep, very long, dreamless sleep, during which I pretended everything was fine when everything was anything but."

"You could lose Alex. You realize that, don't you?"

Iris gave a solemn nod of her head. "But if I don't do this, I'll lose myself. I've protected the two of you all your lives at the expense of my own emotional well-being. You're grown women now. You can take care of yourselves. There is no statute of limitations on murder. Gus can't represent me, as that would be a conflict of interest. But he's agreed to counsel me as a friend and help me find an attorney if I need one. I assume the police will reopen the investigation, and they may very well bring charges against me. I transferred the business to you in case I have to go to prison."

"This is great," Julia said, abruptly pushing away from the table. "We just found our way back together, and now you're tearing us apart again."

She fled the room, seeking refuge on the porch swing where she could think. So what if her mother was unhappy. Anything was better than going to jail.

Recalling her mother's words—*I've protected the two of you all your lives at the expense of my own emotional well-being*—Julia tried to put herself in her mother's shoes. She would do anything to protect Jackson. Including covering up a murder.

Gus came out of the house a short while later. "I put your plate in the warming drawer."

"I lost my appetite," she said, unable to meet his eyes when he sat beside her on the swing.

"I know you don't approve of her decision, but your mother needs us to be strong for her right now," he said, pulling her close.

She rested her head on his shoulder. "I can't lose her, Gus, not after losing Jack."

Gus tilted her chin and kissed her lips gently. "I honestly don't think that's going to happen, Jules, but if it does, I'll be here for you."

CHAPTER THIRTY-SIX

IRIS

Iris and Gus were pulling out of the driveway, on their way to see the sheriff of Colleton County, when her cell phone rang. She heard the fear in her daughter's voice when Julia asked, "Where are you?"

"Just leaving the inn. Why? What's wrong?"

Gus slowed the car and pulled over to the side of the road.

"Alex just texted me. Dad was just rushed to the hospital in an ambulance. It sounds serious."

She gasped. "Are you sure?"

"That's what she texted. I guess we should go to the hospital. I walked to work this morning. Can you swing by and pick me up?"

Iris felt Gus's eyes on her, and she met his gaze. "We're on our way."

Julia was waiting out in front of the shop when they arrived. She jumped in the back seat, and Gus sped off to the hospital. Only a handful of people occupied the ER waiting room. Alex sat alone, gnawing at her cuticles with her eyes glued to the double doors leading to the examining room. Her dark hair was a tangled mess, and she was wearing the silk pajamas Iris had given her the previous Christmas.

Alex sprang to her feet when she saw them. "Mother. How nice to see you. When did you get sprung from the loony bin?" She turned to Gus. "And since when are you a member of this family?"

Iris's body tensed. "Shut up, Alex. This is no time for attitude."

Alex's face registered shock at Iris's authoritative tone. She should've used that tone on her child decades ago.

"How's your father?" Iris asked.

"I wish I knew. They wouldn't let me ride in the ambulance with him. When I asked if I could go back there"—she gestured at the double doors—"they told me I had to wait out here."

"Tell me what happened. Is he sick?"

"He was standing in front of the microwave, cooking his frozen sausage biscuit, when he suddenly gripped his chest and dropped to the floor like the weighted balls we use in my interval training class." She gave Iris a death glare. "This is all your fault, Mother. You should've been at home, where you belong, fixing his breakfast—"

"How dare you!" Iris said. "Until last week, I've made that man breakfast every single day for the past forty-one years."

The double doors swung open, and a frazzled young doctor appeared. "Family for Max Forney," he called.

When Alex shoved her aside to get to the doctor, Iris stumbled into Gus, who righted her. "You can do this, Iris," he said in a low voice. "I'll be out here if you need me."

She smiled a grateful smile. "Thank you, Gus."

She motioned for Julia to go ahead of her, and the threesome followed the doctor in single file to a windowless consultation room. Without making an offer for them to sit, the doctor faced them with a serious expression on his rugged face. "I'm afraid I have bad news. Max suffered a massive coronary. We did everything we could, but his heart was too badly damaged."

"No!" Alex shrieked and bolted out of the room.

Iris could hardly believe her ears. What a twist of fate. She'd been on her way to turn him in to the sheriff, and now he was dead. She pushed aside her emotions and let Iris the Efficient take over. "Thank you for your efforts, Doctor. What happens now?"

"Would you like to see him?" the doctor asked.

Iris had no parting words for her husband. She'd wasted forty-one precious years of her life married to a man she despised.

She lifted her chin high. "No, thank you," she said and turned to Julia next to her. "But you go ahead."

Julia blushed and lowered her head. "I don't care to see him either."

~

Ten minutes later, Iris sat with Julia and Gus in the parking lot with the engine running and the air conditioner blasting, trying to absorb what had just happened. "I can't believe he's dead. If the doctor came out now and told us he'd made a mistake, that Max was going to live, I'd still turn him in. Does that make me a horrible person?"

"I'm a horrible person too," Julia said. "I refused the opportunity to say goodbye to my own father."

Gus locked eyes with Iris in the rearview mirror. "Neither of you is a horrible person. You're honest people struggling to process your grief for a man who was cruel to you. If you ask me, he got off lucky. A pompous ass like Max would never have survived life in prison. And I was determined to put him there for murdering my father." His tone held a quality of loathing she'd never thought possible from him.

Julia peered over the back of her seat at Iris. "Please tell me this business with the sheriff is all behind us now. You didn't kill Gus's father. You were merely protecting your family."

"I guess so," Iris said without conviction. She needed time to come to terms with everything that had happened.

"Glad that's settled." She shifted in her seat, facing forward. "What do we do now?"

Iris inhaled a deep breath as she collected her wits. "You'll go to the shop, and I'll go to Live Oaks to start making arrangements. I'm not Alex's favorite person right now, but I don't want her to be alone, today of all days."

Gus started out of the parking lot. "I'll be at the inn all day if either of you needs me."

They drove toward downtown in silence, each lost in thought. When they parked in front of Lily's, Julia got out of the car and tapped on the back window. Iris rolled down the window, and she leaned in close. "Are you okay, Mama? This has come as a shock to you, and after everything that's already happened."

Iris patted her daughter's hand. "I'll be fine, sweetheart."

"I'm not so sure about that. Alex is a loose cannon right now. What if she sets you off like she did last time?"

"I'm in a much better place than I was a week ago." Iris felt a little shaky, but she felt enormous relief as well. "We probably won't even see each other. Knowing Alex, she's hiding out in the guest cottage, and I'll be in the main house making phone calls."

"If you're sure," Julia said, straightening. "Call me if there is anything I can do."

Iris didn't bother moving to the front seat for the short drive to Live Oaks. When she got out of the car in the driveway, she heard loud music coming from the guest cottage. She started to check on Alex but thought better of it. Her oldest needed her space. She'd give her some time before reaching out to her.

After being away for eight days, Iris worried she'd find the house a mess. Much to her surprise, everything appeared clean and orderly with the exception of the mold growing on the food in the leftover containers in the refrigerator. She threw everything in a yard-size trash bag, brewed herself a cup of coffee, and took it to Max's study. Ignoring the eerie feeling that her husband was watching her, she sat down at his desk and opened the drawer that housed his files. She flipped through the file folders until she found one labeled My Funeral. Inside the file were detailed instructions for the service, burial, and reception. She scanned the typed pages.

"This is exactly the funeral I would've planned for you, Max," she said out loud to the empty room. "Even after four decades of marriage, you had no faith in me. I never lived up to your expectations, but I certainly tried."

She went to the kitchen and placed the file on her small desk in the back corner. After notifying his coworkers at the bank, she called the priest, the funeral home, and the cemetery. Once the funeral plans were underway, she paged Dr. McBride and spoke with him briefly. His calm voice provided the strength and reassurance she needed.

"Despite your differences, Max was still your husband," McBride said. "Take care of yourself, Iris. You don't have to be everyone's rock. We're here for you, anytime you need us. If you sense yourself slipping, check yourself into the hospital for an overnight tune-up."

"I wish it were as simple as getting my oil changed."

He chuckled. "It will be once you get through the funeral and put all this bad stuff behind you. You're stronger than you think, Iris. Keep reminding yourself of that."

She thought about his advice throughout the rest of the afternoon. She cut flowers from her garden for the dining room table, freshened up the downstairs powder room for guests, and organized Max's clothes to take to the funeral home the following morning. When Alex didn't respond to her numerous texts, she walked over to the guest cottage and pounded on the door until her daughter screamed at her to go away.

Around four o'clock, friends and neighbors began to arrive with food and condolences. It was sad to think she'd known many of these women for most of her life, yet none of them had a clue about the trouble in her marriage or her recent emotional breakdown. How blessed she'd been to have Lily, her one true friend, when so many women never had any.

Julia showed up in the delivery van a few minutes past six with several large flower arrangements. Iris helped her unload them from the van and place them around the house.

When they finished, they went to the kitchen for a glass of sweet peach tea. "Go home to your baby. I'll hold down the fort here."

"Gus is keeping Jackson. He insists I have dinner with you."

A wave of relief washed over Iris. "I won't argue. I could use the company."

"We should totally be together tonight. Alex too, if we can coax her out of the guest cottage. Do we have anything to eat?" Julia asked as she crossed the room to the refrigerator.

"Ha. We have enough food to feed all of Beaufort." Iris stood next to her as they surveyed the contents. "I don't know about you, but I could use some comfort food right about now. Helen Vickers brought a platter of fried chicken, and we could heat up some of Sally Beasley's mac and cheese to go with it."

Julia eyed the bag of tomatoes their elderly next-door neighbor had left on their back porch. "And I'll make a salad using those."

"Sounds perfect." Iris grabbed the casserole dish with the mac and cheese. "I'll put this in the oven to heat and open a bottle of wine while you go ask Alex to join us."

"I'm on it." Julia disappeared out the back door and returned ten minutes later. "You can forget about Alex. She's drunk out of her mind. I tried to talk to her, but she refused to let me in and called me names I wouldn't dare repeat."

"Don't take it personally. She's suffering right now." Iris poured two glasses of chardonnay and handed one to Julia.

Julia took a sip of wine. "I'm sorry, Mama, but that doesn't give her the right to be nasty to us."

"No, I guess you're right." She retrieved a roll of herbed goat cheese from the refrigerator and placed it, along with some rice crackers, on a small platter. "Why don't we go out on the veranda and sit for a while. Maybe she'll change her mind. She'll eventually get hungry, and I doubt she has any food in the cottage."

The loud music that had been blasting all day from the cottage suddenly stopped when they emerged from the house.

"Do you think she's spying on us?" Julia asked.

Iris imagined Alex at the window with a pair of binoculars. "Let her. We have nothing to hide."

A cold front had slipped through earlier in the afternoon, bringing cloudy skies with no rain but cooler temperatures. Julia turned on the propane heater, Iris removed a cashmere throw from the basket on the floor, and they settled themselves on the wicker sofa, huddled close together with the blanket draped around them.

"This is not the right time to celebrate," Julia said, "but Arnold Scott called this afternoon. The owner of the warehouse has accepted the offer we made this morning."

"How wonderful," Iris said, pressing her hands together. "It's hard not to get excited over that. We can close at the end of May, which will give us all summer for renovations."

Julia sliced off a chunk of goat cheese, spread it on a cracker, and took a bite. "You should call your attorney tomorrow and have him tear up the papers you signed transferring the ownership of Lily's to me. I doubt he's had a chance to file them yet."

"No way. I was planning to transfer the business regardless. You can pay me a salary. I'll consult with you through your first summer of weddings and help you set up the new store, but once you're settled, I'm going to retire."

"Mama, no!" Julia sat up straight and moved to the edge of the sofa. "I can't take your business away from you."

"You're not taking it from me. I'm giving it to you." She pulled Julia back against the cushions. "Honestly, Jules, having you here to take over Lily's is a dream come true for me. Otherwise, I'd have to sell it, and I'd hate to see it fall into the wrong hands. I've poured my heart and soul into that business, but I want to enjoy my life before old age sets in."

Julia tucked her legs beneath her. "Your work has been your life. What will you do with all your free time?"

"Travel to exotic countries. Heck, I'd just like to see the United States. Who knows? I may learn to play golf or tennis or maybe even bridge."

With a twinkle in her eye, Julia said, "Or maybe the man of your dreams will come along and sweep you off your feet."

CHAPTER THIRTY-SEVEN

JULIA

A formation of pelicans flew over the top of the house and landed at the edge of the marsh.

"I haven't been out on the dock since I got home," Julia said. "Do you think it's too cold to walk down there now?"

"Not if we take our blanket," Iris said, getting up from the sofa and dragging the blanket with her. "Maybe if Alex sees us, she'll come out of the cottage."

Julia's heart broke for her mother, who was so desperately worried about her sister. How Iris could love Alex despite her many flaws was beyond her. While Julia admired her mother for loving her child so unconditionally, she worried that it might be Iris's ultimate downfall.

With the blanket draped over their shoulders, mother and daughter ambled down the brick sidewalk and out the long boardwalk to the end of the dock. They sat with their feet dangling over the edge, sipping wine and enjoying the peaceful evening as the day faded away.

"Tell me about your wedding," Julia said. "I've always wondered why I've never seen any photographs from your big day."

"That's because your father and I eloped. You already know this, because Alex told you. I've been meaning to talk to you about it, but with everything else we've been dealing with, I just haven't found the right time."

"Were you pregnant? Did you lose the baby like me? I know you'd been married a couple of years when Alex was born. At least that's what you always told me."

"I wasn't pregnant. I was a virgin, actually." Iris stared down into the murky water. "Your father insisted I didn't talk about our elopement with you girls. He was embarrassed by my upbringing." Julia listened as her mother went on to describe in detail her life with Ethel after the accident—her lonely childhood, the cinder block house, the lack of money, and Ethel's health issues. "When Ethel's emphysema got the best of her and she was forced to quit her job at the hair salon, I had no choice but to quit high school and get a job. I was only in the eleventh grade."

Her mother's sad story rendered Julia speechless. Iris had always appeared so polished and well bred, Julia had just assumed she'd come from a wealthy family. "I'm so sorry, Mama," she said after a short period of silence. "I wish you'd told me that sooner. I understand so many aspects of our lives better now. But what I don't understand is why Max . . . why Dad was so adamantly opposed to me marrying Jack when he'd been in the same position himself."

"Because he didn't want you to make the same mistake he'd made," Iris said in a quiet voice.

Julia experienced a surge of anger. "He was damn lucky to have you." She drained the rest of her wine. "Whatever. I give up trying to figure out that man. But I never understood why you went along with him when he banished me from the family."

"I tried to stop you the night your father sent you away, but he prevented me from leaving the house. I was distraught after the way he treated you." Iris inhaled a deep breath. "First thing the following morning, I drove to Charleston to your dorm room, but you'd already packed up and gone. Your roommate told me you'd gone to Edisto. I spent that summer driving around the island looking for you, until I spotted you leaving Duke's one day in early August. I figured you would've been five or six months pregnant by then. And . . . well, you were as trim as ever, and I assumed you'd lost the baby. I followed you home. You were living in an apartment at the time, and Jack was waiting for you on the porch."

Julia smiled. "I remember that apartment."

"Watching the two of you together, the way you held each other and kissed, I could tell you were madly in love, that you had the real deal. I made the decision that day not to interfere with your lives."

"In some perverse way, I guess Max did me a favor. By kicking me out of the family, he set me free to live my own life."

"In the same perverse way his death has set me free."

Swinging her legs onto the dock, Julia stood up and offered her mother a hand. "Let's go eat dinner. I'm starving."

They walked back up the dock and were almost at the house when Alex jumped out from behind the garden shed. "Boo!" She burst into a fit of fake laughter. "I got you."

"That's not funny, Alex," Julia said, her heart pounding in her chest. "You really scared us."

"Boo-hoo," Alex said, fake rubbing her eyes with her balled fists.

"Are you hungry, sweetheart?" Iris asked. "We have fried chicken and macaroni and cheese. I thought we could discuss the funeral arrangements over dinner."

Iris's lips were pressed thin, and Julia knew her mother was struggling to retain her composure.

"Actually"—Alex brought herself to her full height—"I came down here to tell you to get off my property."

"You reek of booze, Alex," Julia said. "And this isn't your property. You're drunk and delusional."

Alex grabbed Julia's arm and squeezed with surprising strength. "I said. Get off. My property."

Julia yanked her arm free of her sister's grip. "And I said. This isn't your property."

"Ha. You'll find out soon enough. Daddy never loved either of you. Not the way he loved me. Consider yourself uninvited to the funeral, Mother. You won't be welcomed." Inches from Julia's face, Alex added, "And neither is your bastard daughter."

Iris's face grew scarlet. "How dare you. Julia is Max's daughter, same as you. We'll get a paternity test to prove it, once and for all."

"Don't bother, Mama," Julia said, returning Alex's death stare. "I'd rather pretend that Max wasn't my father and Alex isn't my sister."

"Why, you little . . ." Alex came after her, pulling hair and swinging fists. Alex tackled her to the ground, and they rolled around, kneeing and clawing and grabbing. Alex's rancid breath was near her face as she climbed on top of her, pinning her arms to the ground with her knees. She slapped Julia's face over and over with her right hand and then her left until the sound of her mother's bloodcurdling cry made her stop. With all the strength she could muster, Julia wrapped her legs around Alex's torso and muscled her sister off her.

Julia scrambled to her feet and rushed to her mother's side. Iris was rocking back and forth on her knees with her hands pressed against her ears, mumbling something Julia could not make out. She helped Iris up, wrapped the blanket around her, and started toward the house. Alex was on their heels, throwing gravel at them. "Stay away. This is not your house. It's mine. Daddy and I understood one another. We were cut from the same cloth. Just like the two of you were cut from the same cheap polyester fabric."

"Come on, Mama. You can ride home with me in the van." Julia steered Iris through the house to the kitchen, where she retrieved their purses, and out the back door. She loaded Iris in the van and peeled out of the driveway. Her eyes were wild, and she struggled to catch her breath as she careened around the corner to the inn. Gus was on the porch reading a novel by candlelight when she skidded to a halt in the gravel driveway.

He hurried out to greet them. "What happened to your face?" he asked when he saw the claw marks on Julia's cheek.

"Alex attacked me. She kicked us out of Live Oaks. I'll tell you about it in a minute, but we need to get Iris inside first. She's having another breakdown." Julia slid out of the van and rounded the front to the passenger side.

With Gus's help, she got her mother out of the car and into the kitchen. Pulling a barstool away from the counter, she said, "Sit here, Mama, while I make you some tea."

While Julia brewed chamomile tea, Gus poured her a finger of bourbon into a tumbler. "What's she saying?" Gus whispered to Julia as they stood watching Iris stare at the tea and bourbon in front of her, mumbling the same words over and over.

"I don't know." Julia leaned across the counter, her ear near her mother's lips. "Sounds like she's saying, 'You're stronger than you think, Iris.'" She straightened. "We should call her doctor in Charleston."

Retrieving her phone from her purse, she accessed the contact information and placed the call to the psychiatric hospital. "Please page Dr. McBride and have him call me back. This is an emergency," she said and gave the receptionist her name, the patient's name, and her cell number.

She ended the call and placed an arm around her mother in a half hug. "You're safe now, Mama. You're at the inn with Gus and me. Your grandson is upstairs sleeping in his crib, and you're surrounded by Lily's possessions. We all love you. Please come back to us. What happened tonight isn't real. This is real. We're your family."

When her phone rang, Julia took the call out to the porch. She briefly explained the situation to the doctor. "If I take her to the hospital here, they'll just refer her to you. Should I bring her to Charleston?"

"Let me try to talk to her over the phone first," McBride said. "She and I spoke for a moment earlier this afternoon, and she seemed to be coping with your father's death. When you have an emotionally unstable person, certain things set them off. Until your sister is ready to aid in your mother's recovery, it's best if Iris stays away from her."

"That makes sense, although it won't be easy with the funeral on Friday."

"You did the right thing in calling me, Julia. Now, if you'll put your mother on the phone, I'll try to get through to her."

Julia walked the phone back to the kitchen. "Dr. McBride would like to speak to you," she said, holding out the phone.

"Let's fix her something to eat," Julia whispered to Gus, and they busied themselves with frying bacon and making omelets while eavesdropping on Iris's end of the conversation.

After ten minutes of silence, Iris began to respond to the doctor in a weak voice. "No, you're right. Yes, I understand. I'm stronger than I think." She inhaled deeply and then trembled all over as she exhaled the breath, as though shaking off her problems. "I'm going to make it. I have Julia and Gus and Jackson. And I have my work." She was quiet for thirty seconds before she said, "Will do," and hung up.

She set the phone down on the counter. "It's been a long day. I think I'll go to bed."

"Why don't you eat something first?" Gus said. "We'll have an omelet ready for you in a second."

~

After they'd eaten and Iris had gone to bed, Gus and Julia went out to the porch to unwind.

"How're you holding up?" Gus asked, resting his arm on the back of the swing behind her.

"I'm a little numb, honestly. The man I thought was my father died the night he disowned me, and my feelings for Max . . . well, let's just say I don't care enough about him to mourn his loss. It's hard for me to admit that, but I can't help how I feel."

"No, you can't. Tell me what happened tonight."

She walked him through the events of the evening, careful not to leave out the hurtful things her sister had said. "Alex was drunk out of her mind, and I'm not sure she even knew what she was saying, but she seemed so confident that Live Oaks belongs to her."

"Do you think there's any chance your father left the estate to her and not your mother?"

"I hope not, for Mom's sake, but I wouldn't put it past him. He and my sister were tight. Right now, I'm more worried about the funeral. Should we attend or not? I couldn't care less about being there, but I can't let Mom go alone."

"And I'm not letting you go without me. We'll attend the funeral on Iris's terms. Whatever makes her feel the most comfortable. Whether that means sneaking in the back door or sitting in the front pew with Alex."

"That's not going to happen, not after the way Alex uninvited us tonight," Julia said.

"She'll change her mind once she sobers up and realizes the field day the rumor mill will have if Iris doesn't show up for Max's funeral. Your mother is the darling of this town. He's the ogre."

Julia angled her body toward him. "You never told me that. Does everyone really think he's an ogre?"

"Worse than mean old Mr. Potter in *It's a Wonderful Life.* Let the situation play itself out. Alex needs Iris at that funeral."

"I think you're wrong about that," Julia said. But she was the one who turned out to be wrong.

She was feeding Jackson his bananas and cereal the following morning when she received a text from Alex. **For appearances' sake, we should all go to the funeral together tomorrow.**

CHAPTER THIRTY-EIGHT

IRIS

Iris stayed in bed until after ten on Thursday morning. Every time she opened her eyes, she squeezed them shut again. She could cope with Max's death. It was the hatred she'd seen in Alex's eyes the night before that haunted her. She was teetering on the edge of the abyss. The darkness tempted her, but for Julia's sake, she couldn't let herself fall. Julia was working hard to sort through her own life. She didn't need to contend with Iris's emotional problems on top of everything else.

When she finally dragged herself out of bed, Iris dressed in jeans and a worn fleece pullover and went downstairs to the kitchen. Lettie was at the stove boiling something that looked like lasagna noodles, and Jackson was swatting at the toys in his Exersaucer.

"Morning, Miss Iris." Lettie left the stove to give her a hug. "How you feeling today? I'm so sorry for your loss. I'm sure your husband's death has come as a shock to you."

"You're awfully kind, Lettie. It still hasn't sunk in yet."

"Can I make you some eggs and bacon?"

Iris eyed the fresh pot of coffee. "I'm just gonna have some coffee." Lettie filled a mug and handed it to her. "Where is everyone?" she asked as she added cream and raw sugar to the cup.

"Miss Julia's at work, and Gus is outside." Lettie dumped noodles into a strainer in the sink. "I'm making your favorite vegetarian lasagna for dinner. You don't need to be worrying about food at a time like this."

"Thank you, Lettie. That sounds perfect."

After spending a few minutes with Jackson, Iris went out to the porch. A chill was in the honeysuckle-scented air, and the sun shone bright, glistening off the ripples in the river.

She saw Gus near the marsh, working on his waterside firepit patio. He looked up at her, waved, and set down his shovel. As he came toward her, she noticed his sun-kissed skin and his sweat-soaked shirt clinging to his broad shoulders. The life of an innkeeper agreed with him.

"How're you feeling this morning?" he asked as he approached the porch.

"A little unsteady. But Julia needs me, and I'm determined not to let her down."

"You don't have to be the strong one, Iris. Let us help you through this."

"We'll help each other. Has there been any word from Alex?"

He hesitated, and she knew he was holding something back.

"You can tell me, Gus. I won't fall apart on you. I promise."

"Alex sent Julia a text this morning." He tugged his phone loose from the back pocket of his jeans and handed it to her.

After she read the text three times, something snapped inside Iris, and a powerful rush of anger chased away the lingering threads of hopelessness. She uttered a *humph* as she handed him back the phone.

"What does *humph* mean?" he asked, pocketing his phone.

"It means that I've always given Alex everything she's ever wanted. But that stops today."

"Good for you, Iris. I told Julia last night, you should go to the funeral on your terms."

"I agree! And those terms are nonnegotiable."

~

At precisely eleven o'clock on the day of the funeral, with Julia and Gus on her heels in single file, Iris marched down the aisle at Saint Peter's Catholic Church to the front pew, where Alex was already seated. Iris kept her eyes on the floor in front of her, avoiding Alex's gaze when she sat down beside her. She seethed at the spray of white carnations topping the casket on the altar. A tactical maneuver on Alex's part. Every woman in the congregation would assume the flowers had come from Lily's. Iris admitted to being a flower snob. And carnations were beneath her. Alex had declared war not only on Iris personally but on her business. While she hated the path their relationship had taken, being angry at Alex gave her the strength she needed to stand up to her. The self-loathing and guilt responsible for her breakdown were gone, replaced by a formidable desire to persevere.

Iris skimmed the program while she waited for the priest to begin. Two lines caught her eye in particular: The Forney family invites you to Live Oaks for a lunch reception immediately following the service. A private burial will be held later today. She envisioned Alex standing alone at the cemetery, watching her father's casket being lowered into the ground. She felt pity for her eldest but not sadness. Alex had alienated herself.

The service was dignified, befitting a man of high character and great success but not an abominable creature like Max. Afterward, as they waited for the pallbearers—six of Max's closest friends, whom Iris barely knew—to recess down the aisle with the coffin, Alex whispered to Iris, "I'll expect you to make an appearance at the reception."

The smell of alcohol on her daughter's breath was so strong she took a step backward. Nothing good would come from her daughter's inebriation. "I'm sorry, Alex. I'm not feeling up to it today."

Alex's gaze shifted slightly right to Julia behind her. "You'll come, won't you? To the reception?"

"Sorry. I'm no longer welcome at Live Oaks, remember?"

When the usher motioned for Alex to follow the pallbearers, she spun on her stiletto heels and paraded up the aisle.

Iris lost Julia and Gus in the crowd gathered in front of the church. She was receiving condolences from a small group of the town's most prominent women when she felt a hand on her back. She turned to face Sam Holland, Max's attorney. "Forgive me for intruding, Iris, but I need a word with you in private," he said, and without waiting for her response, he led her to the edge of the crowd.

"I have an urgent matter regarding Max's will that I need to discuss with you." He studied the calendar on his cell phone and then peered at her over the top of his black-frame readers. "Are you available to meet in my office at nine o'clock tomorrow morning?"

Iris's mind raced. Max had never discussed the specifics of his will. As his wife, she assumed the bulk of his estate would pass to her. Then again, she'd been wrong every time she'd assumed anything about her late husband. "I suppose so. Shall I bring Julia with me?"

"Her presence at this meeting would not be appropriate."

Stunned into silence, Iris merely nodded.

Iris walked to the car in a stupor. What could possibly be so urgent about Max's will? And if the purpose of the meeting was to discuss Max's will, why wouldn't Julia be invited? Unless she wasn't mentioned in the will. Alex's words from two nights ago came to mind. *Stay away. This is not your house. It's mine.* She'd ignored her oldest at the time, thinking Alex was merely trying to get under their skin. Could there be any truth to her daughter's drunk rantings? For forty-one years, Iris had cooked and cleaned for Max, raised his children, and kept his dirty secret. She deserved some acknowledgment of her loyalty. But did she even want it?

Julia and Gus were waiting for her at the car. "You don't want to go to the reception, do you, Mama?" Julia asked, holding the car door open for her.

"Not on your life," Iris said, tossing her bag in the back seat. "I fear I wouldn't escape the reception with my sanity intact."

Over the roof of the car, Gus said, "In that case, I'm taking you two lovely ladies to lunch at the Riverview Inn. Lettie is cooking up something special in your honor."

"Perfect!" Iris said, clasping her hands together. "The best food and vista in town."

Lettie had set the porch table with linens and roses from Lily's garden, and she'd prepared a delicious lobster Cobb salad. The warm weather and Miraval rosé did much to improve Iris's mood. While they ate, she told them about her conversation with Sam Holland.

Julia said, "I won't attend the meeting since I wasn't invited, but I'll drive you there and wait for you in the waiting room."

The idea appealed to Iris. She assumed Alex would be attending the meeting, and considering Alex's behavior of late, she hated the thought of facing her oldest alone. On the other hand, she didn't want to burden Julia. "I'm sure I'll be fine alone."

"Sam Holland has a reputation for being abrasive and oftentimes unethical," Gus said. "I agree with Julia. One of us should go with you."

Julia left for the shop right after lunch. Although she had proven herself invaluable, Dani was too new to leave alone for too long. Gus went back to work on his firepit, and Iris stretched out on a chaise longue on the patio with the latest Mary Higgins Clark mystery. The warm sun and wine buzz made her drowsy, and within minutes she fell asleep. She woke an hour later and spent the rest of the afternoon with Jackson. She strapped him into the stroller, and while he stuffed Cheerios one by one into his tiny mouth, she scoured the neighboring streets for houses for sale.

Iris ate a bowl of cereal for dinner and turned in early in preparation for her meeting the next day. She wanted to be ready for whatever surprises Max had in store for her.

With Julia behind the wheel of Iris's Volvo wagon, they left the inn a few minutes before nine for Holland's office. Alex was waiting for her in the reception area with her dark hair pulled back in a loose bun and an emerald silk blouse unbuttoned to reveal her cleavage.

She sprang to her feet when she saw Julia. "What's she doing here?"

Julia stepped in front of Iris. "Chill, Alex. I have no intention of attending your little meeting. I came with Mom to offer moral support. She's been through a lot lately. Obviously, you haven't noticed."

The receptionist, a young woman with a straight face and pinched lips, announced Mr. Holland was ready to see them. Iris and Alex followed the receptionist down a wide hall to the last door on the right. Holland's office was decorated with masculine furniture and leather-bound books lining floor-to-ceiling shelves on two walls. Behind his mahogany desk, a large window offered a magnificent view of the river.

Holland stood to greet them. "Ladies. Please have a seat." He motioned to matching chairs in front of his desk.

"In an effort to save time—I have a busy day ahead of me—I'll get right to the point of this meeting. Alex is already aware of the contents of Max's will. Due to the sensitivity of the situation, we agreed it would be best if she was present for this meeting. There's no easy way to say this, so I'll be frank. Max left his entire estate to Alex. Since you are not a beneficiary, I'm not required by law to conduct this meeting. I'm doing it as a favor to Alex."

"Daddy thought it best if everything went to me," Alex said. "He's counting on me not to squander his family's wealth."

Iris stared at the stranger sitting next to her. She'd known it for years, but she'd been too much in denial to admit it. Her daughter, the woman she'd raised since birth, had turned out to be every bit as cruel as her father.

She returned her attention to the attorney. "And Julia? I gather she's not mentioned in the will either."

"Why would Daddy leave your bastard child anything, Mother?"

"That's not necessary, Alex," Holland said in a warning tone. "Max left no provisions for Julia. I'm not privy to his reasons."

"I don't want you to be destitute, Mother. I'm prepared to give you ten thousand dollars."

Iris burst into fits of laughter. She laughed so hard tears streamed down her face and she tinkled a little in her panties. When she saw Holland and Alex staring at her as though she'd lost her mind, she laughed even harder. She hadn't lost her mind. It had taken over four decades, but she'd finally found it.

She stood abruptly. "Keep your ten thousand dollars, sweetheart. I have no intention of contesting the will. I entered into this marriage with nothing. It's only fitting that I leave with nothing."

She got halfway to the door before she remembered. "Except my clothes and my shell collection. Those are rightfully mine."

"I packed up your belongings for you," Alex said. "Everything is in the trunk of my car."

"By all means. Let's go get them." With a sweeping gesture toward the door, she waited for Alex to walk ahead of her.

When they passed through the reception area, Iris warned Julia with a shake of her head not to ask any questions. "I'm going to get my belongings out of Alex's car; then we can leave."

Few words were exchanged as they quickly transferred Iris's meager possessions—her suitcases, a mountain of hanging clothes, and a cardboard box she assumed contained her shells—from Alex's trunk to the back of her Volvo.

She bit back a sob at the sudden realization that her relationship with her oldest daughter was over. At least until Alex came to her senses. *If* she ever came to her senses.

She embraced a stiff Alex in parting. "Despite everything, I still love you, my darling girl," Iris whispered. "You can always come to me if you need anything."

Iris felt deep sorrow for her child who was so clearly misguided. But she couldn't let those negative feelings dominate her future or destroy her relationship with Julia. She felt trapped on an emotional roller coaster, and somehow, someway, she needed to find a means of escape. She was ready to move on. One life had ended, but another was just beginning.

"Where to?" Julia asked as they exited the parking lot.

"Just drive, please."

"You got it." Julia turned up the music on the country station and rolled down the windows. As they crossed the Woods Bridge to Lady's Island, Iris laid her head against the headrest, closed her eyes, and let the salt air clear her mind.

They made the forty-minute drive to Fripp Island in silence. They had turned around and were headed back when Julia asked, "Are you okay, Mama?"

Iris's lips turned up in a soft smile. "I will be. Maybe not today or tomorrow, but one day soon."

Julia returned her eyes to the road. "What happened at Holland's office?"

"It was a courtesy meeting to let me know that your father left everything to Alex."

Julia stared at her with eyes wide open and mouth slack. "Are you kidding me?"

"I wish I were." Iris squeezed Julia's hand. "I owe you an apology, sweetheart. Your father never believed you were his child. If I'd insisted on a paternity test, things might've been different. You deserve to have your share of the inheritance. For your sake, I'm prepared to contest the will."

"I don't want Max's money, Mama. Jack and I lived a very happy life with only the bare necessities. Seems to me, the only thing the Forney family wealth ever brought anyone is misery."

"You are right about that, my girl." Iris straightened in her seat. "Alex is my child. I'm concerned about her well-being. She's convinced her inheritance is the answer to all her problems, but I don't see how money is going to guide her out of this dark place she's in. I will always be here for her, but I'm moving on with my life. I feel free, like a bird let out of its cage. I'm sure I'll have setbacks along the way, but I feel more like myself than I have since I worked the perfume counter at Tapp's."

As they came off the bridge into downtown Beaufort, Iris tugged on the sleeve of Julia's blouse. "Take a right here. I want to show you something." She directed Julia to take a left on New Street and another onto Craven. "I've always loved this street since Lily and Wiley lived here when they were first married. Pull over to the curb in front of this house." She pointed at a gray two-story Victorian with wide porches. "This house hits the market tomorrow morning. I have the first appointment of the day at nine. If I like it, I'm going to make an offer on the spot before someone else snatches it up."

"Can you afford it?" Julia asked, her eyes on the house.

"Yes, sweetheart. I already told you, I've amassed my own wealth. Nothing like the Forneys' but plenty to last me a lifetime."

"I know what you said. I just want to be sure you're taken care of," Julia said, her face pinched in concern.

"I'll be fine. *We'll* be fine. Would you like to live here with me? It has three bedrooms. One for me. One for you. And one for Jackson."

Julia's eyes met hers. "Oh, Mama, yes! But only for a while. Until I can afford a place of my own."

"Or until a certain redhead asks you to marry him."

Julia blushed. "Don't get ahead of yourself. We're taking things slow."

"The timing for love is never ideal. You of all people should know that."

"I know, but Jack was the love of my life. It seems impossible that I would find that kind of happiness again. I've fallen in love with an old friend. My feelings for Gus are different, softer and more relaxed."

Iris cupped Julia's cheek. "Don't overthink it, darling. True love is a rare gift. Embrace it. You only get one life. Live it."

EPILOGUE
JULIA

The second Tuesday in October dawned crisp and bright. Iris and Julia arrived at Lily's Flower Emporium two hours early to finish preparing for the grand opening. Natural light streamed through the windows, casting Julia in a soft glow as she inspected the display of books and gifts for gardening and entertaining that lined the custom-made shelves.

"These lavender soaps are reasonably priced and would make great hostess gifts." Julia held the basket of soaps out to her mama. "Should we move them to a more visible location?"

Iris took the basket and returned it to the shelf. "The soaps are fine where they are, sweetheart. Stop fussing. Everything is absolutely perfect. Just look at it. We—you and I—did all this." She beamed as she flourished her arms wide at the showroom.

Mother and daughter stood side by side to admire the result of their hard work. A checkout counter with distressed wood paneling on the bottom and black granite on top stretched the length of the longest wall. Oriental rugs in shades of orange and blue were scattered about the random-width oak floors, providing warmth to the renovated warehouse. Galvanized buckets of varying heights with fresh-cut flowers occupied the center of the room, with antique farm tables showcasing a variety of exotic orchids and an assortment of cachepots and terrariums extending from either side.

"We've always made a good team, Mama," Julia said, leaning into Iris. "I loved Jack dearly and I miss him like crazy, but his death is responsible for bringing us back together. Is it wrong for me to feel grateful for that?"

"I believe we would've eventually been reunited one way or another. But good things sometimes come from death. As the saying goes— when one door closes, another one opens. There's no reason to feel guilty, Jules. That's life. I'm only sorry I never got the chance to know Jack. But that's my own fault."

Her voice broke, and Julia put her arm around Iris's waist, pulling her close. "Let's not go there today, Mama. We agreed to focus on the future."

During the past five months, Julia and Iris had spent untold hours talking about and working through everything that had happened. The conversations had deepened their relationship in a way Julia had never anticipated. She smiled to herself as she thought how they had become more like best friends than mother and daughter.

Iris rested her head on Julia's shoulder. "You're right. Today is a happy day. Today we celebrate not only the opening of Lily's Flower Emporium but also our reunion."

Julia spotted Gus and her mother's new beau standing outside on the loading dock with their backs to the door and their heads close together. "We should also celebrate the men in our lives. They deserve some of the credit for our happiness."

"I can't argue with that. Who knew Arnold Scott, Beaufort's most sought-after Realtor, would end up being my soul mate?" Iris nudged Julia with her elbow. "Did I tell you he's taking me to Europe after Christmas?"

"Go, Mom! A romantic New Year's in Europe."

A dreamy expression settled on Iris's face. "I never knew romantic love could be like this."

Julia smiled. "And I never thought I could love again. My relationship with Gus is comfortable because we were childhood friends. But at the same time, it's exciting and new now."

"We're both so blessed," Iris said. "If only . . ."

"Yeah, Mom, I know. If only Alex were a part of our lives. But she's not. At least not right now. After all her talk about keeping Live Oaks in the family, for her to up and sell it to a stranger . . . well, she's clearly not in her right mind."

"I'm just so worried about her. If the rumors are true about the drinking and the married men, who knows what will happen to her."

"I have a feeling we haven't heard the last of Alex. But we can't let her ruin our day." Keeping her eyes on the men and eager to change the subject, Julia said, "What do you think they're talking about?"

She'd begun to think of Arnold as a future father figure, and it thrilled her that Gus and Arnold got along so well.

"Who knows? But they're letting our breakfast get cold," Iris said of the container of coffee Arnold carried and the bag of pastries from Lowcountry Produce in Gus's hand. When she crossed the room and unlocked the door for them, the men reluctantly entered the building.

"What are you two scheming up?" Julia asked as they approached her.

"Oh, nothing really," Arnold said, his eyes on the carton of coffee in his hands.

"Just shooting the breeze," Gus added. But when a blush crept onto his cheeks, Julia knew he was hiding something.

"Mm-hmm," she said, cutting her eyes at him. He'd been acting secretive the past few days. They'd discussed marriage at length, and Julia suspected he was on the verge of proposing. Gus wanted to adopt Jackson, and Julia knew in her heart that somewhere up in heaven Jack was smiling down on them.

"I'd better get outside," Gus said, stuffing a pastry into his mouth and handing Julia the bag. "I need to water the pansies before our first customers arrive."

With a quick glance at the clock over the door, Arnold thrust the container of coffee at Iris. "I'd better help you, Gus. We don't have much time," he said, even though they had nearly an hour before the opening.

Iris and Julia watched them go, waiting until they had exited the building for the outdoor garden area before bursting into laughter.

"That man of yours has developed quite the green thumb," Iris said. "Being a full-time innkeeper suits him."

"He is in his element entertaining his guests, cooking breakfast for them, and having his champagne receptions in the afternoon. I hope some wealthy woman doesn't steal his heart."

"There's only one woman for Gus. You should know that by now."

"I do. And I'm the luckiest girl alive."

"Yes, you are. Now, let's finish our work before the masses arrive."

Iris and Julia hustled about the showroom, sweeping the hardwood floors, Windexing the doors, and plucking wilted flowers from the bins.

When Arnold and Gus finally came back inside a few minutes before ten, the staff—Dani and the two middle-aged women Julia had hired to satisfy their expansion needs—had arrived. They stood in position at the checkout counter as a large crowd began to gather on the loading dock for the opening ceremony.

At precisely ten o'clock, with her mama at her side, Julia stood tall and proud as she clipped the red ribbon with the oversize scissors. She stepped out of the way so the shoppers could migrate inside.

They were nonstop busy all day long with wave after wave of customers coming to inspect their new digs and product offerings. In the late afternoon, Lettie brought Jackson for a planned visit, and he toddled about on his chubby little legs, a helium balloon tied to his wrist.

They laughed when he moved from one galvanized bin of flowers to the next, pausing at each to sniff the blooms.

Iris's eyes twinkled as she watched her grandson. "Looks like somebody inherited our love of flowers."

Julia nodded. "Another Forney to carry on the tradition."

Gus and Arnold moseyed into the building from the garden area and joined Iris and Julia in the center of the showroom beside the cut flowers. Gus scooped Jackson up. "Hello there, little man. I have a question I'd like to ask your mommy. Will you help me?"

Jackson nodded, his blue eyes bright.

"Let's pick out a flower for her. Which one do you want?" Jackson pointed his tiny finger at a bin of coral-colored lilies.

"Good choice." Gus removed the lily from the bin and dropped to his knee in front of Julia, setting Jackson on his feet beside him. "Julia Forney Martin, will you marry me?"

Julia let out a nervous giggle as she glanced around the showroom. "Are you seriously doing this right now with all these people watching?"

He presented her with a black velvet box. "Does this look like I'm serious?" he said, opening the box.

Julia's hand flew to her mouth at the sight of the brilliant-cut diamond.

"This ring belonged to my father's mother," Gus said. "And Dad gave it to Mom when he asked her to marry him. Lily would want you to have it. And I'd be honored if you'd accept it. So, I'll ask you again, will you marry me?"

Unable to find her voice, Julia bobbed her head up and down. As the few remaining customers erupted in applause, he slipped the ring on her finger. He got to his feet, wrapped his arms around her, and planted a hard kiss on her lips.

When Jackson ran toward them, Iris scooped him up and embraced Julia and Gus in a group hug.

"What about me?" Arnold asked, edging his way into the hug. "I want in on the action."

"So that's what all the secrecy was about this morning," Julia said, giving Gus a playful slap on the shoulder.

Gus winked at Arnold. "I had to let my best man in on the secret."

When Iris let out a sob, all gazes landed on her in concern. "I'm fine," she said with tears streaming down her face. "I'm simply overwhelmed with joy. I only wish Lily were here to share in our happily ever after."

ACKNOWLEDGMENTS

I'm grateful to the many people who helped make this novel possible. First and foremost, to my editor, Patricia Peters, for her commitment to excellence and for making my work stronger without changing my voice. To my agent, Andrea Hurst, for her guidance, her sound advice, and her friendship. To Danielle Marshall, editorial director at Lake Union Publishing, for having faith in me and for her continued support and encouragement. To Gabriella Dumpit, author relations manager extraordinaire, and the amazing Amazon marketing team. To Nicole Pomeroy, my production manager, for polishing the manuscript for publication, and to Haley Swan and Kellie Osborne, my very skilled copyeditors.

A big thank-you to my beta readers—Alison Fauls, Mamie Farley, and Kathy Sinclair—for taking interest in my work and providing invaluable feedback and to my behind-the-scenes team, Geneva Agnos and Kate Rock, for all the many things you do in managing my social media so effectively. I'm appreciative to Tim Galvin, Richmond architect, for answering my many questions about architecture, Karen Stephens for advice on real estate, and Betsy and Moultrie Dotterer for background information about Edisto and the surrounding island. A special thank-you to Caroline Wallace and her parents, Caroline and John Trask, natives of Beaufort, South Carolina, for providing names of restaurants and background information on Beaufort.

I am blessed to have many supportive people in my life who offer the encouragement I need to continue the pursuit of my writing career. I owe a huge debt of gratitude to my advanced review team, the lovely ladies of Georgia's Porch, for their enthusiasm for and commitment to my work. To Leslie at Levy's and the staff at Grove Avenue Pharmacy for helping my books make it into the hands of local readers. Love and thanks to my family—my mother, Joanne; my husband, Ted; and the best children in the world, Cameron and Ned.

Most of all, I'm grateful to my wonderful readers for their love of women's fiction. I love hearing from you. Feel free to shoot me an email at ashleyhfarley@gmail.com or stop by my website at ashleyfarley. com for more information about my characters and upcoming releases. Don't forget to sign up for my newsletter. Your subscription will grant you exclusive content, sneak previews, and special giveaways.

ABOUT THE AUTHOR

Ashley Farley is the bestselling author of the Sweeney Sisters series as well as *Sweet Tea Tuesdays*, *Magnolia Nights*, *Beyond the Garden*, *Nell and Lady*, and other books about women for women. Her characters are mothers, daughters, sisters, and wives facing real-life situations, and her goal is to keep readers turning pages with stories that resonate long after the last word.

In addition to writing, she is an amateur photographer, an exercise junkie, and a wife and mother. While she has lived in Richmond, Virginia, for more than two decades, part of her heart remains in the salty marshes of the South Carolina Lowcountry, where she grew up. Through the eyes of her characters, she captures the moss-draped trees, delectable cuisine, and kindhearted folks with lazy drawls that make the area so unique. For more information, visit www.ashleyfarley.com.